Melissa Oliver is from south-west London, where she writes sweeping historical romance and is the winner of the Romantic Novelists' Association's Joan Hessayon Award for new writers for her debut in 2020, *The Rebel Heiress and the Knight*. For more information visit www.melissaoliverauthor.com, and follow Melissa on Instagram @melissaoliverauthor, X @melissaoauthor and Facebook @melissaoliverauthor.

THE LADY'S BARGAIN WITH THE ROGUE

Melissa Oliver

MILLS & BOON

First published in Great Britain 2025
by Mills & Boon, an imprint of HarperCollins*Publishers* Ltd,
1 London Bridge Street, London, SE1 9GF

www.harpercollins.co.uk

HarperCollins*Publishers*, Macken House, 39/40 Mayor Street Upper,
Dublin 1, D01 C9W8, Ireland

The Lady's Bargain with the Rogue © 2025 Maryam Oliver

ISBN: 978-0-263-34504-9

01/25

This book contains FSC™ certified paper
and other controlled sources to ensure responsible forest management.

For more information visit www.harpercollins.co.uk/green.

Printed and Bound in the UK using 100% Renewable Electricity
at CPI Group (UK) Ltd, Croydon, CR0 4YY

To my three fearless gorgeous girls.

Always be true to who you are.

Chapter One

1882

You're a Bawden-Trebarr, Eliza, never forget that. It courses through your veins, giving you strength, fortitude, resilience and courage. Attributes that are incredibly important, especially for a woman, and something that our forebear, Elowen Bawden-Trebarr, exuded in every way. So never forget that. And never forget who and what you are...

With her mother's words turning around her head, Lady Eliza Carew née Bawden-Trebarr stood in awe of the huge four-storey building that wrapped itself around the corner of Bury Street, in the St. James's area of London. An area littered with many gentlemen's clubs, except this was unlike all the others.

The Trium Impiorum, or Three Wicked Devils, was the most notorious and exclusive gaming hell in the whole of the country, let alone London, as were its scandalous owners, the Marsden Bastards.

Eliza glanced up at the imposing redbrick building with its bay and arched windows, ornate columns and intricate cornices framing the windows on each floor. She took a deep breath and stepped inside the grand entrance, her heart hammering against her ribs, and blinked several times in surprise.

Well, now, this was not what she had imagined when she'd considered the interior of the Trium Impiorum, not that she knew much about such establishments. Heavens, but the gleaming black-and-white mosaic-tiled floor, with the walnut wainscoting in the hallway, was not very different from any palatial town house in Mayfair. Eliza tentatively ambled along to the large open reception hall with a sweeping stairway to the side, towering potted plants on ornamental stands dotted around, her eyes flicking to the many servants busily cleaning and polishing the dark mahogany furniture. This indeed was not what she'd envisioned a villainous lair belonging to the Marsden brothers might look like. Indeed, it could be the entrance to many sumptuous grand houses rather than the interior of one...

'May I enquire as to the nature of your business here, miss?' One of the doors had opened to reveal an older well-dressed man, with a streak of white running through his hair and a matching neatly trimmed grey beard. Not quite what she had expected of one of the proprietors of Trium Impiorum, not that it mattered.

'I have come to see you in person, Mr Marsden, since I haven't received a reply to my many correspondences to you.' Eliza decided to give the man her most winsome smile in the hope that it might charm him. Sadly, it failed to do so. The man gave her an impatient look that one might adopt when dealing with a rather recalcitrant child. 'Again, I must insist in enquiring who you are and why you are here at the Trium Impiorum.'

'I am Lady Elisabeth Bawden-Trebarr and I believe I have already answered you as to the reason why I am here.' Eliza straightened her spine and attempted to look as stiff and starchy as this man. 'Now, would you please do me the courtesy of granting me a moment of your time…in private, Mr Marsden?'

'I am Mr Hendon, the major-domo of the club.' The man looked her up and down before continuing on with a bored, dismissive voice. 'And if you wish to speak with Mr Marsden, I would recommend that you write again and ask for an audience with him. But I should warn you that he is an extremely busy man and therefore cannot guarantee that you will gain any moment of his time…in private or otherwise.'

'But…'

'The Trium Impiorum is no place for a young woman to visit on her own, either. It will not look well on you.'

Oh dear, this was not going quite to plan but then Eliza was not the most forceful of people, despite her exalted Bawden-Trebarr name and the blue blood that coursed through her veins. Perhaps it was more a trickle in her case, nay a drop, because at this moment she did not feel particularly strong nor in any way courageous. In fact, she felt…

'I shall see you out, my lady.' The man ushered her back towards the hallway and the front door that she had taken a long time dithering outside before finally opening. But she was desperate. So very desperate.

'I think not. I have already written many times to Mr Marsden and gained no response.' She twisted back around to face the man and gave him another smile, this one real. 'But I will have my say, Mr Hendon. And I shall cheerfully stay here all day and all night, until I do. Indeed, I will not leave. Please do convey this message to Mr Marsden, if you will.' Eliza sat gracefully down on a handsome wooden barrel chair, which was probably more expensive than everything she owned put together.

The man must have heard something in her words or perhaps because she was not cowed by him, that he finally relented. The major-domo inclined his head before leaving the reception hall, only to return a few minutes later with the message that Mr Marsden would see her briefly, with the caveat that he could only offer the length of time it took for him to drink his morning coffee. And that would be all. How magnanimous of him. Her impression of the man was not favourable in the least, and this just made it sink even lower.

Eliza followed the major-domo up the gleaming wooden staircase, her eyes flicking to the trompe l'oeil paintings running up the length of the walls, which gradually revealed carnal depictions slowly and deliberately. Only once she had reached the first-floor landing could she see the provocative images as they were meant to be seen. Sprites and cherubs engaged in acts that no sprite or cherub should ever be found in. Indecent, scandalous, shameless but strangely beautiful. Strangely alluring. Still, Eliza could feel herself blushing as Mr Hendon caught her staring, making her quickly look away, clutching the handle of her battered leather portmanteau a little tighter. They walked the length of a long, dark hallway and stopped outside a door. The major-domo knocked, which prompted a low, brooding voice from the other side to eventually answer and permit them to enter.

'Lady Elisabeth Bawden-Trebarr is here for you, Mr Marsden,' the man said before leaving the dark and soulless room scattered with strewn foolscap and ledgers all around the large desk. Goodness, if Eliza thought the major-domo was foreboding, he was nothing compared to the man sat on the other side of the mahogany desk hidden in the shadows, deliberately, it seemed. Good grief, how very dramatic. It seemed as though Mr Sebastian Marsden was set on frightening Eliza into fleeing and all before he'd even finished his coffee. Not very chivalrous, but then the Marsden Bastards were not known for their chivalry. The room fairly crackled with tension, which was really ridiculous since Eliza had never even met him before.

'Thank you for seeing me,' she muttered, nervously shifting her weight onto one foot and then the other. And when Sebastian Marsden failed to respond, she continued to fill the silence, which was not always such a good idea. 'You have a beautiful—' *gaming hell, place of vice and debauchery* '—establishment.'

'Do I?' Heavens, but the man's voice was low and menacing. It fairly sent a shiver through her. 'How so?'

'W-well, the interiors are quite elegantly arranged and the trompe l'oeil wall paintings are…' Good grief, but why did she have to mention those? 'They are quite interesting.'

'Did you take a long, hard look at them before forming your interest, then?'

'Well… I…'

'Yes?'

'Nothing.'

'So, you have come all this way to say nothing?'

'Of course not.'

'Are you trying to make me guess the reason for your visit, then?'

'Are you trying to intimidate me?' she blurted out before she could stop her unruly mouth.

Silence once again filled the room for a long moment before the man spoke again.

'Intimidate you? If I wished to do that, then you would certainly know about it, miss. And I'm not in the habit of intimidating women. This here is me being friendly.'

Friendly, was it? Good Lord, if that were true, then she would never want to be this man's enemy. 'How very obliging of you, sir.'

'Allow me to be frank. I am only being this obliging, this friendly, since you, Miss Bawden, made quite a nuisance of yourself when you threatened to sit at the entrance of my club until I agreed to this meeting. You see, it would not do to have my patrons nor my staff exposed to a witless lone woman entering the Trium Impiorum, seemingly lacking in sense and propriety as she sat in wait for me.'

Witless? Lacking in sense and propriety? Eliza could feel her ire rising but managed to tamp it down.

It would serve no purpose to act all missish because of this man's insults. Not when there were far more important matters at hand. Far more at stake.

'Friendly indeed,' she said sweetly, ignoring his provocation. 'And in the spirit of that friendliness may I say how glad I am that you agreed to see me this morning.'

He picked up his cup and took a long sip of coffee. 'The time is ticking away, Miss Bawden, so say whatever it is you have come to say. But be hasty about it.'

Eliza had just about had enough of Mr Marsden's unpardonably rude behaviour. 'It's Lady Elisabeth Bawden-Trebarr and the usual courtesy afforded a woman who enters a room is to stand, before offering her a seat.'

Mr Marsden lifted the small cup once more and took another long sip of his coffee, his whole silhouette shrouded in the shadowy darkness before placing it down slowly. His head moved up and down as though he was studying her intently, probably wondering how it was that a supposed lady was clothed in such shabby apparel, had such a dowdy appearance. 'I see. So, you have come barging into my club to teach me manners, Lady Elisabeth Bawden-Trebarr?' His low voice drawled out her name slowly and with so much scorn, that she almost gasped. Almost.

'Yes, it is a bit of a mouthful, isn't it? Although I

do prefer Eliza to Elisabeth…' She prattled on as she often did when her nerves started to show. 'And I'd rather use my maiden name of Bawden-Trebarr than my married one, especially now that my husband is dead, which is rather a relief because he is…that is, he *was* rather awful.'

The man sat on the other side of the desk leant forward, his features finally coming into view and knocked the air from her chest. Why, Sebastian Marsden was so…so very dashing, with a wicked gleam in his dark, almost obsidian-black eyes, impossibly sharp cheekbones and features that sat in perfect symmetry. He was quite simply the most breathtakingly beautiful man she'd ever seen. Eliza gasped; she could hardly help it this time.

'If you have quite finished gaping at me, my lady,' he said with a hint of amusement.

She could feel herself burning with shame. 'I would never gape…'

He raised his brow but didn't contradict her. Not this time, as they both knew that she had.

'In any case, I doubt that you came here to inform me of my shocking lack of manners or that you despised your late husband. Dear me and in private, too.'

'Well, no. That is not it at all.' She pushed her wire-rimmed spectacles back up the bridge of her nose. 'And manners cost nothing, sir.'

'*Mr* Marsden or just plain Marsden would do, my lady. And tell me, have you come here to offer your services?' A choked sound escaped her lips, as he paused momentarily before speaking again. 'To teach me manners?'

'Of course not, you're a…' Oh, dear, but why could she not hold her tongue?

'I'm a…?'

The future Earl of Harbury… Or rather he would have been had he, along with his brothers, not been declared illegitimate years ago. But none of that was Eliza's concern. She hardly cared who this man was except for what he now held in his hands. Her property.

'A businessman,' she said instead. 'A shrewd one at that, if one is to believe all they say about you.'

'Oh, and what is it that *they* say?'

'Many things, Mr Marsden. But perhaps I should get to the point of my visit.'

'I wish you would.' He steepled his fingers together, his elbows on the table as he made a study of her. 'However, since I have been reminded several times of my manners, would you care to take a seat?'

'Thank you.' She masked her surprise at this sudden pleasantry and sat down on the chair in front of his imposing desk.

'I am in a charitable mood, Lady Eliza, as last night

was particularly profitable.' He poured more coffee into his cup. 'May I offer you some?' Eliza declined, watching his large hands complete the task. 'Now, how may I be of service to you, Lady Eliza, bearing in mind that time is still of the essence?'

'It is your business acumen that I hope to appeal to, Mr Marsden. And your sense of fairness.'

'And you believe me to be fair, do you? Is this also something *they* say about me, as well?'

'I hardly know.'

'Ah, so you assume that I am fair?'

She smoothed the creases of her overcoat. 'I do not know what to think. But I hope that I, too, am magnanimous enough not to judge a person from idle gossip.'

He smiled, seemingly enjoying her response. Well, that certainly was a first. 'But you do want something from me, do you not?'

'Yes…yes, I do.'

'Good.' The side of his mouth kicked up. 'Because you can dress it up to appeal to my business acumen, as you put it, but I think it best if you say what it is that you actually want from me.'

'Before I do, may I ask why you would sit in the relative darkness in broad daylight?' Her spectacles had slipped down her nose again, as she gazed at the drawn curtains blocking out all the sunlight; the only source of light in the small room coming from the small oil lamp on his desk and the crackling fire in the hearth. 'It really isn't good for your eyes to attend to those ledgers in such reduced light and I should know.'

Judging from the look on the man's face, Eliza knew that she had gone too far in imparting her observations. Yet, it was something that had bothered her from the moment she had entered this dark, rather sparse and messy room.

'And how is it that you should know?'

'Do you always do that?' Eliza frowned. 'Ask a question after being asked one yourself? In any case, my eyesight has always been poor and deteriorated further after years of reading lurid Gothic tales beneath my blanket.'

He leant forward, his large hands spread on the desk. 'Are you ever going to get to the point of your visit, Lady Eliza?'

'Oh, yes, of course.' She smiled nervously. 'Well, let me see, how best to proceed. You see, I believe that my late husband owed a lot of money to you, Mr Marsden. Indeed, he owed a lot of money to many tradesmen, establishments and creditors, many of whom have since been paid. However, he used something to pay off his debts to you that should never have been used, as it belonged to me.'

'And what exactly was that, my lady?'

'The deeds to my ancestral home, Trebarr Castle.'

The man's brows shot up in surprise. 'Yours? You're Ernest Carew, Viscount Ritton's Countess?'

She nodded. 'I was, Mr Marsden. I am now his widow.'

And thank God for it. However, Eliza did not appreciate Sebastian Marsden looking her up and down again, this time as if to ascertain whether she had once been a countess, something she had largely been in name only, since her late husband, Ernest Carew, had rarely treated her as a wife, much less his countess. After a disappointing wedding night, her late husband had viewed her with barely disguised contempt, disparaging everything about Eliza, from the way she looked, *remarkably plain*, to the clothes she wore, *drab and dowdy*, to her interests and her many causes, *mannish and unnatural*. Purely because Eliza was fascinated by the natural sciences and ancient worlds, as well as her interests in politics, social improvements and suffrage for women. Ernest had raged with indignation at everything she did and everything she said. Eliza was apparently too astute, too clever for a woman, far too opinionated and always had a ready reply. In time, nevertheless, he'd worn her down and those opinions and ready replies had eventually dried on her lips. Along with that, his indifference and revulsion of Eliza threw him into the arms of his many mistresses, not that she'd cared since it meant that he indulged in every licentious pursuit while she was left with her many committees and her books. Yet, it was after his death that Eliza discovered the true extent of his debts. One of which had been settled with the only thing that truly mattered to her—Trebarr Castle and all the land attached to it. And she wanted desperately to get it back. Because she might then get her mother back. Her mother, whom Ernest Carew had sectioned in a women's asylum over two years ago.

'I might not resemble a countess in your eyes, Mr Marsden, and frankly, I don't care either way. All I want are the deeds to Trebarr Castle.'

'In exchange for what, Lady Eliza? What could you possibly give me to settle that debt and buy back the deeds to your crumbling old estate?'

'The only thing that you would naturally accept—money. If you could tell me how much he owed you, then I'll arrange to pay it back to you within an agreed time period. In return, I would like the deeds to my castle and all the land attached to it.'

'As easy as that?' Sebastian Marsden watched her for a moment, before a slow smile curled on his lips. It wasn't a particularly nice smile; indeed it was cold and calculating. 'Without offending your sensibilities, Lady Eliza, I suggest that we dispense with the subterfuge.'

What?

'I do not know what you mean.'

'Don't you?' He raised a brow. 'I think you're bluffing, my lady.'

'I… I would not know how.' What on earth was the blasted man speaking about? 'Although, this would be the perfect place to hone such skills.'

'Ah, but you are a far cleverer woman than you let on.'

'Am I?'

'Indeed. You come here in this state, wearing clothing that has been mended more times than you'd probably care to remember, antagonise my staff, antagonise me, for the love of God, and offer to pay Ritton's debts in exchange for deeds? While this has all been somewhat amusing, you and I both know that your late husband was not only a desperate gambler and a profligate, but he also did not have two pennies to rub together.'

'Good of you to notice, especially my apparently shabby appearance.'

'I notice everything.'

She tilted her head and studied him. 'I suppose you must when one considers this establishment.'

'Undoubtedly. I gather details about everything and anything that might prove useful to me and mine.

I pay attention, and avoid swindlers, charlatans and cheats. At all costs.'

Eliza narrowed her eyes. 'And do you believe that is what I am?'

'I have yet to ascertain that, since I know very little about you.'

'As I do about you, Mr Marsden. What I can tell you is that I would have welcomed avoiding cheats and swindlers but alas, could hardly do so, when I was married to one.'

'A regrettable mistake.'

It had been. But how could she have known what kind of man Ernest was until it was too late? Like her father, who'd pushed hard for the match, Eliza had been taken in by his easy charm and affable manners.

'Oh, yes, but we women rarely get the choices and freedoms that men get.'

'Ah, so you're a radical?'

'And if I am?'

'Nothing.' He shrugged. 'Just another observation.'

Eliza sighed. 'As women, we are even more powerless once we're married, with our person and our possessions given over to our husbands, no matter how proficient we are with the finer details. This needs to change.'

'It does and yet it is also exactly my point, Lady Eliza.' He took another sip of his coffee and set it back on its saucer. 'I may believe you to be far superior to your conniving wastrel of a husband, but I cannot believe that while he sold every earthly possession that had not been entailed to his estate so that he could pay off his debts, you, Lady Eliza Bawden-Trebarr, you have somehow managed to raise ten thousand pounds so that you can buy back your fairy-tale castle? Would you honestly have me entertain such nonsense?'

'It is not nonsense and it is not a fairy-tale castle, Mr Marsden,' she ground out through gritted teeth. 'While it might seem like a crumbling old relic, my ancestral home means everything to me.' Eliza leant forward, gripping the edge of the table with her gloved hands, clinging to the hope that it might give her some semblance of support as she felt the balance of this discussion slowly slipping away under the weight of his derision. 'Trebarr Castle has been in my family for generations and as the last surviving custodian of a castle with such significant historical importance, it is beholden on me to ensure that it's restored to its former glory. To preserve its history and its tradition as a legacy for future generations.'

He started to clap slowly. 'A very impassioned speech, my lady,' he murmured, inclining his head in apparent mock deference. 'However, castles, even those steeped in tradition, afforded some inflated importance because they had once been a part of some revolt or had a king stay under its turrets, are just rock, stone and whatever medieval mortar was used. Nothing more.'

She paled. 'Trebarr Castle is far more than that to me.'

'Is it? Will it put food on your table? Will it clothe you? No, I think not.'

'If this is what you believe then why would you accept it in lieu of the money Ritton owed you?'

'Because I am no fool, my lady. I know precisely how much the land that comes with that pile of crumbling stone and mortar is worth. The Trebarr estate sits on premium Cornish land and is worth more than ten times what your dearly departed husband owed me.'

'And what exactly would you do with it?'

'Do you really want to know?' No, she did not but sat there waiting for his answer, anyway. 'I could tear it down and flatten it, and build luxury hotels on the cliff instead.'

She felt faint. 'And you would beggar me in the process, rather than allow me to pay back what he actually owed you?'

He gave her a rueful smile, one that she itched to wipe off. 'I am a businessman, Lady Eliza, as you pointed out, and a shrewd one at that. Besides, and I hope you do not take offence, but how could an impoverished widow such as yourself hope to manage to raise such a sum?'

Eliza flushed with embarrassment. God, how lowering. 'All I ask is for you to allow me the opportunity to do so, Mr Marsden. Within an agreed time. I may not have the money yet but I am confident I can raise it.'

'How, my lady? How exactly do you propose to raise ten thousand pounds?'

No, Eliza would not tell him that. Not just for fear of being laughed out of the room but because it was her last trump card. One that even her late husband knew nothing about, otherwise he would have done everything in his power to find it: the Trebarr treasure...

Eliza needed to find the map, decipher the code and go in search of the treasure, the legend of which had been handed down the generations along the female line, since Elowen Bawden-Trebarr herself. Or so the legend claimed. Her mother had filled her head with stories about two star-crossed lovers—the great Simon Trebarr and Lady Elowen Bawden, who overcame their family's enmity and forged their union with a love so strong it transcended time itself. And the treasure they had left their descendants was supposed to be so vastly significant; a princely sum, if it even still existed, that Eliza knew she had to at least try to recover it.

It might seem futile, it might seem insurmountable,

but it was all she had. Indeed, it was her only hope. And all she asked for was a chance. A chance to find the treasure, so she could not only win back Trebarr Castle and restore it, but have enough money to get her mother out of Helshem Asylum and make a home for both of them. Yes, it seemed quite impossible, but Eliza was prepared to die trying.

She pushed her spectacles up the length of her nose again, her fingers shaking as she did so. 'I hope you do not take offence either but that, Mr Marsden, is none of your concern.'

'Then in that case I cannot help you.'

Oh dear, this was slowly unravelling. 'Please find it in your heart to help my situation. I am not asking for much.'

'You do not get to determine that, my lady. And frankly, I care not for traditions and preserving legacies of so-called great families of these isles. They are meaningless to me. They are part of the past and I am more interested in the future, in commerce, industry and progress.'

'But, Mr Marsden…'

'I'm afraid I cannot acquiesce to your wishes, Lady Eliza. I am sorry for your situation but it is not of my doing. Nor is it my concern.'

God, the man was insufferable. Eliza stood, her fists clenched to her sides, her nostrils flared. She couldn't remember the last time she was this angry. 'It seems that you are as heartless as they say you are, Mr Marsden. It seems everything they say about you is true after all.'

'Yes, it seems that it is.' He also got up, uncurled his long limbs slowly like a sleek panther and stood towering over her even when he clasped the edge of the table that separated them and leant forward. For the first time since she had stepped into this room, Eliza took in the size, the breadth, the sheer magnitude of the man, with his broad shoulders encased in a tailored single-breasted frock coat, with its matching waistcoat, four-in-hand tie and fitted trousers, and all in the same sombre black. All except his stiff turn-down white shirt. His black eyes glittered as he matched her anger with his, adding even more fuel to the fire. 'And by the by, Lady Eliza Bawden-Trebarr, I sit in the darkness because it soothes me. It's my home. It belongs to me but this is no Gothic tale, it is mine.' He knocked back the remainder of his coffee. 'We're done here.'

Chapter Two

It had been three days since Ritton's countess, *Lady* Eliza Bawden-Trebarr, had come into his domain and shaken Sebastian Frederick Leopold Marsden to his very core. Three days since he had been unsettled by her unexpected visit to the club. Somehow, and this was something Sebastian did not quite understand, he actually felt guilty for turning the woman away after she had come to plead her case, which was not like him at all. He never cared about the wishes of the upper order; what the *haut monde* thought was their due. Not even an impoverished countess.

After all, he'd been publicly ousted as the Earl of Harbury and declared to be illegitimate along with his two brothers after the death of their beloved father many years ago. And that had naturally ensured Sebastian maintained such firmly held beliefs. Indeed, the shame of how it had all come about had given him a focus for all the wrongs that had been done to his family. It had given him a way to direct all of his bitterness and resentment towards the very people who'd scorned him and his brothers, Dominic and Tristan, and their mother.

Yet, he had once been a part of that world; he'd been one of them. Wealthy, handsome, young and a leader among his peers, he'd thought that there was nothing that he could ever have want or need of. Sebastian had been coveted by men and women and been destined for greatness. As the future Earl of Harbury, and head of a powerful dynastic family, he had been born with a silver spoon in his mouth.

But oh, how the mighty had fallen…

He would never forget that terrible time when their whole world came crashing down. It had been during the summer term at Eton, after he'd been informed of his father's sudden death. And soon, after rushing to Harbury Hall, Sebastian had found his uncle presiding over a meeting with his father's solicitors clutching a marriage certificate that had oh, so mysteriously come to light, proving beyond all doubt that their father had been a bigamist. Overnight, everything had changed. He was not even allowed to grieve for their father properly in their home, as Sebastian and his brothers were stripped of everything they'd known; their whole lives altered irrevocably. And with the death of their gentle and loving mother barely a year later, the three boys had been left to fend for themselves and forced into the unknown, their future uncertain.

Yet, after all that bleakness, all that heartache, Sebastian had somehow managed to drag them all out of relative poverty, through sheer will and determination. And eventually, the three brothers had had enough capital to open Trium Impiorum—their home, their reason for being, their whole existence. Out of the ashes of doom and all that. Indeed, the exclusive gaming hell tucked away behind St. James's Place, where the rich, the idle and the powerful came to indulge in vice and sin, meant everything to Sebastian and his brothers. It gave him a huge sense of satisfaction to take from the same men, the same peers and idle fools who had once taken from him. No, the irony of that had never been lost on any of the Marsden Bastards…

Which made his reaction to Lady Eliza Carew née Bawden-Trebarr all the more surprising. The woman's husband had not only been a wastrel but a despicable cheat, swindler and everything he loathed in a peer. His drunken fall from a horse resulting in his early death, being just as pitiful. And though Sebastian had never met the woman until she had come barging into his club, he could not help but feel sorry for the young widow, who had obviously found herself in reduced circumstances. Not enough, however, to acquiesce to her outlandish proposal to regain the deeds of the vast Cornish estate now that it belonged to him. It seemed entirely implausible that the lady could get her hands on that amount of money, in any case. And yet, there had been something more that he'd seen in those pretty hazel eyes of hers, magnified by the strangely endearing round wire-rimmed spectacles, that troubled him. It was her desperation. A desperation that he knew all too well. And it did not sit comfortably with him. Not at all.

'Ah, are you still brooding over Ritton's widow?' His brother Dominic, closest to him in age, leant against the open door, *his open door*, with his arms crossed over his chest and an annoying grin on his face. He must have walked into his office without Sebastian realising.

Damn!

'How were last night's takings?' he muttered, ignoring Dominic's jibe.

'Good. Excellent even.' He rubbed his jaw. 'Although Harbury was here again wanting to discuss certain family matters with us, as he put it.'

'Oh so we're family now?' Sebastian scowled. 'And why was I not informed of this?'

Their cousin Henry Marsden had lately inherited the Harbury Earldom after the death of his father and then years later their uncle. The same uncle who had orchestrated their demise. The same man who'd brought about the claim to prove that Sebastian and his brothers were bastards and therefore not legitimate heirs. All in order to take the Earldom for himself and his heirs; not that Sebastian truly believed their cousin Henry had had any part in it, and not that the claim hadn't been true. That was what had pained Sebastian the most. That their father had indeed been a bigamist. That he had lied to them. That it had all been true. He had caused all of that devastation and the early death of their mother. Whether or not he'd meant it was neither here nor there.

Dominic shrugged. 'I didn't inform you because I didn't want to disturb your meeting with Marrant.'

'But I would still have liked to have been informed.'

'Well, I'm telling you now, Seb.' Dominic slumped into a chair and dragged his fingers through his hair. 'And besides, I've handled it.'

Sebastian sighed, not wanting to get into an argument with his brother. His meeting with his bookkeeper had taken up so much of his time during the night that he could not attend the floors. And although the club was doing well, they still remained financially stretched, with most of their profits ploughed back into the business. However, that did not mean that he shouldn't be informed of important news such as the arrival of their cousin to the Trium Impiorum. 'Well, what did Harbury want?'

'The usual. He wants us to cease buying all the unentailed assets that dear Uncle Jasper was forced to sell.'

Yes, their uncle's mismanagement of the Earldom had been a gift from the gods and one that Sebastian and his brothers had welcomed and used to their own advantage. It had started when a few unentailed properties and parcels of land belonging to the Harbury estate came up for auction. Which neatly fell into the hands of the Marsden Bastards soon after. A transfer of ownership that Sebastian had enjoyed taunting his uncle with before he'd died, after everything he had put them through. Especially his gentle and kind mother, who had never gotten over the disgrace of her husband's bigamy. Their uncle could have chosen to protect her; he could have chosen to look after his nephews. Instead, he'd thrown them out of their home, condemned them all to live in near poverty and shunned them, pretending that they no longer existed.

Oh, yes, Sebastian had welcomed this well-deserved retribution, by taking what he could from the Harbury estate, brick by brick. While Henry may not have been responsible for his father's actions, he was still his damn son. And neither Sebastian nor Dominic nor for that matter, Tristan, owed him any of their loyalty.

'You should have told me earlier, Dominic. I always want to be informed of any possible trouble or otherwise, at the time it actually occurs.'

Yet, for all his conviction in knowing that this was Harbury's due, it still sat uneasily with Sebastian when he knew he was judging Henry for what Jasper Marsden had done. Which, despite it all, was wrong and was unfair to Henry. But then, as he'd explained to Eliza Bawden-Trebarr only a few days ago, he had never claimed to be *fair.*

In any case, none of it was Sebastian's concern. He would waste no further time thinking about Henry, the Harbury estate or this unfamiliar and unexpected feeling of guilt that had gotten hold of him today.

'I'll try and remember that next time Harbury comes here, which he said he would keep doing until the day you agree to grace him with your presence, as he put it.' His brother grinned. 'Which brings to mind another thing, Seb.'

'Oh, and what is that?' he said on a long sigh.

Sebastian was tired, that was all. It was obviously the meeting with the young widow that had ruffled him far more than he liked to admit.

'A bit of a problem, actually,' Dominic muttered. 'Which needs our attention.'

'Can it wait?'

'I don't think so.'

Sebastian rose and scrubbed a hand across his face irritably. 'Very well.'

The truth was that Eliza Bawden-Trebarr may have presented herself as a dowdy bluestocking despite her relatively young age, but she did have spirit. She might have been desperate in coming here to plead her case, yet she had not cowered before him when doing so. No, the widow had not been afraid of him, even when he had hidden in the dark in an attempt to conclude the meeting as hastily as possible, which he'd failed to do. If anything, it had made her more inquisitive, tilting her head in that strangely endearing way she had, and asking more and more impertinent questions.

May I ask why you would sit in the relative darkness in broad daylight?

Good God, that one had flummoxed him, and for a moment he'd thought about throwing her out. He never allowed anyone to get under his skin or to get too close, especially someone who seemed to be as perceptive as this woman. It had made Sebastian order one of his men to follow her to her residence after she'd left the club—a small town house on the skirts of Chelsea—just to prove that she hadn't been a hoax. An old mistress out to see what she might gain through Sebastian. He had looked into Eliza Carew née Bawden-Trebarr's situation further and confirmed that she was whom she'd said she was and had been living modestly for a woman who'd once been a countess. Meaning there could be no possible way for her to obtain the amount of money required to pay back her late husband's debt. So why come here in the first place? It made little sense.

Charity...that was probably the most likely explanation. Like all members of the haute monde, the *lady* thought to use her wiles to somehow gain the deeds of her estate for nothing. Or perhaps appeal to his sense of honour and fairness. But he'd soon disabused her of that belief. No, he was no longer the man he'd been destined to be. Instead, Sebastian, as well as his brothers, had fashioned new paths for themselves that straddled an ambiguous existence with no need for virtues such as fairness or honour.

Sebastian snapped his head around towards the window as a sudden loud noise of people shouting and chanting from the street below broke through his musings.

'What the hell is that commotion?'

Dominic strolled towards the window, pulling the curtain to the side and peering outside. 'Ah, that's the problem I was referring to.'

Sebastian scowled. 'Which is what, exactly?'

'Possible trouble, or otherwise.' Dominic nodded towards a small crowd that had gathered just outside the entrance of the Trium Impiorum. 'Your friend has returned. Lady Eliza Bawden-Trebarr, and this time she has not come alone.'

What the devil?

'That termagant is no friend of mine.'

'Interesting, as Lady Eliza contradicted that notion when she approached me a moment ago, introduced herself and appealed to me to summon you, her afore-mentioned *friend*, down.'

'Summon me...?' Good God, she had a nerve. 'This isn't funny, Dominic, and I don't care what she called me! I want to know what the woman wants.'

'The same as before, I should imagine. She mentioned that since her "friendly chat" with you proved unsuccessful, she was resigned to come back here again and try and persuade you. And she would not leave until you agreed.'

Sebastian swore long and low under his breath. 'Well, she will be disappointed once again.'

Dominic smirked, clearly enjoying this. 'You'd best see to her, then.'

'Couldn't you? And while doing so, remove her person from outside the club?'

'I think not as the women she has come with would certainly have something to say about it, and some of them look like they might just bite.'

'What women?'

'Come and see, brother. It seems the lady has brought

reinforcements.' Dominic pulled the curtain back more, allowing a long beam of light to stream into his office. 'Ritton's widow is trouble.'

'That, she is,' Sebastian said through clenched teeth before storming out of the room.

He rushed down the stairwell, bypassing some of his workers who must have had the foresight to jump out of his way as he stomped through the reception area and pushed both of the entrance doors with force, making them fly open.

Sebastian scanned the crowd on the pavement and road just outside the club. Two dozen or so women held banners and shouted slogans, while clusters of on-lookers stopped in their tracks to see what was going on. His eyes flicked around until he spotted the one woman he'd been looking for. The one responsible for whatever the hell this was supposed to be. He tugged the edges of his fitted overcoat irritably as he climbed down the few steps and made his way towards Eliza Bawden-Trebarr.

'What in blazes is this?' he roared as he approached her.

The woman spun around to face him. 'And a good day to you, too, Mr Marsden.'

'This is far from being a good day,' he muttered, dragging his fingers through his hair. 'I would like to know the meaning of this.'

'Oh well, you see, I happened to inform some of my friends from various women's groups of my sad plight. They naturally then decided to lend me their support.'

'Your *sad plight*? Well, that is a misrepresentation if ever I heard one.'

'Oh come now, Mr Marsden, can you not comprehend my situation? Can you not listen to my reasoning?'

'So I am unreasonable because I did not agree to your mad scheme?'

'It is not a mad scheme. It is a desperate attempt to right the wrongs that I believe have been done to me. Surely, you of all people can understand that.'

She was once again saying words that resonated with him; words that made him feel uncomfortable in his own skin. 'And why should I understand that?'

'Because of your past and how you had to overcome it.' The woman shrugged. 'I am trying to do just that, Mr Marsden. Overcome and survive.'

'And by that you mean to take me to task?' He waved his arms towards the various women gathered outside the club. 'By creating all of this?'

'No, I never intended for it to become *this*. It has got rather out of hand. But you see, I mentioned my predicament to a friend and then word must have got around. I had no notion that so many would turn up.'

'Somehow I find that hard to believe,' he muttered through clenched teeth.

'Oh, but it's true.'

'It seems that I underestimated you, Lady Eliza.'

She nodded in apparent agreement. 'Many do.'

But Sebastian was not many. He was a man who prided himself on always being one step ahead of everyone, including an oddity like the woman before him. It was one of the main reasons why the Trium Impiorum was as successful as it was. Because of his attention to detail and always being vigilant. Yet, in Eliza Bawden-Trebarr's case, he had got it spectacularly wrong.

Sebastian looked at the placards the women were holding. One had *Clean London of this pernicious evil* just about fitting it on the placard. Another had *Gambling is evil*. Another that it was *a sin*. As well as *Women resist the wickedness of gambling* in large letters.

If that wasn't bad enough, the women were also shouting slogans. *"No to gambling, no to vice."* And *"Resist this evil from our lives."*

He exhaled through his teeth. 'Who in God's name are these women? And why, for pity's sake, won't they stop this incessant clamour?'

Eliza smiled sweetly and pointed at the small group of disapproving women. 'That group with the placards

about the betterment of morals are the Ladies Association of Social Justice and Moral Correction, who
I admit are a bit stuffy but are rather vocal and think
of themselves as crusaders. I have to say that they invited themselves but were insistent on coming to warn
others of the many dangers of gambling.'

Sebastian pinched the bridge of his nose, trying
hard to keep his temper in check. 'And the other
group, dressed in all that pale froth and lace. The
younger women?'

'That group is one that I am part of and is led by
my friend over there, Miss Cecily Duddlecott. I can
see she is arguing with your brother, whose acquaintance I've just had the pleasure of making,' she said,
nodding towards a young dark-haired woman engaged
in a heated debate with Dominic. Of course, Eliza
Bawden-Trebarr didn't bat an eyelid over anything
that was going on. 'Cecily and I formed the TWERM.'

'The what? Dare I ask what that is?'

'The Women's Enlightened Reform Movement.'

God give him strength. 'Well, whoever the hell you
all are, I want you to leave now, Eliza,' he snapped.

'I do not believe that I gave you leave to use my
given name, Mr Marsden.'

He purposely took a step closer, crowding her. 'And
I did not give you leave to create havoc outside my
doors, *Eliza*.'

This close, he could see the freckles dusted lightly across her nose and cheeks, as though it formed a map, a language he suddenly wanted to decipher. His eyes took in her appearance, again dressed in greys and unflatteringly modest clothing. Yet, her poise was as impeccable as it was elegant. And her little jaunty hat, fixed to the side of her head, did little to cover her glorious hair, pinned and pulled into a tight, neat bun. Good Lord, but it was the most unusual colour, pale and luminous like spun gold. How had he thought her unremarkable or even ordinary? At first glance perhaps, but a further look made him realise that she was uncommonly lovely. His eyes dropped to her full lips briefly before he looked away, disgusted that he'd noticed all of this about her at that precise moment.

Thankfully, she appeared unaware of his errant thoughts as she raised a brow and crossed her arms. 'I am sorry to create this unrest just outside your hallowed doors. However, I do wonder how a gaggle of women standing outside will affect your business. What will your patrons think? What of the satirists, cartoonists and the newsmen once they get wind of this? It does not bear thinking about, Mr Marsden.'

How had this woman outmanoeuvred him so easily? 'You are enjoying this, aren't you?'

'Not in the least. But as a means to an end, it is quite effective, don't you think?'

Whatever feelings of admiration he'd had dissipated instantly. Eliza Bawden-Trebarr was a harridan. A termagant. A vixen. 'What I think is that you should leave now and take this caterwauling group of shrews with you.'

'Now, now, Mr Marsden, there's no need for such language and besides, you can hardly remove us in person.'

'Shall we put that to the test?'

'Stuff and nonsense. You do not own the roads.'

'Try me.'

She took a step forward so she was standing directly beneath him, pushed her spectacles up her nose and glared at him. 'You wouldn't dare.'

'Wouldn't I?' He bent his head so that his nose was mere inches away from hers, as he clenched his fists tightly and resisted the urge to touch her. Her scent teased him. A scent that was fresh and reminded him of the morning dew in spring. He gave himself a mental shake just to dispel such errant thoughts. 'I can get my men out here right now and instruct them to remove every one of you women from the vicinity of the Trium Impiorum. Drag you all away by any necessary means if need be.'

Her eyes glittered with a sudden blaze of anger that was extinguished just as quickly. How interesting. Eliza seemed to be a woman who kept her emotions on a tight leash. 'You would, however, refrain from doing anything so deplorable.'

'Would I now?'

'Yes, because a gentleman would never do such a thing.'

'And as I told you before, I am no such thing.' He let out an exasperated breath. 'Now go, and take these women's groups and ridiculously named associations with you.'

'I think not. I think I shall stay. Indeed, we shall all stay all day and all night until you finally agree to my terms, Mr Marsden.'

'That is blackmail.'

'I'd imagine that someone like you would be used to something like that.' She tugged on her gloves and shrugged. 'I'd say that for *a lone witless woman seemingly lacking in sense and propriety*, I have rather outdone myself.'

Sebastian marvelled for a moment at the cheek of her as she threw back his asinine insults from their first encounter. But only for a moment. 'Why are you doing this, Eliza?'

She pushed her ill-fitting spectacles along the bridge of her nose and frowned. 'You gave me little choice. And by the by, it's Lady Eliza Bawden-Trebarr to you!'

As she turned to move away, in an obvious attempt to dismiss him, Sebastian caught her by the elbow and stilled. Unable to move, shocked by the contact, the warmth of the touch, even through the layers of clothing, he just stared at the point where his hand wrapped around her arm. It momentarily stunned him. And he, Sebastian Marsden, was not a man who had ever been flummoxed, especially by a bespectacled, delicious-smelling bluestocking partial to ill-fitting apparel. Yet, she was doing just that. This mere slip of a woman.

He dropped his hand, as though he'd been scorched by the touch, and took a step back, needing a little distance from this irritating woman. 'What will it take to make you leave?'

'You know precisely what I am after, Mr Marsden. Allow me the opportunity to pay back my late husband's debt in exchange for the deeds to Trebarr Castle.'

'How? How would you acquire such a vast sum?'

'What does it matter as long as I pay back the debt?' She narrowed her eyes. 'Is it so that you can somehow scupper my progress?'

'And why on earth would I do that?'

'How is one ever to know what is in your head? For instance, I still cannot understand why you continually refuse to allow me the opportunity to pay back Ritton's debts.'

'Because I know there is no way in which you can do it, Eliza.'

A slow, mischievous smile spread on her lips. 'O ye, of little faith.'

'It is more the absurdity of what you're proposing than any lack of faith.'

'Then put it to the test, Mr Marsden. Give me six weeks and if I fail to get your ten thousand pounds then Trebarr Castle and all its land is yours to do with as you wish, and with my blessing.'

Somehow Sebastian did not quite believe her. The woman was certainly trouble. And yet, he needed to get her as well as all these other women away from Trium Impiorum as soon as possible. Away from St James's. In this, she had played a masterful card and had been quite correct when stating how bad the publicity would be for the club. As Eliza had so eloquently put it, the ridicule that this news would garner would spell indefinite disaster if this charade was allowed to continue for much longer. 'If I agree to this, you will leave and take these damn women's groups away from my club.'

'Of course, Mr Marsden.'

He narrowed his eyes. 'I don't trust you, Eliza. There is some mischief here, something shifty at play that I just can't put my finger on.'

Her jaw dropped as she looked indignantly at him. 'There's nothing of the sort. I am just a woman trying to make her way in the world.'

'Somehow I think you are the sort to get on regardless.' Even so, Sebastian knew that he would agree to her terms, and with that decision made, an invisible weight fell away from his shoulders. In any case, in this he had little to lose. 'Very well, if you keep your word and leave now, I shall grant you two weeks to pay back the debt.'

'I need more time than that. Four weeks.'

'Three and that is my final offer, Eliza.'

'But that is still not enough.'

He stuck out his hand. 'That is all I am willing to offer. So will you take it?'

Eliza glanced at his outstretched hand and then at him, before nodding and slipping her gloved hand into his. 'I will, although I still have not given leave for you to call me by my given name.'

A ghost of a smile touched his lips. 'I think we can drop the formalities, don't you?'

She raised a brow as she slipped her hand into his. 'Ah, so you permit me to call you Sebastian, then?'

He gripped her hand and immediately felt the heat from her skin, despite the fact she was wearing leather gloves. This was the second time that this had happened when he'd inadvertently touched her. He swallowed uncomfortably. 'No...no, you may not.'

Sebastian let go of her hand abruptly and clenched and unclenched his own several times in an attempt to rid himself of that damnable warmth. That elusive touch. What the hell was wrong with him? It was her, the woman, standing just before him.

'Three weeks, Eliza, that is all you have. Now, I would like you to leave this area as agreed and take all your women's reformists groups with you.' He spun on his heel and strode away needing not a little distance from Eliza Bawden-Trebarr but quite a lot more.

Chapter Three

It had been one week since Sebastian Marsden had finally agreed to allow Eliza the chance to pay back Ritton's debts. One week, and yet she was still no further along in her quest since that day when Sebastian Marsden had stood in front of her outside Trium Impiorum and glared and glowered at her, surrounded by all the women's groups and associations, until he had finally and surprisingly relented.

It had initially been rather amusing watching him as his panic and frustration grew; so much so that she had thought smoke and fire would billow out of his ears and flared nostrils. God, but she had enjoyed sparring with the man. It was probably churlish of her to do so but he'd tested and challenged her to the point that she'd felt invigorated afterwards. In just the same way as she always did after a brisk walk in Hyde Park. And of course, it didn't hurt that he was far more attractive than she remembered after that first encounter in his office. He was the epitome of a handsome if not doomed hero in one of those lurid novels she'd used to read. Tall, dark, brooding; a little too brooding, perhaps. Actually, if Eliza considered him in the cold light of day, the man scowled at her more than anything else. And his almost obsidian eyes were actually a very dark shade of grey-blue like clouds during the heaviest of thunderstorms.

In any case, it was a good reason not to trust her reaction to him when he was near. He annoyed her despite the sparring, and he was far too dangerous to her peace of mind in a way that Eliza couldn't quite fathom. Besides, how could anyone be that beautiful to look at, with all that chiselled perfection, smell that heavenly of lemons, bergamot and sandalwood, yet be someone whom she would happily throttle? The man was abominably rude and exceedingly vexing but at least he had eventually agreed to her terms and given her time to find the money.

Three weeks…

With seven of those days already gone and only fourteen left! Never mind Sebastian Marsden's panic, hers was starting to make her want to reach for the smelling salts. What on earth was she to do? There had to be something…yes, yes there was…to remain calm and concentrate on the task at hand. Which meant attempting to understand the conundrum that was before her on the wooden table…

Eliza looked at the Bawden-Trebarr heirloom, a beautiful ornate small casket box made from inlays of different wood and decorated with the faded colours of the two Cornish houses—of Bawden in gold, brown and blue, and Trebarr in gold, light blue and verdant green. The casket box, which of course would not open to reveal its secret.

It was tightly closed with a solid metal lock hasp screwed to the lid and fastened to a lock plate, which was attached to the side front. The metal lock plate itself was fashioned to look like the *Morvoren* or the Cornish legend of the Sea Maiden, which had been in some way significant to Eliza's ancestors, Elowen and Simon Bawden-Trebarr. But aside from the exquisiteness of the design, the intriguing aspect to the box was that there was no keyhole and no apparent key to open it with. So yes, it was indeed a conundrum. The only way that Eliza believed it might open was if there was a metal disc of the exact design that would fit on top of the lock plate, and when pressed would release the metal lock.

It was Eliza's mother who had given it to her before being forcibly admitted into Helshem Asylum and warned Eliza to keep it safe and not allow anyone to take it from her, especially not Ritton. And this was something that Eliza had managed to do, keep it hidden away in an old worthless box in the attic of their London home until after his death.

Even now, Eliza could recall her mother's words as she gave the box to her.

It was commissioned by Simon Trebarr for his beloved, Elowen. And within the box itself they placed a secret, which has remained intact for hundreds of years, Eliza, and has only been passed down the generations through the female lines. It is said that the treasure contained inside is only to be used if any of Elowen's ancestors are ever in dire need. If that happens, you must find that which would open the box first. Never forget that, daughter dearest, for it is not so easily found...

Meaning this was going to be far more challenging and difficult than Eliza had first believed. The legend of the Bawden-Trebarr treasure was that it had always been kept as a secret, and was devised by Simon and Elowen on their marriage as a way to protect their daughters and all those who came after them.

Yet, for all Eliza knew, the so-called treasure that was apparently hidden inside the box might have been taken years ago. After all, Simon and Elowen had lived in the fourteenth century, so whatever treasure they'd had hidden away that this box led to, might be long gone by now. And yet, if it had been taken, then why go to all the trouble of having the box sealed again and having the thing that opened it so difficult to find? It was rather like having two treasures to discover—one that she hoped would lead to the other.

It all seemed impossible and showed how desperate Eliza was for her to pin all her hopes on *this* to pay back Ritton's debt. But with no other plan in place, this very risky venture was all she had at present.

Perhaps Sebastian Marsden had been right after all, when he had stated that she was bluffing about being able to pay back his ten thousand pounds. How was she going to find even half of such a sum? The man would think her mad if he knew that *this*…this search for the Bawden-Trebarr treasure was the only solution to her woes. Still, she would not give up—not yet.

Eliza glanced at the table with all her notes, findings and books neatly piled up on one side and the box on the other. The answer to the riddle must be here somewhere but first she had to get the bloody thing open. And she had tried everything, to no avail. The only logical solution was that there was a metal plate somewhere that was made especially to fit the lock plate, cut and soldered in the shape of the Morvoren. However, everywhere she had looked from the British Museum to the Ashmolean in Oxford, there had been nothing in any public collections that looked remotely like it. Aside from rushing to Oxford, Eliza had also spent the past week visiting every pawnshop, antique warehouse and vendor in London as well as a handful in neighbouring counties but was once again left disappointed. It was like searching for a needle in the proverbial haystack.

Of course, Eliza could just take a hammer to the box and break into it and risk destroying whatever was hidden there, which would be quite a pointless exercise. No, she had to find a way.

'Any luck?' Her friend and cofounder of The Women's Enlightened Reform Movement, Cecily Duddlecott, or Cecy as she liked to be called, walked in with one of her footmen, carrying the tea tray.

'No.' Eliza slouched in the chair and sighed. 'Sadly not.'

'Then some restorative tea might be in order.' She directed the tray to be set at a side table before sitting on the small floral settee beside it.

This was Cecy's domain—two adjoining small but pleasant rooms decorated with feminine pinks and blues unlike the rest of the austere dark house that her friend shared with her older unmarried brother, Stephen. The jutting chimney breasts in each room with the matching intricately carved wooden fireplace gave the rooms warmth while plump soft cushions and the Aubusson rugs added a touch of sumptuous comfort. The rooms opened out to pristine gardens at the rear, promoting the necessary need for serenity within the heart of the city. A serenity that was far from how Eliza was presently feeling.

She frowned as she stared at everything on the table. 'I cannot help thinking that I am missing something vitally important.'

'You have been saying that for some time, Eliza.' Cecy poured the tea and passed the cup and saucer to her. 'Have you thought of the possibility that whatever fits the lock might not be here in London at all? Why, it might not be in England. For all you know it could be lost, damaged—indeed anything could have happened to it.'

'Yes, thank you for that.'

'Oh, I do not mean to be pessimistic in any way. However, it is best to be pragmatic.'

'I know, which is why I have traced the lock plate capturing every detail and took it to a brass founder near St Pancras to have it moulded.'

'Oh, Eliza, you didn't go all the way to St Pancras on your own, did you?'

This was always a point of contention with Cecy, which was rather silly when it was Eliza who was the widow and her friend, whom she had met all those years ago at the Ravendean's School for Young Ladies, who had never married. Cecy had instead been allowed to follow her dream of being one of the first female students to attend Lady Margaret Hall, Oxford, by her forward-thinking parents, something that Eliza would have desired above all else for herself. However, her father had prohibited it and encouraged her to marry Ernest Carew, Viscount Ritton.

You will be a countess, Eliza, just as a young woman of your lineage should be... Her father had repeatedly said that when she had tried to convince him otherwise and yet, the irony of where that got her never failed to amaze her. Being a countess had, in fact, brought nothing but misery and strife. All ending with her situation as it was, and everything to lose if she did not manage to find the money to pay Mr Marsden.

'Of course, I did not go there on my own. I took Willis.'

'Still, you must take care, Eliza, especially when visiting less salubrious parts of London.'

'I am aware, Cecy.' Willis, who was her housekeeper Gertie's son, thankfully lent himself to being the man about the place despite being only sixteen years old, on the account of his height and brawn.

'Even so, I do worry about you traipsing all over London with just a boy for protection.'

'Thank you for your concern but I can look after myself.'

'I know you can, Eliza, but after visiting the Trium Impiorum and taking its enigmatic owner to task, dare

I wonder whether you are now taking far too many risks?'

'By that you mean behaving in a manner that is reckless, impulsive or something far worse?' she asked wryly.

'Never that.' Cecy sighed. 'However, I think a little caution will go a long way. After all, I can imagine that a man like Sebastian Marsden could be provoked too far.'

'I have no wish to provoke him in any way,' she said a little too defensively.

'From where I was standing that day, I wasn't sure whether the man wanted to kiss you or throttle you.'

Kiss her?

Eliza was equally appalled and intrigued by such an idea. Not that it was remotely plausible for a woman as unsophisticated as she was to have a man like him want to kiss her. And she certainly didn't need to be reminded of her encounter with Sebastian Marsden. Annoyingly, she had been thinking about him far too often as it was, which would not do.

'Nothing of the sort. He's just a man used to getting his own way. And I'd soon as throttle him myself, for all his imperious and arrogant manner.'

The man might be enigmatic and far too handsome for his own good but he also stood in the way of her getting Trebarr Castle back. Not that Sebastian

Marsden believed that she could do it. No, by giving her three weeks to come up with the money he was merely humouring her, assuming she'd fail, anyway and more importantly, using it as a way to get her off his back. The day Eliza could prove him wrong by paying the blasted debt owed to him could not come soon enough! She would then be done with this, all of it. And the only way to achieve that was to get this box open without damaging it.

Eliza peered at the box using her magnifying glass to look more closely at the smaller details of the lock plate, hoping she had not missed anything. 'In any case, I cannot see how you noticed that when you were engaged in such a heated argument with Sebastian Marsden's own brother.'

Cecy flushed. 'Yes, well, he was nothing but a rude, obnoxious scoundrel.'

Eliza suddenly felt a wave of guilt rush through her, knowing that she had inadvertently allowed her friend to be exposed to such behaviour. If Cecy's brother Stephen got wind of it then he would prohibit further outings. And where would Eliza be then? She had few friends as it was. 'Oh, I'm sorry you had to experience that.'

Cecy shook her head. 'Don't worry. I put the man firmly in his place. Abominable rogue!'

'I'm sure you did.' A faint smile curled at her lips. 'It seems that it runs in the Marsden family.'

'Quite.' She took a sip of tea and placed the cup back on the table. 'But it puts me to mind of another family, Eliza. Your husband's cousin, the new Viscount Ritton, Ronald Carew, came sniffing around here looking for you.'

Eliza grimaced and rubbed her forehead. 'And at my lodgings in Chelsea while I was away according to Gertie.'

'He's convinced that you made away with the Ritton silver, or something that belongs to him. He cannot believe that he's inherited an empty shell of an estate. That there's nothing whatsoever left in the coffers.'

'Well, it has naught to do with me. Indeed, he can believe what he likes. The new, and not much improved, Ritton seems to be just like his predecessor and frankly it means nothing to me.'

'Even so, if he gets to hear about this box or even that there's a possible whiff of treasure attached, I cannot say what he would do.' Her friend sighed impatiently. 'Eliza? Are you even listening to me?'

'Of course, I am.' She sighed. 'Ronald Carew doesn't concern me in any way. This box is mine, given to me by my mother, and it has nothing to do with the Ritton estate.'

'Yet, he could still cause you trouble, which is why taking Willis here and there will simply not do.'

'Surely not,' she teased, raising a brow. 'I cannot recall going anywhere as thrilling as *here and there*.'

'This is no time to jest, Eliza. I do not trust Ronald Carew,' she said, rubbing her forehead with her fingers. 'Perhaps I should speak with Stephen about you using one of our servants.'

'Please, Cecy, that is not necessary.'

It was bad enough that Eliza was all on her own apart from Willis and his mother, the ever-faithful Gertie, who had been with her since she was a young girl, as well as relying on the few friends she had, such as Cecy. But it was quite another to be beholden to Stephen Duddlecott, who just about tolerated Eliza, believing her to be a bad influence on his sister. If only he knew the half of it! Ever since the deaths of their parents over a year ago, Mr Duddlecott had become increasingly protective of his unmarried sister. A little bit too protective, in Eliza's opinion. It was as if those years that Cecy had studied at Oxford had never actually happened, and God knew what her brother would say if he knew about Cecy's involvement in their women's group. Yet, she could not begrudge the man for caring; at least Cecy had someone who looked out for her. Stephen Duddlecott might be a pompous bore but at least he took pains to ensure his sister's comfort. And the man had never questioned the fact that his sister had turned these rooms at the back of his grand Belgravia home into a meeting place once a month for The Women's Enlightened Reform Movement, although in truth he was quite unaware of what went on and believed them to be doing some charitable endeavour or other. Even so, Eliza was happy to come and do her research here from time to time, since her own lodgings in her modest Chelsea town house lacked the library resources as well as the space. But she drew the line at using some of Stephen Duddlecott's servants.

'Come now, Eliza. I'm only concerned for your well-being.'

'I know and I thank you for it.' Eliza sighed, glancing at her friend and offering a weak smile. 'But I simply don't have time to fret. However, I shall promise that I will take care, in particular when I visit the less salubrious parts of London. There, are you satisfied?'

'For now, yes, it will have to do.' Cecily returned her smile. 'So tell me all your findings since I last saw you.'

Which was when they had been together outside the Trium Impiorum with The Women's Enlightened Reform Movement as well as the other groups creating quite a stir. Where Sebastian Marsden had apparently looked as though he might either throttle or kiss her.

Heavens. And why on earth was she even pondering on such an absurdity? And at such a time. Cecy must have it all wrong in any case.

Eliza cleared her throat. 'As I mentioned, I've commissioned a mould to be made to fit the lock plate in the hope that it might open the vexing thing. However, that unfortunately is as much as there is to say about any findings.'

'Surely, it can't be as bad as all that.'

'In all honesty, I'm not certain about anything at the moment. All I have done is to have a mould made from a tracing I made of the lock plate. Nothing more.'

'It is an inspired idea,' Cecy said encouragingly. 'Really, it is.'

'It is my *only* idea.' She sighed and shook her head. 'I am starting to worry that I will run out of time.'

'Come now, don't lose heart. Chin up and all that.'

Eliza slumped back in the chair in a very unladylike manner. 'I am trying, I really am, but this is starting to be quite impossible. And the thought of going back to Mr Marsden with empty hands, proving that he was right about me all along, is intolerable, Cecy.'

'Yes, but why would you care about his opinions?'

She sighed. 'I don't know. It's more that I cannot stand the idea of him getting the better of me.' Eliza flicked her gaze to Cecy, who was studying her intently, and looked away. 'Of course, all that matters to me is getting the Trebarr estate back. That was the only reason I approached Mr Marsden in the first place, and where my dealings with the insufferable man begins and ends.'

Cecy smiled, nodding. 'Of course.'

Eliza turned her mind back round to the box, not wanting to linger on anything to do with Sebastian Marsden. 'And to achieve that I need to work this lock out.'

Her friend got up and moved towards her, pulling out another chair and sitting beside Eliza, brushing her fingers over the lock plate. 'It's strange but I can't help thinking that I have seen something that looked just like this before and quite recently, too. Here in London.'

Eliza blinked in surprise. 'You haven't said this before.'

'No, but I've been turning it over my head while you were away.'

'And?' Eliza muttered, hoping not to sound too excited.

'And what?'

'Where do you believe you have seen it?'

'Well, that is just it, Eliza, I cannot recall.'

Her heart sank. Cecy was probably mistaken in her assumption that she'd seen it.

'I know what you're thinking, that I'm probably

mistaken, but Eliza, this odd, irregular shape is not something one forgets.'

'It's not an odd, irregular shape, Cecy. It's the shape of a Morvoren.'

'A Morvoren?'

'Yes,' Eliza said. 'Surely, you've heard me talk of it before? The stories my mama used to tell me about the Morvoren, or sea maidens, as well as other myths and legends.'

'How funny. I never realised the lock was in the shape of a sea maiden but yes, now that you mention it, I can see it.'

'Exactly, you can see the long, wavy hair and the long, swirly flick forming her fishlike body. It even has the detail of her scales.'

'It's quite unusual, memorable, really. I just wish I could recall where I saw it.' Cecy rose and ambled over to the small table to retrieve the three-tier cake tray filled with dainty finger cucumber sandwiches, small cakes and fluffy scones.

'Never mind, it might come back to you. In any case, the Morvoren legend has long been associated to the Bawden-Trebarr history and also with this casket box.'

'I hadn't realised.' Cecy sighed and placed a floral porcelain side dish on the table beside Eliza's tea cup and saucer. 'Anyway, allow me to offer you some sandwiches and scones. There's also a pot of clotted cream and some strawberry conserve.'

'Thank you but the tea is quite sufficient.'

'You haven't had a bite to eat since you arrived, Eliza. And you cannot think on an empty stomach. Come, at least have some of the scones, which were baked today. They're Cook's speciality.'

'Very well.' Eliza split the still-warm scone on the plate and spread the thick strawberry jam generously all over before adding a dollop of clotted cream and spreading that evenly on top. Sinking her teeth into the pillowy softness of the warm scone, jam and cream and taking a bite of the sweet concoction was something she hadn't realised she needed until she started eating. Cecy was right; she needed sustenance if she was to be able to think. 'Compliments to your cook, Cecy, this is delicious,' she said, licking the crumbs from her lips. 'As good as any I've had in Cornwall.'

'Cornwall?' Cecy's eyes widened as her fingers touched her forehead suddenly. 'Cornwall...of course, it's Cornwall! That is the connection. That is where I had seen it!'

Eliza wiped her lips with a handkerchief and blinked. 'What on earth are you talking about?'

'Your sea maiden, your Morvoren.' Cecy stood and clapped her hands together excitedly. 'I remember where I saw it, Eliza. I remember it well! It was at a private viewing of the "Cornwall Collection" by an acquaintance of Stephen's, Sir Algernon Bottomley, which we went to see a couple of days ago at the British Museum. He was showing a collection of geological and botanical findings such as fossils, corals, brachiopods as well as artefacts from the local areas of *Cornwall*.'

Eliza also stood facing her, grabbing her friend by the shoulders. 'Are you certain, Cecy?'

'Yes! I am. I remember out of all the bits of stone, limestone and semiprecious bits and pieces, there was a small collection of beautifully carved and moulded sea maidens—one that looked exactly like your Cornish legend of Morvoren and engraved on a metal disc. That could be the piece that might fit onto this lock plate.'

'Yes, it could very well be the thing. Oh, Cecy, you're a marvel!' Eliza hugged her friend. 'A private viewing at the British Museum, you say? How can I meet this Sir Algernon Bottomley?'

Cecy's smile slipped from her lips and she started to chew on them instead. 'Ah, but there is just one little snag with his collection. You see, what we saw at the museum was a preview of what Sir Algernon is about to take to the Royal Society, with a lecture set for some time this week.'

'When?' Her brows furrowed in the middle. 'When is the lecture happening?'

'I am not certain but I do believe I saw something about it in the newspaper.'

Cecy rushed out of the room only to return with a batch of the week's newspapers, which they started to tear through, trying to find the date for the lecture. Finally, they found it and as Cecy had said it was indeed set for that very week. Two days hence, on Wednesday to be exact, at half past three at the Royal Society.

'Well, that settles it. I shall visit Sir Algernon and try and convince him to…' To do what, exactly? Part with an artefact that was part of his collection? No, that just wouldn't work; the man would never agree and she hardly had anything that might entice him to do so. A more drastic action was needed.

'Oh dear, I do not like that look on your face, Eliza.' Her friend shook her head slowly. 'It's the one that always spells trouble.'

'Oh, not trouble. That is one thing I wish to avoid.' Eliza smiled, her shoulders sagging in relief for the first time in ages. 'Come now, we have only two days and there's a lot to do.'

'I do believe that there's something that you've forgotten.' Cecy looked at her with apprehension. 'The Royal Society and in particular, Sir Algernon, does not permit entrance to women and especially not to his estimable lectures. Heaven forbid that a woman might comprehend his advanced observations. After all, our tiny brains might actually explode from all that knowledge. When I went with Stephen to view his collection at the British Museum, the man was as obsequious towards my brother as he was contemptuous of my presence.'

'Abominable!' Eliza exhaled through her teeth in annoyance on her friend's behalf. 'In that case, I shan't feel guilty for what I intend to do at his lecture.'

'Oh, dear God, Eliza, dare I ask what that might be?'

She smiled. 'Why, to find the correct Morvoren seal that fits the lock plate and steal it from under his very nose.'

Cecy sighed and shook her head. 'Do be serious, dearest.'

'Oh, I am. But I need your help as there is much to do and little time to do it. Come on, Cecy.'

And so it was that two days later, after the mould that Eliza had commissioned failed to open the lock plate of the box, she put her plan into motion. Her big plan. Thankfully, Eliza did manage to gain entrance to Sir Algernon Bottomley's private viewing at Gresham College as part of the Royal Society with a forged letter of recommendation from Cecy's brother Stephen, and dressed as a young man. Well, maybe a very young man with the austere clothes borrowed from another friend's younger brother. Indeed, this part of the plan had gone exceedingly well. Far better than she had initially thought.

And with this part complete came the far more arduous part of locating and then stealing the Morvoren seal, without any of the other guests noticing. In fact, this was what Eliza dreaded the most as she had to wait and formulate a strategy. Which was challenging enough without the presence of the last person Eliza had expected to find there. And the last thing she'd needed. For there, attending the lecture, was her nemesis, Mr Sebastian Marsden.

Chapter Four

Sebastian could not quite believe his eyes. Perhaps he was imagining it; perhaps he was going mad; but there in the stuffy lecture hall sat… No, it couldn't be *her*, could it?

He had come to the Gresham College with his youngest brother, Tristan, to hear a lecture given by Tristan's old Cambridge tutor, Sir Algernon something or other, when he'd noticed a young man coming inside the lecture hall and taking a seat at the back, closest to the door. Nothing out of the ordinary, except that the chap was the oddest person he'd ever seen in every way.

It was his manner, his gait and the general way he held himself that seemed strange somehow. Apart from constantly fidgeting and sitting in an awkward manner, there was something about him that did not seem quite as it should. Something almost feminine, which wasn't that unusual as there were many such young men. But it was something more. Sebastian couldn't quite put his finger on it but the young chap definitely looked familiar, which made him wonder where he'd seen him. Perhaps he had visited the Trium Impiorum; perhaps he'd been sitting at his gaming tables or had drunk himself into a stupor…but no. He did not believe it was that.

Apart from the tawny moustache and side whiskers and the ill-fitting suit, the young chap looked surprisingly like a certain bluestocking who had plagued him recently. A maddeningly annoying woman who had blackmailed him into giving her three weeks so that she could find ten thousand pounds to pay back her late husband's debt. Perhaps the chap was in some way related to Eliza Bawden-Trebarr, although from Sebastian's research into her he'd found nothing that mentioned any living male relatives.

Strange, but the more Sebastian studied the man the more he realised how much he resembled Eliza. He even had the same round wire spectacles that kept slipping down his nose. And the chap kept pushing them back up his nose just like Eliza did…

Good God, it couldn't actually be her, could it? Sebastian kept his eyes peeled to the *chap*, watching everything he did, hoping to determine whether he was finally going mad or if he was, in fact, staring at a mad woman instead. And just when he was about to look away, convinced that perhaps he'd made a mistake, it happened. Sebastian watched from his seat as the *chap* reached across and unbuttoned his waistcoat, pulling it open and scratching his chest over his shirt. Of course, he wasn't scratching anything but adjusting something and it wasn't really his chest at all, but quite clearly the outline of a taped breast! From where Sebastian sat, slightly to the side of the semicircle arrangement of chairs, and with the beam of light from the window, he could just about make out the tape wrapped around the woman's bosom.

He swore under his breath as he realised that he'd been right all along—it *was* Eliza Bawden-Trebarr who was sitting there at the end of the hall, seemingly without a care in the world. The woman must be as addled as he'd initially believed her to be for her to come all this way so that she could attend a boring lecture dressed as a young man. What the blazes was wrong with her? What on earth was she up to now? Oh, yes, mad, quite mad. He wanted to march over to her and demand answers but knew that he would have to wait. He'd have to bide his time.

The room suddenly erupted into applause, signalling the end of the lecture and an invitation to view some of the collection that Tristan's old tutor had been droning on about.

'You didn't have to come if you found it so boring, Seb,' his brother whispered from beside him.

'I didn't find it boring.'

'Then why the hell have you been staring at the door to the side there instead of at Sir Algernon, who was actually delivering the lecture?'

'A speech that you wrote, Tristan.'

'Which I was happy to write, Seb, but that is neither here nor there.'

'My apologies. I was, or rather I became, quite distracted.'

'With what, exactly?' His brother rose and shook his head. 'I can't imagine anything here that might distract you.'

'Nothing, as it turned out. I thought I saw someone I knew but I was mistaken.' Sebastian stood and clasped his brother on the shoulder as he looked back to where Eliza had been sitting, but the chair was now empty. Damn! The woman must have gone somewhere but where? Sebastian darted his gaze in every direction but could not see her. It was difficult in this sea of black suits, dressed as she was.

'Come, let's go and see the collection itself. Unless you'd rather get back to the club?'

Tristan seemed a little prickly, a little nervous, since this seminar with its lecture and viewing was something he had been closely involved in. It mattered to him, all of this—science, geological discoveries, engineering and technological advancement, the Royal Society...academia—in a way that he did not share. Above all else, Tristan worked hard for it, wanting something outside of the Trium Impiorum much to Sebastian's and Dominic's dismay. Both of them had always known that there would come a time when their youngest brother would outgrow the club and would eventually follow his own path. His interests and his intellect demanded a different pursuit, one which did not involve them. Which was understandable, after all that was what Sebastian had always wanted for his brothers: to be able to be in command of their own destinies. But that did not mean he was happy about it. For now, however, Tristan was still keen to hold on to his duties at the Trium Impiorum even though Sebastian knew that it would not be forever; there was an inevitability about this fleeting time they shared.

'Of course, I want to see this collection of yours, Tris.' He pasted a smile on his face. 'Come, lead the way.'

As soon as they entered the adjoining salon, Sebastian spotted Eliza with her back to the whole assembly, looking at one of the glass cases in the collection.

'Apologies, Seb, but Sir Algernon is summoning me over. Allow me introduce you.'

Tristan's old tutor stood in the middle of the room,

surrounded by a group of men, hanging on his every word. Evidently, the stuffy old man wasn't quite finished delivering another speech, but now needed the brilliance of his erudite brother to lend him a little gloss, hoping it might rub off on him.

'You go ahead. I shall join you in a moment.' Sebastian smiled at his brother, who nodded and walked over to stand beside his tutor and field more questions regarding the Cornwall Collection.

But of course, it was *Cornwall*! That was what had brought the woman here... Cornwall. It could be no coincidence that Eliza Bawden-Trebarr was present at Gresham College attending a lecture by the Royal Society about a collection devoted to the same county that her beloved estate was located in. But to what end? And why had she gone to such extremes of dressing as a man just to attend a lecture? Surely, it had nothing to do with her Women's Reform group? No, the more Sebastian thought about it, the more he was convinced that it was not. Which meant that there had to be another reason she was here, dressed as she was. Eliza must have come especially in search of something and it was likely that whatever it was, it was here and part of this very collection. But then again, failing that logic, there was still quite a strong possibility that the woman was completely addled in the head. There was only one way to find out... Sebastian looked over at the back of Eliza and smiled coldly before ambling towards her.

He stood beside the woman as she studied whatever it was in a glass case before her. So intently that she hadn't realised his approach. He stole a quick glance at her, noting that the trousers and jacket she'd donned hardly concealed her shapely feminine bottom. It was quite ridiculous that anyone here could mistake her for a man.

'I am not sure what your game is, Lady Eliza Bawden-Trebarr, but your presence here is unbelievably reckless—even for you,' he whispered.

Sebastian could see from the soft gasp that escaped her lips that he'd surprised her, but not enough to make her give herself away. He could begrudgingly respect the fact that she continued to keep her head low as she looked at the glass case, apparently still studying the artefacts it contained.

'Why are you here, Eliza?' he continued quietly. 'What could possibly have captured your interest that would make you come here dressed as you are?'

'I could ask you the same question, *Sebastian*,' she chided.

'Ah, how lovely. I see you're as quarrelsome and belligerent as I remember.'

'Do you make a point of remembering me?'

God, but the woman had cheek. 'In every detail.

You see, I now have a policy of making certain I vet every young woman who enters my club just in case they're the type who believe that they can blackmail me.'

'Very wise, although if I were you, I'd avoid becoming petulant and unscrupulous in your dealings with them. They might then avoid having to blackmail you in the first place.'

'Are you so adamant to poke the lion, Eliza?' he murmured, tapping a tattoo on the glass with his fingers before spreading them wide on it, mere inches away from hers.

'I assume you are the proverbial lion?'

'Did I say that?'

'Not in so many words.' He moved closer to her, his side brushing against hers before she continued to speak. 'Although, I would hope that I'm astute enough not to do something as foolish as that.'

He stared at the glass case looking for clues as to why she might be here but finding nothing of note. 'Apparently not astute enough to know how foolish it is to come here dressed like this.'

'Shoo! Will you not just go away, Mr Marsden? I do not have time for this.'

'Did you…did you just *shoo* me away?' It seemed that even after such short acquaintance, Eliza Bawden-Trebarr never failed to surprise him. And not in a good way. 'Because I would wager that that would be the most foolish thing of all.'

'Well, you would know all about wagering. And for goodness' sake, keep your voice down,' she hissed.

'How you dare to speak so to me.'

He felt her tense beside him. 'As I said, I do not have the time for this...whatever this is, Mr Marsden. And if you won't leave then I shall.'

As Eliza started to move away, Sebastian reached over and stilled her by placing his finger across her hand—her gloveless hand. The moment he touched her the inevitable spark of heat seemed to spread from that singular spot and travel up his arm and disperse throughout his body. What on earth was it about her? It disconcerted him, unnerved him, how something so innocuous could cause such a reaction. In one way it fascinated him; in another this surfeit of feeling horrified him and made him want to pull away. But he didn't. He kept her firmly in place with that one finger and marvelled instead at the graceful slender hand with its neat, short nails, stained with ink. Despite the softness of her skin beneath his, they were bare hands, working hands, used to toil and trouble but nevertheless aristocratic hands. How she could even think that her small, feminine hands could pass as anything other than belonging to a woman, he'd never know.

'I cannot imagine why you keep on making the

same mistake, Eliza. Believing that you can do just as you please at any time.'

'I do not know what you mean.'

Was it his imagination or did her voice hold a sudden breathless quality? Was this touch affecting her as much as it was affecting him? But then why would he care? So what if she also felt some sort of strange pull towards him. It mattered not. A woman like Eliza should never rouse an interest in him. And yet, she did. That was what appalled him the most. The fact that he found her attractive despite Eliza being a *lady*. She'd been a damned countess and was still part of the upper echelons of society, even if she was now having to live within reduced means. And that was what was unacceptable to him. For a man like him should be drawn to a woman like her.

'Can you not guess?' He grazed his finger along her ridiculously soft skin, stroking up the length of her index finger and down again. Slowly, slowly, wanting to put it to memory. 'First, you come uninvited to my club making demands, then you blackmail me into an agreement I am still not particularly happy with. And now I find you here dressed wholly unconvincingly as a young man so you can hear a lecture and view this frankly uninspiring collection. And for what reason, I wonder?'

'Not uninspiring and not altogether dressed unconvincingly, either. I gained entrance, did I not? I fooled everyone here.'

'Not quite everyone, Eliza. I saw through this little ruse immediately and anyone looking closely at you would come to the same conclusion. So yes, unconvincing. Now, why are you here?'

'It is not your concern.'

'It has something to do with Cornwall, has it not?' Eliza tried to pull her hand away, which meant that he must be correct about her reasons. He wrapped his fingers around hers and clasped them tightly against the glass case. 'I thought it did. And it has also got a connection to Trebarr Castle.'

'Let go of my hand, *Sebastian*. People will see.'

'Not until you answer a few questions, Eliza,' he retorted coldly. 'And yes, people might witness such familiarity between us. From calling each other by our given names to this, holding hands.'

'People will talk and you know that is not something you invite willingly, Mr Marsden.' The coldness in her tone matched his. 'Especially since you seem to have forgotten how I am dressed.'

'As if I could.' He gripped her hand tighter and pulled her to his side, his head bent low as though he were also studying all the small artefacts in the glass case. Thank goodness this case faced the tall bay window so that their backs were to the gathered men behind them. 'What is it that brought you here, eh? There's something here in this case, isn't there? Something that has made you once again take such drastic actions without a thought to your safety, your reputation, or your status. Are you always this reckless?'

'Those things matter to me as little as they matter to you. Now, let me go.'

'No, you shall not set the terms here. Not this time, Eliza.'

She did not speak for a long moment as though weighing up the predicament that she'd found herself in. It was obvious that Eliza had not expected to find him here, or for that matter, be caught searching for something in this glass case. Eventually, she spoke. 'Very well, but I cannot speak with you here.'

'Then where?'

'There you are, Seb.' Tristan ambled towards them, making Sebastian remove his hand from Eliza's and take a step away from her. 'Won't you introduce me to your friend?'

'*Edmund* Bawden-Trebarr at your service.' Eliza lowered her voice, which Sebastian had to admit sounded a bit like a young man, possibly an odd-looking one unless Tristan bothered to look closely. She stuck out her hand for his brother to shake.

'Tristan Marsden.' His brother clasped Eliza's hand. 'How did you find the lecture, Mr Bawden-Trebarr?'

'Insightful, sir, insightful. I have a keen interest in Cornwall since I'm from that part of the world, you see.' Eliza had somehow contorted her mouth, making her jaw jut out, and changed the way she stood to more closely resemble a young man. How preposterous, how unbelievably farcical, this was. 'Anyway, I shall bid you gentlemen a good afternoon. I really must be off.'

'Ah, but before you go, *Edmund*.' Sebastian grabbed the woman's arm. 'About that private matter we needed to discuss?'

'Never mind that, old chap. We can see to it another time.'

'No trouble at all. I'd rather conclude our dealings now if you don't mind...*old chap*.'

His brother glanced from one to the other and raised a brow. 'I see that I have interrupted your discussion with er... *Mr Bawden-Trebarr*.'

Ha, so Tristan was starting to pay attention and could see that *Edmund Bawden-Trebarr* wasn't quite as he seemed. That *he* was actually a *she*. The woman by his side seemed to sense this, too, which meant that Sebastian would have to act fast if he wanted to get answers from her in case she bolted out of here. 'Not at all, Tris, but if you wouldn't mind directing us to a small chamber for us to conclude our discussion?'

'Of course. There is a small room that should serve

your purpose. Outside the hall, back to the main foyer, the third door on your right. All the other chambers and rooms on the ground floor will otherwise be locked.'

'Good. Thank you, this shouldn't take long.' Sebastian gripped Eliza's elbow, ushering her away. 'Come along, *Edmund.*'

'You're holding on to me too tightly,' she muttered from the corner of her mouth.

'I have to, in case you get ideas about running off, Eliza, or stalling this discussion even further.'

'I wasn't going to do that.'

'Oh, yes, you were. I'd rather not take any chances where you're concerned.'

They did not speak again until they reached the door of the room, off the main vestibule, which he opened with one hand and practically pushed her inside with the other. Sebastian blinked as he flicked his gaze around the room, which was not quite a chamber at all but a small storeroom, with a few tables with strange scientific instruments on them, extra chairs stacked together and some bookshelves packed with ledgers and boxes. Apart from the large window there was no other light and the room was exceedingly cold.

He turned to face the woman who had been causing him far too much trouble lately and frowned. 'Well, are you going to explain yourself, Eliza?'

'I suppose I must since you have made clear your intent to interrogate me to all and sundry.'

'My brother is not all and sundry.' He folded his arms across his chest and glared at her. 'Now, tell me why the hell are you here?'

'As you said yourself, I have a keen interest in the county of my ancestral home. Cornwall and everything Cornish holds a special place in my heart—its unparalleled beauty, its very rugged and wild landscape, the blistering wind along the cliffs, the sea battering against them below.'

'Balderdash, Eliza! Spare me the poetic soliloquy.'

'It's true. This small yet important lecture reminds me of home and of everything I miss about the county. And while I lack the necessary funds to go back to Cornwall at present, this was a rather good alternative.'

He shook his head. 'You expect me to believe this tosh?'

She shrugged. 'I do not care either way, Mr Marsden, but it is the truth nevertheless.'

He stepped in front of her, crowding her as he rubbed his chin. 'You would have me believe that your love for Cornwall propelled you to somehow gain an invitation to this frankly boring lecture that contained nothing remotely of unparalleled beauty, and come here in disguise just to assuage your apparent homesickness?'

She nodded. 'Indeed. I could hardly come as my-self since women cannot attend these lectures, ergo the reason for my disguise.'

'It is a terrible disguise.'

'So you have mentioned but it did seem to fool most of the men in that hall, apart from you. Well, and your brother.' She sighed through her teeth. 'And now that we have established everything, I think we've con-cluded this discussion. Good day to you, Mr Marsden.'

As she made for the door, he made a grab for her. 'Not so fast.'

'Will you stop manhandling me incessantly? I have answered your questions despite finding you exceed-ingly impertinent.'

'Impertinent, am I?' He started walking towards her, making her step backwards.

'Very much so. Furthermore, you're…' The woman fairly squeaked when her back hit the wall, her feet catching a small desk as she moved and making the box on top of it fall with a clatter of noise, the con-tents crashing to the floor.

He scowled at her. 'Now, look what you have done. I should imagine that has alerted everyone to our pres-ence here.'

'Good. I've had enough of your insolent, ill-mannered and frankly boorish manner.'

'You have such a way with words, don't you? Not that I agree with being referred to as boorish. The others, though, I'll accept happily.' He stepped closer, placing one hand on the wall above her head, effectively pinning her against it. And with the other he started to peel off her moustache, side whiskers and the other bits and pieces of her terrible disguise.

'Ouch!' she cried, rubbing the side of her face and chin. 'Will you stop it? I still need the whiskers when I leave this blasted place.'

'No, you don't. You fool no one with or without them.'

She narrowed her eyes. 'I know what you're about. You're attempting to intimidate me again.'

'And why would I do that?'

'For some nefarious reason of your own, no doubt. But I shan't fall for it. For I tell you that it won't work, Sebastian.'

His lips quirked into a smile; he couldn't help it. She was highly engaging if not strangely endearing at times. He leant forward, catching her chin between his fingers and tilting it up. 'Do you know you do that, Eliza? Every time you get flustered and annoyed with me, you call me by my given name.'

He watched as a pink hue washed across her face,

drawing out the dusting of freckles on her nose and cheeks, and he had a sudden compulsion to brush the tip of his finger across them. Annoyed with his musings he spread his hands against the wall further away from her, just to avoid such a temptation.

'Since you make free of my name, I think it only right that I call you by yours. And I have only ever been flustered and annoyed with you, so that is neither here nor there.'

'Believe me, the feeling is mutual.' He bent his head so that they were now practically nose to nose. 'Now, I shall ask you one last time, why are you here?' When she did not respond, he continued to speak so that he could get some sort of reaction from her. 'You have come looking specifically for something here. Something to do with Cornwall and something that was in that glass case, I believe. I want to know what it is and why you seek it.'

He watched as she sank her teeth into her plump lower lips, her brows furrowed as though she was weighing up whether she should disclose all of it to him or not. She lifted her head and shook it defiantly just as they heard a disturbance in the hall outside the room.

'I say, did one of you hear where that crash came from?' a man's voice boomed from outside.

Damn!

Sebastian groaned inwardly as he screwed his eyes shut for a moment. What dashed bad luck. He opened them again to find Eliza's eyes pleading with him to remain quiet.

Well now...

'You know, Eliza, as far as I'm concerned, an institution such as this should admit women through its hallowed halls, as you call it. But they...' he whispered, pointing to the door. 'They do not.'

'Do you take me for a simpleton?' she hissed. 'Naturally, I wouldn't be dressed like this if I didn't know that.'

'Quite.' His lips curled upwards. 'And if you do not tell me the real reason why you're here, then sadly I'll be forced to tell them that there is a woman in their midst. Imagine what it would do to their delicate sensibilities.'

'You wouldn't dare.'

'Oh, I would.' He grinned, enjoying this far too much. 'You have *five* seconds to tell me...'

'Of all the insufferable, presumptuous men I have ever had the misfortune to meet, you, Sebastian Marsden, are without doubt the...'

'*Four*... You are running out of time. I do hope you don't make a habit of it.'

Her jaw was clenched so tightly, he was worried she might inadvertently break a tooth. 'You annoying, infuriating…rogue. You blackguard… You, you knave… You rantallion fopdoodle.'

'*Three*… My my, you're inventive with your insults. And you don't know what rantallion means.'

'I do since you're standing right in front of me.'

Sebastian had to stop himself from laughing out loud, finding it too much that Eliza had just insulted his manhood without even knowing it, judging by the confusion on her face. '*Two*… Oh dear, is that the Gresham men I hear outside these walls? Do you want such influential men to know of your true identity? Tsk-tsk, it shan't look well for you. What with you being a *lady* and all.'

'Stop it.'

'Not until you tell me the truth, Eliza.' He raised a brow. 'Well?'

'No, I think not.'

'Alas, you give me no choice… *One*.'

Just as Sebastian opened his mouth to speak, Eliza rose on her tiptoes and pressed her lips firmly to his, surprising and silencing him at the same time. He was too stunned to move, too shocked that the woman had resorted to…to this.

Good move, Eliza, he wanted to say, begrudgingly admiring her audacity. Of their own volition Sebastian's arms curled around her small waist, pulling her tighter towards him as he heard the muffled shouts and cries from somewhere behind him, as the door to the room began to open. He no longer cared, even as he made certain that his much larger body obscured her identity from the men's gazes behind them. Pompous fools the lot of them. But none of it mattered. The only thing that did matter was that Eliza Bawden-Trebarr was kissing him. And just as shocking was the fact he was kissing her back…

Chapter Five

Eliza looked from one brother to the other as they sat inside the closed carriage in total silence. They were making the short journey back from Gresham College in the city to The Trium Impiorum in St James's from what she had understood. Not that she had been actually informed of any of it. The two Marsden brothers had acted swiftly and bundled her out of the storage room as fast as they could to avoid any further embarrassment, with all those men from the Royal Society glaring at her as though she was a veritable She-Devil once they realised that a woman had infiltrated their precious male-only institution. And by keeping her head down, her face covered and the two much larger men on either side of her, she had somehow managed to leave Gresham College pretty much unscathed.

She glanced across to Sebastian sitting in the corner with his eyes turned away, looking out the window, and she sighed, quickly dropping her gaze to her hands clasped tightly together in her lap.

Well, perhaps not quite unscathed…

Dear God, but what had she done? She had hurled herself against Mr Sebastian Marsden, pressing her mouth to his just so she could silence the man from uttering her name! Of all the ridiculous schemes that Eliza had ever been a part of, that had to be the worst. What in heaven's name had she been thinking? The trouble was that she had not been thinking at all; indeed, she had not given any thought as to where she was or what she was doing. None whatsoever. The only thing that had seemed to matter in that moment was that the blasted man was so impossible she'd felt obliged to prevent any more words from being uttered by those same lips she had kissed. And she had momentarily succeeded. She had shut him up, surprising him as well before he had kissed her back… He'd kissed her, Eliza Bawden-Trebarr, back!

As well as all that, she now knew the feel of his lips on hers; incredibly soft. She now knew the shape of his mouth as it covered hers, slipping and sliding as he'd kissed her. She also knew what it felt like to be held in his strong arms. And what it was to be crushed against him, so that she could feel the ripple of warmth emanating from his skin despite all their layers of clothing.

Good Lord. She could feel herself getting warm just thinking about it!

Eliza was, however, mortified to recall the look of absolute shock and disgust on his face as Sebastian suddenly came to himself and realised who it was he was kissing against the wall in the back of the storage cupboard with disapproving spectators looking on in the hallowed halls of Gresham bloody College. No wonder the man couldn't even bring himself to look in her direction now. And Eliza was somehow supposed to sit in this carriage and pretend that none of it had happened, as though she was perfectly amenable to returning to his gaming club and explaining the reasons for "all of it" to him, even though she had walked out of the Cornwall Collection without being any closer to getting hold of the seal fashioned in the shape of the Morvoren.

It was the excitement of finally locating the thing in the first place that had made her careless. It had made her unaware of Sebastian Marsden's approach as she was staring at the Morvoren seal until it was too late. And really, she ought to have known better; she ought to have been on her guard when she'd spotted the man in the audience. But Eliza had been complacent, believing that he couldn't possibly see her. Why should he? Her disguise was supposed to have worked; it was supposed to shield her from his notice. But notice her, he had, and at the most inopportune moment. When she'd been quietly jubilant at finally, finally finding what she had been searching for all these months ever since Ritton's death. Eliza ought to have slipped away the moment she had found the seal, so that she could then devise a way to come back and filch it, but instead, she'd continued to stand in front of that glass case, waiting for trouble in the form of Sebastian Marsden to arrive and torment her. So much so that she'd ended up losing her mind! Dear Lord, the man was maddening, and infuriating and arrogant; abominably so. He took particular delight in vexing her again and again. Yet, she was loath to admit it but well, the man could certainly kiss a girl senseless!

Eliza flicked her gaze to the younger Mr Marsden—*Mr Tristan Marsden*, who resembled his older brothers greatly except for his lighter hair and cerulean blue eyes that she detected behind the metal-rimmed spectacles similar to her own. Tristan looked just as furious as his brother but for obviously different reasons. He would naturally blame her and possibly his older brother for embarrassing him in front of his Royal Society peers. From her understanding it seemed that he was in some way connected with the lecture and curating the artefacts from Cornwall. And well, for that, Eliza could hardly blame him. She had caused all that uproar along with the young man's own brother, so his scowl was well placed.

'I wish to convey my deepest apology, Mr Marsden,' she said with a small smile, hoping to coax one out from him in the process.

'While I might at a push accept your apology, Eliza, it does not in any way mean that you can renege on your explanation for all this madness,' Sebastian Marsden muttered coolly.

'Then it is a good thing because my apology was not directed at you but your brother.' Her retort earned her a flash of a grin from Tristan, who then inclined his head at her.

'I thank you, my lady.' The young man regarded her with a faint smile before continuing. 'And was it really true that you were there because you were desperate to see the collection?'

'Oh, very desperate, Mr Marsden.'

'What? Tristan, you cannot seriously believe any of the nonsense she spouts.'

'*She*, however, is telling you the truth, Mr Marsden,' Eliza said, ignoring the elder Mr Marsden and keeping her eyes fixed on the younger man. 'I was enraptured by Sir Algernon Bottomley's fascinating lecture, and as for the artefacts of my beloved county, all I can say is that they were sublime, truly sublime.'

A surprised laugh slipped from Tristan's lips as he

shook his head. 'I had not realised that was the real reason for your presence at the lecture, my lady.'

'I can believe it. Your brother did rather paint me in a very unfavourable light,' she said, softly ignoring Sebastian indignantly huffing and puffing in the corner. 'You see, I have always been particularly taken with everything that hails from my native Cornwall. From the artefacts made from Cornish granite, sandstone and slate to the majestic native flora and fauna and of course the agate gemstone, or the *vicus crystallis* in all the opaque colours that can be found.'

'I am amazed and honoured by your interest, my lady.' Really, Tristan Marsden was rather more mannerly than his brusque and frankly hostile brother. And handsome, too, in a boyish manner with that flop of brown hair over his eyes and that one dimple that popped in his cheek when he spoke so earnestly.

'Oh, it's far more than just merely an interest, Mr Marsden.' She leant forward. 'You see, Cornwall is in my blood. It's made me into the woman I am today.'

Tristan glanced at his older brother uncomfortably at the mention of bloodlines and belonging, which made Eliza feel a stab of regret briefly before he turned his attention back to her.

'Then I can appreciate why you would want to attend the lecture today, my lady.'

'Oh, yes, and please do call me Eliza.' She smiled broadly.

'Very well, Eliza. As long as you call me Tristan.' Dear me, but had Sebastian just growled at them? Irascible man. She would continue to do him the courtesy of pretending he was invisible even though the man took up most of the space in the carriage as he sat back against the plush leather squabs.

'And again I would like to extend my sincerest of apologies to you for causing all that distress at Gresham College, Tristan.'

'Please.' He waved his hand. 'Think nothing of it. I'd like to think that I'm progressive enough, Eliza, to believe that women should have the right to be admitted into such institutions as Gresham College and the Royal Society. I hope that one day soon this will be the case, so that you can come and enjoy the lectures and seminars without having to resort to such extremes as you were forced into.'

Eliza immediately warmed to him. He was so refreshingly honest, so naturally pleasant, so amiable and accommodating...

'Bah, no one can force Eliza Bawden-Trebarr to do anything. She's as obstinate as an ox!'

Unlike his infuriating older brother.

'Take no notice, Tristan,' she muttered, refusing to look in Sebastian's direction despite the obvious provocation. 'I'm afraid that your brother doesn't much approve of women like me.'

'Women like you, eh? Troublesome, meddlesome, infuriating minxes? Is that the type you refer to?' Sebastian snarled.

Eliza gasped loudly and screwed her eyes shut, covering them with her fingers.

Tristan stared at his brother with incredulity and horror. 'Good God, Sebastian! I have never known you to be like this. That is totally uncalled for. I insist that you apologise to Lady Eliza this instant.'

'No, no, that will not be necessary,' she said quickly between sniffling and peering gleefully at Sebastian from beneath her fingers. And found the man was staring right at her, his eyes sparkling with a flare of anger, his brows risen. Oh dear, he was not amused. But did Eliza care? Not one scrap. She needed to get Tristan on her side, especially since he was the one who was connected with Sir Algernon Bottomley's Cornwall Collection.

Of course, that was it! Eliza was suddenly struck by a marvellous idea. What if she could manage in some way to convince Tristan to help her borrow the Morvoren seal, even temporarily, just so she could finally open the Bawden-Trebarr box and find out the secrets it possessed? He could then take it straight back to the collection and no one would be any the wiser.

Well, other than Sebastian, who now looked as though he could read everything that was going through her mind, and by the slow shake of his head, he was telling her that he knew exactly what she was up to.

What is your game?

Sebastian had asked her earlier and quite frankly she had not known how to respond. She still didn't. The last thing she wanted to do was to confide in him, as he'd think her even more addled than he already did. Eliza could just see his face now if she explained the truth to him as he expected her to; from the reason why she had been at Gresham College, to the Bawden-Trebarr treasure—the very treasure that she was pinning all her hopes on finding so she could pay back the debt to him and recover her estate. If she told him everything, she'd risk not only his ridicule but would also likely never hear the end of his sardonic laughter as he'd mock and pity Eliza for her hare-brained scheme. As well as that he'd probably rescind their agreement to give her time to pay back the money. No, she could not tell him any of it but then she didn't know how she was supposed to avoid doing so. Especially as he was keeping a close eye on her in case she *bolted* as he'd put it.

Of course, Eliza could attempt to trust him and ask for his assistance. After all, the man had protected her when they were caught in the storage room, and he had assisted her out of the college, shielding her from the hostility of the glowering gentlemen. And he had kissed her back as well, which was neither here nor there, since it must have been a lapse in judgement, just as it was for her.

'Either way, my brother's comment was unpardonably rude, my lady... Eliza, so allow me to apologise in his stead.'

'You are too kind, Tristan.' She reached out and placed her hand over his and smiled. 'Your brother has been thoroughly provoked today otherwise I cannot imagine he'd ever mean to be so unthinking and impolite, especially to a gently bred woman.'

Sebastian flashed her a stony glare but did not respond. His temper she sensed was stretched so thin that it might snap at any moment, and despite everything she did not want to aggravate him into doing that. He had helped her after all.

'Even so, he should not have taken out his bad mood on you, Eliza. It was hardly your fault.' They both ignored Sebastian's indignant grunt as he shook his head and turned to look out the window again. 'Anyway, I do hope you managed to see the various agates that were on display before your unfortunate discovery.'

'Yes, I particularly liked the display of the sea maiden artefacts. There were so many fascinating exhibits that I noticed, from the medieval boxwood hair comb, to those little tins. All with the distinctive *Mor-voren* design on the pieces.' Eliza bit into her bottom lip knowing that this was her one chance to get Tristan invested in her scheme, while his older brother's attention was diverted elsewhere. 'But there was one in particular that I was studying for a…a pamphlet, an essay, if you will, that I hope to write, in regard to Cornish myths and legends. However, unfortunately, I did not get to take in all the details and intricacies of it, since I was interrupted while I was making my study and putting it to memory. Alas, I attended the lecture with nothing to document it.'

'Oh, I see, that is most unfortunate.'

'Yes, it was rather.' She nodded. 'Very unfortunate.'

Tristan rubbed his jaw in the same way that she'd witnessed his brother do when he was pondering on something. 'They were quite special pieces. Exquisite, really, and I was rather pleased to be able to include them in the collection, much to Sir Algernon's disinterest, who viewed them as historical fripperies.'

She weighed up again how much she ought to say, how much she should disclose and how much she should hold back. Trust, after all, was not something that came easily to Eliza having had it abused by others far too often. And yet, if she said nothing then she was likely to lose whatever sympathetic ground she had gained with Tristan.

'Not everyone can see the value, the true worth of artefacts associated with myth, legend and folklore but those relics, those fragments from a bygone era, are imbued with stories that matter, the stories that give us hope and bind us together collectively. Indeed, they give us a sense of who we are and where we have come from.' She shrugged before continuing. 'I suppose that is why they're so important to me. And why I'm grateful that you had the foresight not to dismiss them as mere historical fripperies, Tristan.'

The moment Eliza lifted her head she knew she had revealed a bit too much about herself as both men were now staring at her intently. Even Sebastian, whose earlier irascible hostility seemed to have been replaced by a strange wistfulness, as though he was recalling now something that he'd forgotten, something perhaps from his own bygone era. A time, possibly, when he might have been free from the worry, obligation and responsibilities that pinned him down as they must do now. A time when he had been cosseted, looked after and cared for. And in that one single moment Eliza perfectly comprehended him, this surly, proud and rather imposing man. She could empathise with the man who'd had little choice in being foisted with the heavy burden of duty and responsibility. After all, she had had a similar experience when her father had encouraged her into accepting a loveless marriage, just because it came with a noble title. None of which she had actually wanted.

Just as swiftly, however, the man turned away, just as she did, annoyed with where her musings had quickly travelled to, and at thinking of anything other than the task at hand—to get the Morvoren seal back.

Tristan coughed and cleared his throat, drawing her attention back to him. 'Yes, that was why I knew I had to find a way to include those pieces. For the er…reasons you so eloquently mentioned.'

He really was a lovely young man, and Eliza hoped that she could somehow encourage him to take pity on her cause and help her. He was, after all, the only person who could.

She sighed deeply in rather a dramatic manner and heard Sebastian snort. Eliza ignored the man. 'But alas now I doubt I would be afforded another chance to capture their likeness.'

'Please do not despair, Eliza. I worked very closely on the collection and can always come up with a scheme for you to have another chance to capture the likeness of those artefacts, as you put it, for your research.'

She raised her brows, genuinely touched at his generosity. 'You can?'

'Yes,' he muttered, covering her hands with his. 'If anyone can, it is I.' He paused to smile almost triumphantly, knowing he was the one to solve Eliza's dilemma before continuing. 'The pieces you're interested in can be brought to you for your attention but only for a short while before I have to return them.'

Eliza gripped his hands in hers and returned his smile. 'Oh, that's wonderful, Tristan, you are such a marvel. I am so indebted to you. Really, I am.'

'I hate to intrude on such glad tidings but I cannot sanction you to help Eliza, Tristan. Not until I have a full understanding of her reasons for being at Gresham College.'

His brother frowned. 'But you heard the lady's reasons.'

'Did I?'

'Yes. They might not be to your liking but Lady Eliza explained herself quite admirably.'

'Well, I am gratified that you are able to bestow such admiration on the lady, Tristan, but I am not so easily convinced.'

Eliza rolled her eyes. 'But that is only because your brother has allowed his dislike of me to govern his judgement.'

'Judgement? Dear me, but you are quite outside of enough, Lady Eliza,' Sebastian said coldly, brushing his hand up and down his face irritably before he leant towards her. 'I cannot believe you would stoop this low to get what you want. But enough of this obvious attempt to beguile and mislead my brother. It is intolerable.'

'How dare you. I am doing nothing of the sort.' She was outraged even though she knew deep down that the man might be a tiny bit correct. But God above, *beguile*? She could never do that, since she knew not how. And all that aside, Eliza was not that unscrupulous.

'You might fool him but you do not fool me, Eliza.'

'Sebastian! What are you about?' Tristan scowled at his brother. 'It's outrageous that you continue to show such unwarranted incivility towards Lady Eliza. I cannot comprehend you.'

She flushed as she placed a hand on Tristan's arm. 'I am certain that your brother has your best interests at heart, but he would have you believe that I am trying to take advantage of your involvement with the Cornwall Collection and that, more than anything else, is rather unfair.'

'It is indeed.' Even in the relatively dim enclosed space of the carriage she sensed the growing tension between the brothers.

Glancing at Sebastian so stiff, so terse, as he sat there almost in disbelief that a mere woman was, heaven forbid, challenging him, Eliza wondered whether he might have suited being a military man instead of a gaming hell owner, barking orders and demanding to be obeyed. And in a sense perhaps that is what he did, anyway, since he was the king of his domain, exuding absolute authority, with his brothers as his lieutenants. So it must gall him that his youngest brother was presently chastising him with his mutinous behaviour.

'Ah, so you're telling me that you believe Eliza managed to cajole me into giving her time to pay back her late husband's debt so that she could regain her precious estate in...yes, Tristan, *Cornwall* of all places. And yet, this has nothing to do with the fact she came dressed as a man to your lecture and take note of the intricacies of some artefact or other because she now has time to write an essay? Come now, you cannot believe this rubbish.'

'Even so, I share the same view about these artefacts as Eliza does.'

The man grimaced. 'Surely, you don't believe all this guff about *fragments from a bygone era*, which are apparently *imbued* with some story or other that somehow matter?'

'I do, yes.' The younger man shrugged.

'Then more fool you. All this nonsense about finding hope... It's nauseating enough to cause indigestion.'

'Surely you're not mocking me, Mr Marsden?'

'No, I am saying that you're a fraud, Eliza.'

'That is not true.' She gasped, taken aback. 'But you, sir, are a cynic. How very unfortunate that you view the world as you do.'

'I prefer to be called a realist. It is far preferable than having some sentimental romantic view of the world. Otherwise, one of these days you might just get your fingers burned unexpectedly.'

'And who says that they haven't already been?'

Sebastian caught her fingers in his hands, lifted them and nodded before dropping them unceremoniously. 'I am.'

'How dare you?' she said in a clipped tone, trying to tamp down her anger. For some reason this annoyed her far more than anything he'd ever said to her in their short acquaintance. 'You make such assumptions about me, about my past, yet you know nothing at all about the life I have lived,' she muttered quietly.

This somehow stunned the man into silence as he locked eyes with her, as though trying to decipher the truth in what she'd just stated. Not that she cared one jot. The man could go to the devil for all she cared but found that in this moment where the air fairly crackled between them, where they were confined in such a small airless space, where they were locked in some sort of battle of wills, it was suddenly impossible to avert her gaze. She drew in a long breath, steadying her heartbeat and allowing a little of the curiosity that she'd always held about Sebastian Marsden to creep in. He was holding himself perfectly still, tempering his emotions, his judgement and rationale to hold on to his steadfast beliefs. Careful, always so very careful not to give himself away. His face was almost inscrutable, all but the glint in his eyes and the twitch in the corner of his mouth.

'No,' he muttered, eventually breaking the strange, awkward silence. 'I would never dream to pretend to know anything about your life, Lady Eliza. However, I can make a fair assumption about you and anyone else who holds on to the past as though it is something that is living and breathing, imbuing it with such a force of feeling and sentiment that it overflows with a surfeit of emotion.'

Eliza was becoming so angry that she could feel herself getting hot. 'You assume far too much.'

'Do I?' he asked coldly.

'Yes, for that surfeit of emotion and feeling that you so evidently abhor goes into creating beauty. It goes into creating art. And if we're really lucky some of that manages to stand the test of time and become fragments from a bygone era, which again binds us to the same surfeit of emotions that initially created them, whether you like it or not. It speaks to us with a voice so that we might understand, that we might better appreciate what it meant, and contrary to what you believe, it's a voice devoid of sentiment.'

He fixed her with an unblinking gaze that made her feel as though she were stripped bare, which was hardly helped by such a rousing passionate speech.

Tristan coughed again, drawing her gaze away from his older brother. 'I, for my part, would be very happy to help you, my lady,' he said, breaking through the tension between them making Eliza blink and look back towards the younger man. For a moment she had forgotten that Tristan Marsden was even there. But he was. Indeed, he was the one who could help her with her predicament, if only she did not need to get around the older brother as well. She should be trying to be far more accommodating and certainly remorseful rather than constantly going toe to toe with the man and aggravating him further. Eliza wouldn't be surprised if she had all but ruined her chances despite Tristan's intentions. None of it could happen if Sebastian prohibited him from helping her. But by God, his condescension, his general dislike of her, was difficult to bear, even though she knew she ought to disregard it. The fact that the man found her so wanting bothered her more than it should, but she knew that was because it felt far too familiar. It was a sentiment shared by most men she came into contact with, except perhaps Tristan, who seemed more of an anomaly.

The carriage suddenly came to a halt, signalling that they'd arrived at the Trium Impiorum. 'You are in luck, Lady Eliza,' Sebastian drawled, the earlier intensity between them all but dissipated. 'It seems that my brother is willing to help you and bring you these fragments of history that you're so keen to observe.' He opened the carriage door and stepped outside and motioned for his brother to follow suit. 'However, you shall come here to do so, under my supervision, where I can in turn understand what you are about, especially since I have been reminded how very little I actually know about you.' He took a step back and addressed the groom. 'Carter, drive Lady Eliza home. Until tomorrow evening at six, I bid you good night.'

Chapter Six

Sebastian could not remember the last time he'd been so thoroughly outmanoeuvred with the aid of his youngest brother, no less, and by a damned infuriating woman bent on creating chaos wherever she went. Eliza Bawden-Trebarr had unequivocally ruffled him from the moment that he'd seen her dressed so ridiculously at Gresham College to having to steal her away for a private chat in the store room, to that surprising kiss, which just for a moment had made him revel in having the woman finally in his arms so he could learn everything about her; from her scent, the taste of her mouth to the feel of her magnificent curves so exposed to his touch in that scandalous attire. And then he'd remembered who it was he was holding, who it was that he was kissing and where they happened to be.

Bloody hell!

He could not recall the last time that he'd felt so unnerved. It had left him visibly shaken and unable to even meet her eyes in that confined carriage as she'd simpered and smiled at Tristan. He was so outraged to be duly dismissed that for one mad moment, he'd wanted to hurl his brother out of the carriage so that he might continue with where they'd left off with that kiss. Madness indeed. The more time he spent with Eliza, the more he wanted to know more about her despite how much she aggravated him. The woman was undisciplined, impulsive, impetuous and impossible. And the fact that he'd acquiesced to her wishes to study those *fragments from a bygone era* that she'd supposedly gone to Gresham College for was astonishing. But even more so was the uncertainty that flickered across her features as she'd attempted to decipher everything about him, as though he was also a puzzle she needed to solve.

And all because he hadn't shared that sentimental nonsense about how relics and artefacts from the past somehow possessed a link to the present. By showing anyone, apparently, who they were and where they were going like some sort of invisible map to a safe and happy destination. He'd never known such wide-eyed naivety and in a woman who should know better after being foisted into a marriage with such a reprehensible chancer. And still, she had not learnt that lesson. Sebastian did not know whether that was a flaw or a strength of her character. That despite everything that life had thrown at her she still viewed it with hope… Still believed in possibilities. Eliza saw the value, the true worth of things, and wanted to discover all its myths, legends and so on.

A surfeit of emotion and feeling might create beauty and art as Eliza had argued so fervently, but when all was said and done, these artefacts were just things—useless things that people who could afford them stuffed into their houses. They did so in the vain hope that all that beauty and art might transcend their existence, giving some meaning to it and yes, link them with another time and another place. But their inflated importance was only a vehicle to exercise their wealth and nothing more. Another way to show the distinction between people who could afford things and those who could not. Besides, what did the poor, the destitute or hungry care about any of that trifling nonsense? What art and beauty could they discern when owning a lot of worthless *stuff*? Unless of course they could get a bob or two for it from people who shared the same views as Eliza. That was what it all amounted to—how much things were worth in cold, hard cash. Nothing more.

When Sebastian, along with his mother and brothers, had their lives turned upside down after the death of his father, they'd scrambled around to take a handful of stuff that reminded them of who they once had been. A link to their old lives. But all it had ever done was to serve as a reminder of everything that they had lost. It had only served to destroy his mother in the end. And the day she was buried, the three brothers got rid of every last remnant of their old lives, either by selling them off or throwing away all those relics from that bygone era. Everything except three jewelled daggers that his father had made, one for each of his sons. And the only reason they'd kept those was because of their usefulness when they were forced to rebuild their lives.

Other than that, Sebastian hadn't needed any reminders of the past. They'd forged a new life and built Trium Impiorum from scratch, knowing for certain that this was what they were always destined to be.

Yet, when Eliza had spoken about old relics and how they could be used almost as a way to unlock the past, he'd felt the pull of her words and suddenly felt himself transported to a different time and place back when he was thirteen during that golden summer when he'd gone fishing with Dominic and their father at a lake in Harbury Hall, their ancestral home. Except, it was no longer that, and it should never have been theirs in the first place.

And that reminder stunned Sebastian into behaving yes, in an unpardonably rude manner to Eliza. She might be difficult but she had not deserved that. His egregious anger was not really meant for her but for another. So he'd thought of the first thing he could do to make it up to her—he'd invited her here to look at the artefacts that Tristan had furtively brought over from Gresham College for her to study at her leisure. Which meant that in a very short time Sebastian would have the pleasure of her company once again. Something he'd wished to avoid, especially since Tristan had been called away by a matter to do with his research paper, and Dominic was organising the main rooms ready for that evening's gambling. Meaning that once again he'd be alone with her.

Sebastian glanced at his desk with the handful of velvet boxes filled with artefacts lined up in a row, which had taken Eliza's interest and frowned. He could not help but think that something about this was still not as it should be. He couldn't quite put his finger on it, but still could not determine what her interest could possibly be in all this stuff. After all, he had agreed to give her three weeks to pay back her husband's debt, yet she still had time for a farce that she'd concocted yesterday, all to take in the beauty of this? No, he was missing something and he promised himself that before she left his office today, he'd be closer to finding out what Eliza was about. But he would do it by employing a different approach. Since thus far, their interactions had been nothing short of a disaster.

A loud, assertive knock on his door brought his attention back to the imminent arrival of his guest.

'Enter.'

Mr Hendon, his major-domo, opened the door to his office and ushered the vexing woman he'd spent far too much time thinking about inside his room. 'Lady Eliza Bawden-Trebarr here to see you, sir.'

'Thank you, Mr Hendon. Could you possibly see to some refreshments?'

'Yes, sir,' the man said as he inclined his head and left, closing the door behind him, leaving him alone with Eliza.

'Good afternoon, Mr Marsden.' For once Eliza was dressed fashionably. Even if it was still a little austere, she had definitely made far more of an effort than before, aside from the Gresham College debacle, which didn't really count.

She was dressed in an elegant dark teal-coloured skirt cut fashionably but without the usual fuss and frivolity so many other women adored, bar a few rows of satin ribbons sewn at the hem. Her fitted jacket buttoned up to the neck was in the same matching colour and was offset with a military-style ribboning on the front bodice with fringing on the epaulettes; seemingly the only extravagance she'd allowed. Her glossy pale blond hair had been pulled into a neat chignon with a small hat trimmed with black netting and ribbons in the same shade as her outfit secured to the side of her head.

Sebastian noted that once again she'd come to his premises with her huge battered old portmanteau as though she was staying for the night. The thought of which made him feel far too warm around the collar.

'Lady Eliza.' He pasted a smile on his face and nodded. 'Please take a seat. I'm glad you could make the appointment.'

She raised a brow before gingerly sitting down on the leather chair in front of his oak desk. 'Thank you. I hardly had any choice in the matter.'

He perched on the edge of his desk and rubbed his chin absently. 'No, I don't suppose I gave you much of a choice in anything. Before we start, I would like to apologise for my behaviour in the carriage yesterday. I was, as it was pointed out to me, unpardonably rude.' He shrugged. 'Forgive me?'

The woman actually looked shocked and slightly bewildered, possibly wondering how a man like him had managed to offer an apology to anyone. This gave him pause waiting for her to realise that he was actually in earnest. That this wasn't some ruse to disparage her in any way. Whether she believed him, however, was another matter altogether. In the end, those good and proper manners that Eliza clung on to for dear life won out. 'Thank you but it's really not necessary. I believe my own behaviour was hardly beyond reproach. In fact, I would like to extend an apology in return.'

'Accepted.' He nodded briskly.

'I am very grateful to Tris…your brother, Mr Marsden, and to you of course for facilitating this…this viewing for me, especially as I caused so much trouble at Gresham yesterday.'

Ah, so they were both attempting to be civil for a change. Well good, even though it did plunge them into the unknown, as they seemed to skirt around one another, not knowing how to go about it.

'Not at all,' he muttered, finding this sudden awareness between them far more awkward than it needed to be.

'In truth, I thought your brother might also be present.'

'Tristan sends his apologies but he had to see to an urgent matter that needed his attention this evening.'

'I see. Well, I'm indebted to you both. Without your approval and agreement to this today, none of it would be possible.'

Sebastian sat back against his chair and contemplated the woman sitting in front of him. He looked to see whether it was rancour or sarcasm that she was attempting but found nothing in her manner to suggest that. Was this some new strategy of hers? This apparent demureness, which was wholly at odds with whom he believed her to be. He wasn't certain and she must have realised this as she pushed her spectacles up the length of her nose before explaining. 'I can see that I've surprised you but I hope you know that my gratitude is sincere.'

'I do now.' He smiled faintly before clearing his throat. With the pleasantries behind them he wanted to get this over and done with. And as quickly as possible.

'Shall we commence?'

'Yes.' She nodded excitedly as Sebastian stood and opened the four velvet boxes one by one to reveal the sea maiden artefacts that had taken Eliza's fancy.

He heard her gasp as each one came into view, making her stand as well.

He watched her in fascination as her eyes glittered with excitement just as a child might when receiving a gift on Christmas Day morn.

'What is it about these particular knickknacks that has you in such rapture?'

She raised her head and blinked behind those spectacles of hers. 'You wouldn't understand.'

He chuckled dryly. 'I suppose after yesterday, I can't blame you for thinking that but I am actually intrigued.'

Eliza worried her bottom lip before shrugging, evidently coming to a decision. 'The truth is that I have always been interested in folklore and mythology, especially...' Eliza suddenly looked a little uncomfortable, seemingly catching herself before she revealed more.

'Especially?' he said, encouraging her on.

'Especially myths, legends and fables that capture the inner workings of the heart. Stories such as Tristan and Isolde, Hades and Persephone, Leyla and Majnun, Radha and Krishna, and of course, Romeo and Juliet.'

'Ah, so happy tales?' he asked sardonically.

'I suppose at their very core they all share the same notion of the tragic love story. Stories that explore the intensity of emotional connections that nevertheless are destined to doom.' She paused for a moment as she studied something that looked like an elaborate comb, frowning before placing it back on his desk. 'Ultimately, though, these stories serve as a warning about the perils of forming such...such dangerous and misguided attachments.'

So he was not the only cynic when it came to matters of the heart. But perhaps for different reasons. Sebastian did not believe in marriage, let alone love, after the disastrous example of his own parents and the terrible consequences of their ill-fated union. And he was in no hurry to make the same mistakes as they had. After all, there were very few people he trusted and depended on; never mind allowing himself to be foolish enough to give his heart to a woman, someone faithless and capricious. It was not something he'd ever wanted for himself. Besides, he was content with his life as it was, and there was no reason to complicate it unnecessarily with a wife... It was not as though he didn't have the same healthy appetite as any other red-blooded male, but sex and marriage were not mutually exclusive. Not for him, anyway...

That, however, did not seem to be what Eliza's aversion to—what was it again?—ah yes, *emotional connections* was all about. For her, it clearly stemmed from her unhappy marriage to Ritton and not for the first time, Sebastian pondered on the nature of that marriage. Had the blackguard broken her heart? Had he even cared for her? Evidently not.

'So how do those items fit into your interest of mythological tragedies?' He nodded at the various artefacts depicting sea maidens and mermen.

'Mythological tragic love stories,' Eliza corrected before continuing. 'These knickknacks as you call them are part of a Cornish folklore that, yes, end just as tragically as the others. This beauty is Morvoren, a sea maiden, and is part of a story called the *Mermaid of Zennor*,' she murmured, tracing her fingers up and down an irregularly shaped metal disc with an engraving of a maid with long, flowing hair and a tail that swirled and formed part of the shape of the seal. 'Legend has it that a beautiful strange maiden with long white flaxen hair arrived in the village of Zennor, near the Cornish coast, and settled her sights on a handsome young man by the name of Matthew Trewella. Morvoren opened her mouth and sang to him with a voice as beautiful as a songbird and enticed him, pulling him more and more under her spell.'

'So, it was love at first sight?' he mused.

'Does such a thing exist?' She shrugged. 'In any case, Matthew followed Morvoren out of the village and towards the cliffs overlooking the sea. Needless to say, after he left to follow Morvoren, he was never seen or heard from again. But according to legend if you visit the coastline near Zennor on a stormy day, you might just hear Morvoren and Matthew singing an ode to one another. The wind carrying their voices into the air.'

'Very touching.'

'Or possibly it's more of a cautionary tale.'

Sebastian reached out and cupped her gloved hand gently and heard a small gasp escape from her lips as he lifted it to inspect the seal she was holding. It was an impulsive thing to do and he wasn't certain why he had. Only that he couldn't help touching her when she spoke like this. So wistful, so pensive, as though these relics and the made-up tales woven around them were somehow more interesting and more important than her own life, her own experiences. That they were more real to her than anything else in her life.

But as always, a visceral burning heat bloomed and spread from where they touched innocuously to every part of his body. And all from a chaste touch. Sebastian didn't have a name for this or why it happened but it was incredibly disconcerting. It must be that being this close to her reminded him of the previous day in that storeroom when he'd held Eliza, kissed Eliza, wanted more from Eliza, preferably for her to be naked in his bed.

Sebastian could not understand his reaction to her and had wondered over and over about this odd visceral attraction to her. It did not make any sense; she was someone he'd never normally find attractive and yet he did. He very much did…

He bent his head to take a little closer look at the seal before dropping her hand, clenching and opening his own hand several times, trying to get rid of the strange residual heat. 'And the caution that was gained from this tale?'

'Not to trust a stranger.'

'Of course.' Well, he could certainly agree with that.

And knowing that they had this in common, this inability to trust, inability to rely on others, this self-sufficiency that meant there was little room for anyone else in their lives apart from a select few, his brothers in Sebastian's case, made him suddenly inexplicably uncomfortable. He didn't want to have this connection to this woman and he certainly did not want to feel any heat from a mere touch on a gloved hand.

He cleared his throat and scowled, watching her with her face bent low towards the artefacts she so revered lined up on his table. 'Is there anything I can assist you with?'

She lifted her head and gave him a small, awkward smile. 'As a matter of fact, yes. I don't suppose you have a pot of ink and a quill I can borrow. I seem to have left mine at home.'

He fetched a pot from his desk drawer and rose to sharpen a blunt quill for her, placing them both on the table, gratified to be doing something other than having these damned disagreeable musings.

'Thank you.' She unclasped her portmanteau and peered inside and groaned. 'Drat, I seem to have also mislaid a sheet of foolscap. It's so unlike me to be this absent-minded.'

'Not to worry. I think I can spare a sheet,' he said, moving to the small wooden chest of drawers at the side of the room. 'Ah, it seems that I don't have any in here. Would a small unused notebook suffice?'

'I thank you but I cannot accept a whole notebook

from you. A single sheet would suit my needs far more.' She rose. 'I shall return after visiting a local stationer.'

'Sit, Eliza. You do not need to go anywhere. I shall go and enquire about finding you what you need. Please, I insist.'

'I am putting you at an inconvenience again, Mr Marsden, but thank you.'

'It's quite all right, and in any case, I should also enquire about where the refreshments have got to. If you'll excuse me for a moment.'

'Of course.' She stood as well and gave him another winsome smile.

'Oh, and Eliza, while I have made free of your name as have you with mine once or twice, I think you should call me just Sebastian from now on, don't you?'

He noted the colour rise in her cheeks as she nodded. 'Thank you, I shall… Sebastian.'

Chapter Seven

Eliza blew out a breath she hadn't realised she'd been holding and absently rubbed her fingers against the back of her gloved hand as though it might erase the feeling of Sebastian's touch from just a few moments ago. Feeling a little dazed, she slumped back in her chair and pushed these unwanted feelings away as she didn't have time to ponder on any of it now. Not when she only had a few precious minutes with the Morvoren seal before the man would return. It irritated her that she was considering something wholly unrelated, when the excitement of finally having the seal in her grasp should be all that mattered. Especially after she had deliberately managed to get Sebastian to leave his office so that she might attempt to open her box with the metal engraved seal on the table as expediently as possible. Even so, she still felt that sting of guilt pierce through her for deceiving Sebastian and just when he'd unexpectantly begun to behave with civility towards her. But it could not be helped.

Lifting the box out of her portmanteau, she grabbed the Morvoren seal from the table and slid it into place in the lock plate. She felt her excitement bubble inside and took one deep breath before pushing the seal down and hearing the distinctive click as it slotted into place before releasing the metal lock.

'Eureka,' she muttered with a little laugh, 'it worked!'

Behind her she heard the sound of a slow clap and knew instinctively who it was. She swallowed uncomfortably, waiting for his acerbic retort.

'May I offer my felicitations, my lady,' Sebastian drawled, making her title sound almost like an accusation. 'Because we now come to the real reason for your interest in all that *stuff* that you so eloquently described earlier, do you not think?'

She shut her eyes momentarily and shook her head. 'The explanation I offered for my interest in the Morvoren was just as I said, Sebastian.'

He walked around and perched on the edge of the desk to face her. 'Perhaps, perhaps not.'

'Yet, it's nevertheless the truth.'

'What? Even the part about the *surfeit of emotion* that you insisted needed to be injected to create art? That, too?'

'Yes, even that.'

He gave a short, hard laugh. 'But you also decided to keep vital information from me for whatever reason. However, I would like to know everything, if you please, Lady Eliza.'

The presumption of the man in believing he had a right to know everything about her situation was galling and yet, Eliza instinctively knew that he was due some explanation. Her sense of fairness demanded that he did after everything he had done for her, even if it had been begrudgingly granted.

She rubbed her forehead and sighed deeply. 'How to explain.'

'In the usual manner, I'd expect.'

Eliza felt his eyes on her and found that for once she couldn't meet them. She didn't want to see the usual glare of disapproval and censure with an added wariness that she could hardly blame the man for.

'Well?' he said. 'I am waiting.'

She gripped her hands together tightly to prevent them from shaking. 'I realise that and hope that you might understand once I tell you everything.'

Could he, though? Could Sebastian Marsden be able to appreciate that she had never meant to misguide him intentionally? After gaining three weeks to pay back the debt, she'd never wanted him to know how she had planned to do it, knowing full well what his response might be. Ridicule and disbelief. But now, being caught in this unfortunate manner, she was forced to tell him, anyway.

'No, Eliza, you do not get to request any understanding from me. I shall judge for myself and make my own decision.'

'I expect you would.'

'I would, yes. So, would you like to explain now or do you need a little more time to consider your answer?' he said, raising a brow. 'Shall I help? For instance, you can begin by explaining whether you meant to filch this seal yesterday from under the noses of all those stuffy academics? Was that the intention of your ruse?'

'Yes,' she said quietly. 'I had to. There was no other choice.'

'Ah, *choice* is an interesting word, Eliza, do you not think? For instance, I could choose to be as accommodating to you as I have been from the first time you entered this room, making outrageous demands of me. Or I can choose to take that box that you're clutching so tightly and have you thrown out of here. I can even choose to terminate the agreement we made regarding the payment of Ritton's debt so you could gain your precious estate back.'

She paled, her heart beating so fast as she lifted her gaze to finally meet his cold stare. 'Very well. The truth is that I have been looking for this seal ever since

Ritton's death, never wanting him to suspect what this box might mean to me.'

'Which is what, exactly?'

'Something rather special and personal.' She took a deep breath before continuing. 'But he…he took such a perverse enjoyment from tormenting me, much to my shame, and took anything and everything away from me if he believed it to be of some importance to me.' From people to possessions, it had mattered not to the late viscount. 'Which is why I had to hide this box, with the search of this seal beginning in secret the day after his burial and in earnest after my imposed mourning period was over. However, until recently, I had no luck in locating it.'

'I see.' His eyes had filled with such bleak fury that she wondered at the cause of it. Wondered whether it could possibly be what she had said about Ritton's behaviour towards her that had put that blaze of anger in his eyes. After a long moment, Sebastian addressed her again. 'How did you know it would be part of the Cornwall Collection?'

'My friend, Miss Cecily Duddlecott, remembered seeing something like it at a preview of the collection at the British Museum.'

'And did your friend also see fit to attend the collection in disguise as you did?' he asked sardonically.

'No, Sebastian, she didn't have to because she attended with her brother, who provided her with an escort. I, however, had no such thing, and with the presentation to Royal Society at Gresham College predictably prohibiting women, there was little else I could feasibly do if I wanted to see for myself whether the seal was the one I had been looking for or not.'

'I see. And it must have been a surprise to have encountered me there.'

'It was.' She nodded, swallowing uncomfortably. 'I did not know that you would also be in attendance or that your brother was involved with the collection.'

After a long moment, Sebastian spoke again but his earlier asperity seemed to have faded. 'So, you thought to come in disguise to somehow take this seal.'

'Yes.'

'To what purpose?'

'To open this box, as nothing else would, and believe me I have considered many possibilities. For it to open, however, it had to be the original seal.'

'I see.' He crossed his arms over his chest and studied her for a moment. 'And what is so unique about this particular box?'

'As I said, it's a family heirloom.'

'Indeed.' He sighed in apparent frustration. 'You have explained all that well enough, Eliza. But I cannot help thinking that there's more to this than merely keeping your family heirloom from Ritton's grasping hands.'

'Yes,' she said quietly.

'And will you not tell me? Can you not explain the reason that you needed to have this box opened?'

This was the part that Eliza was dreading. The part that would confirm what Sebastian already believed about her; that she was quite mad, foolish or whatever else he'd think about this outrageous scheme. For if she disclosed why the box needed to open, she would also have to explain what she hoped to gain from what she might find inside it.

'You would think me addled...' Eliza looked up and caught a bemused gaze before adding, 'perhaps even more so than usual.'

'Ah yes, I forgot, you must know me so well through our...handful of exchanges.' He raised a brow. 'And no, I don't actually think you're addled, Eliza. I think you're a clever woman bent on getting your way by any means—and if you need to lie and cheat to accomplish that, then so be it.'

'That's not true.'

'Then tell me everything, so I might understand.'

'I... I...' How could she explain all the ugly sordidness of her marriage to Ritton.

'Does any of this have to do with paying back the debt you owe me?' Her eyes snapped to Sebastian's.

She felt herself flush as she scrambled to think of what to say, which was unnecessary since he responded instead. 'I shall take that as an affirmative answer.'

Eliza took a deep breath before continuing. 'The truth is that this box was given to me by my mother before Ritton condemned her to an asylum, Sebastian.'

'Did you just say that Ritton put your mother in an...an asylum?'

She nodded. 'As I explained earlier, he liked to torment me by taking away anything that he...he deemed important to me. That, unfortunately, included people. And my poor, powerless mother was one such person who became a pawn to his schemes and when he found her unbiddable, when he believed her to be interfering in our marriage because she challenged his treatment of me, he had her locked away. Indeed, it was remarkably easy to do as no one dared question a viscount.'

'Dear God, Eliza.' He leant forward and placed his large hand on hers, giving it a gentle squeeze. 'It's a good thing that Ritton is dead. Otherwise, I'd kill the bastard for thinking that he could bully women in the way that he did you and your mother. It is something that I cannot abide...not ever.'

Eliza was stunned, unable to take in Sebastian's sudden gesture of support for the situation that had been foisted on her. And after his earlier antipathy this was far more surprising than she could ever have imagined. Her gaze dropped to his hand covering her gloved one. She could once again feel a warmth bloom in every part of her body from this one contact, this one touch, and yet what made Eliza unwittingly grateful was that Sebastian seemed concerned…for *her*. Genuinely, possibly, surprisingly, without doubt. She realised then that this gruff man was far more than he appeared. He cared deeply for people and things; from how he behaved towards his own brothers to this sympathy he offered her now—given to a woman who'd constantly frustrated and exasperated him. It somehow made her want to weep, especially since no one, save her mother, had ever cared that much for her before.

'Thank you,' she whispered, feeling a little moved.

'There are many things that people assume about me, my character and the life I choose to live, but one thing I will not accept is a man who'd exert his power over a woman. So, please do not thank me, Eliza. I'm sorry that you were forced into such an unpleasant situation. I'm sorry you were forced to endure him.'

'As am I,' she muttered, feeling a little exposed, a little vulnerable, knowing that this protectiveness had caught him unexpectedly on the raw just as it had her.

'And your mother, she is…she is still alive?'

'Yes, she is still there even now after Ritton's death.'

She swallowed uncomfortably. 'So, you see, what I am trying to do here is as much for her as it is for me.'

He nodded and removed his hand from hers. 'Will you tell me the rest?'

And just then Eliza understood implicitly that Sebastian Marsden deserved to know everything about the legend of the treasure and what she hoped to do with it. Perhaps it had been the manner in which he'd given her his unequivocal support and comfort by something as innocent as holding her hand. Perhaps it was his understanding and empathy, telling her that he could not *accept a man who'd exert his power over a woman*, while he must still have been annoyed with her deception, that made Eliza realise that he should know all of it. Indeed, it would be a relief to finally get it off her chest.

If he then took the decision that she was absurdly foolish in pinning all her hopes on this then so be it, but at least he'd know the truth. At least he would know the reasons for it and why she wanted to find the treasure, pay back the debt and get the Trebarr estate redeemed. And far more importantly, free her mother.

'The box contains secrets that indicate the whereabouts of the Bawden-Trebarr treasure—a legend within my family that my ancestors have hidden for over four hundred years.'

'I beg your pardon?' he muttered, his jaw dropping. 'Did you just say the Bawden-Trebarr...*treasure*?'

She smiled and nodded. 'Yes...yes, I did.'

Sebastian stared at Eliza for a long time, allowing the moment to stretch, unable to quite believe what he had just heard. After so many revelations this afternoon...this was her apparent explanation? A lost treasure! No wonder she hadn't wanted to tell him any of it.

'Allow me to comprehend this. Your whole scheme of paying back the money Ritton owed me has rested on...hunting for treasure?'

'A legendary treasure, yes,' she said quietly as though admitting a terrible confession. 'A four-hundred-year-old treasure, to be precise.'

Sebastian laughed in disbelief; he couldn't help himself. Of all the hare-brained schemes he'd ever heard, this had to top them all. It was breathtakingly absurd in its naivety. Like one of the long-ago games he'd devised with his brothers as rapscallion boys causing havoc in Marsden Manor, playing pirates on the hunt for looted treasure.

'I know it's difficult to understand. I know it might seem like madness but it is what I have been planning for a long time.'

Sebastian's eyes lingered on her face before dropping to the box she'd been holding. After everything that Eliza had disclosed, he didn't have the heart to deny her this. He could not bear to deride her dream. Her determination and the patience that she must have had in willing it all to come together was not only commendable but also unbelievably incredible.

Hell, it was all incredible but dash it all, a treasure? She was hunting for bloody treasure, of all things?

Sebastian had been prepared to act accordingly when he'd encountered her in this office not half an hour ago when he'd found her furtively hovering over that box of hers with the seal in her hand pushing it into something. He knew then that she had wanted to get him out of this room to do whatever she needed to do. But this? He could never have expected any of this.

'Let me understand you, Eliza.' He dragged his hand through his hair. 'You seek a four-hundred-year-old family treasure?'

'Yes.'

'All to pay back Ritton's debt?'

'Yes,' she said again.

'But how can you be certain that it still exists, if it ever did?'

'I don't.'

'And even if does, why was it not found years, decades or even centuries ago?'

'I do not actually…know that it wasn't.' She shook

her head slowly. 'The legend of the treasure has only ever passed down through the female line. And according to my mother, my ancestors intended for the treasure to be sought only when their female descendants have an actual urgent need for it.'

'Which you do.'

'Yes,' she whispered, before lifting her head and squaring her shoulders. 'I must try.'

Sebastian laced his fingers with the fingers of her pristine kidskin-gloved hand and frowned. She must be desperate as well as determined to go through with such a scheme. But it showed him Eliza's resilience, fortitude and courage, that even after she'd been knocked back time and time again by her reprobate of a husband, she was still willing to find a way to gain back her dignity and family honour. Virtues that were evidently very important to her.

Even her attire seemed to have been purposely chosen to appeal to his vanity. It was as though she was seeking affirmation and to appease his opinion of her should he find out about this treasure. Or perhaps to prove that she was sane despite her desperation.

The truth was that he'd anticipated one outcome, confident that he knew how to handle the situation, but then had been handed quite another. And it had left him feeling curiously bereft, as though he'd been knocked off his normal axis. More than anything, he felt furious that a woman, and one like Eliza Bawden-Trebarr, had felt she'd need to resort to this to regain her standing in the world. And he'd had the nerve to lecture her about having choices, when in reality she'd had very little choice over the situation she'd been forced into. The injustice of it all made him angry, with himself just as much as with everyone else.

Sebastian almost wanted to give her the damn deeds to her estate and wish her well with it. But no, he strongly doubted she would accept it and it wasn't what they had agreed, in any case. If he simply gave back her castle, Eliza would naturally believe that he'd want something from her in return and that would never do.

'I know that it seems like madness,' she muttered again. 'But this…plan is the only one that I have.'

Meaning it was all she could do. Sebastian suddenly felt jaded knowing full well how the world treated a woman like Eliza, who was not quite the same as the usual accepted notions of femininity, of what she should be and how she ought to behave. And he could see quite clearly how someone as quick-witted and intelligent as Eliza would threaten the masculine pride of a man like Viscount Ritton. No wonder he'd resented her. No wonder she'd hated him.

It made him burn with anger that Eliza had to resort to this subterfuge to gain the peace that she craved.

Had she not said that at their first encounter here in this very room? And hadn't he, a man who prided himself on his sense of fairness and justice, dismissed her, possibly like every other man in her life had done? God, but he felt heartily ashamed of himself.

Nevertheless, he would help her in getting her mother out of whatever asylum Ritton had stuck her in. The utter bastard. Everything she'd said about her late husband only confirmed what he knew of him, but Sebastian could never have imagined that the man would be as bad as this. To take enjoyment from belittling and bullying not just any woman but a woman who should have had his care, his protection and his respect if not love, was as cruel as it was unforgivable. He was glad that she was well rid of that monster. Which made him ponder on what she would have done had he not perished. Good God, what if the man hadn't died unexpectedly? Would Eliza have waited indefinitely as she worried about her mother withering away in an asylum and powerless to do anything about it? And to think only half an hour or so ago, Sebastian had been ready to throttle Eliza, believing that she was determined to deceive him yet again when he'd come back into his office to find her furtively fixing the seal to her heirloom of a box… Which apparently led to treasure. It was ludicrous. Truly ludicrous.

'Knowing your tenacity, I can well believe that you

have been planning this for a long time, Eliza. In fact, your patience is admirable. However…'

He watched as her shoulders slumped. 'You wish to rescind the agreement we made?'

'No, Eliza, that is not what I was going to say.'

She looked a little bewildered. 'Then what?' She sighed deeply. 'Forgive me, but I don't understand.'

'I would like to help you in any manner I can.'

He watched Eliza's bewilderment, as she blinked repeatedly behind those ill-fitting spectacles, give way to a slow smile that curled around her lips but without the usual cynicism and doubt. It made her look so young, so damn guileless and innocent, that it almost took his breath away. He wondered whether he deserved this smile. It spoke of hope and faith—virtues that he didn't know he could accept from her. And they weren't something he could easily give in return, either, despite his sudden impulse to help her, which was not like him at all. Sebastian stared down at their entwined fingers and frowned, realising that he should not have touched her, even if he still wanted to take her into his arms and press her close. Hold her, so that he might be able to erase the difficulties that she'd been forced to shoulder on her own. But that would not do. No, he did not need a complication like that in his orderly life, and holding Eliza, kissing Eliza, or doing anything other than keeping matters cordial between

them would lead them down a path that he had no in-
clination to travel along. This pull of attraction, for
that was what was simmering between them, had to
be quashed now for both their sakes.

Sebastian released Eliza's hand and crossed his
arms over his chest to stop himself from touching
her again.

'You would like to help...me?' Her brows furrowed
in the middle. 'May I ask how?'

He shrugged. 'First, if you would allow me to know
the details then I would be happy to help you with your
mother, Eliza. I can make enquiries on your behalf.'

'You would do that for us?'

'I would.' He watched as she looked at him in surprise.

'Why?'

'Because I cannot accept the injustice of it all. I cannot stand the fact that a powerful man chose to inflict
so much pain and suffering on women in his care, just
because he could. It was cruel of Ritton to do so.' It
also reminded Sebastian about his own mother, who
had been plunged into an untenable situation, forced
to accept the ignominy of her husband's deceit after
his death, stripping her of everything she knew and
sending her to an early death. 'Believe me, Eliza, I
understand what you went through more than you can
possibly know.'

Eliza's gaze lingered on him for a long moment before she nodded her thanks. 'It was cruel, yes. And… and your offer is very generous,' she muttered awkwardly. 'I'd be very much obliged to you, Sebastian.'

He gave her a small smile, hiding the fact that he, too, was feeling a little uncomfortable with this newly found accord between them. 'It would be my pleasure. Although I cannot promise anything at present, I shall try my best to start the process of getting her out. I may be a gaming hell owner but I do have some influence as well as a few influential men who owe me a favour or two.'

'Thank you.' She reached across and placed her hand over one of his, which were still crossed over his chest.

He dropped his gaze to where her small gloved hand lay over his for a long moment before having to pull his attention away. He cleared his throat. 'As for the rest, we can discuss that tomorrow afternoon at your convenience.'

'The rest?' She frowned. 'To what are you referring?'

Sebastian's eyes flicked to the box in her hand and then back to her face for what seemed the hundredth time since she had explained her outrageous plan, and the absurdity of it suddenly struck him again.

This was how she had thought to pay back Ritton's

debt, and to get her castle back… This, a treasure. She thought to find it within the three weeks she'd negotiated—an ancient treasure from hundreds of years ago that had probably already been found. Had already been squandered. Yet, Eliza was pinning all her hopes on finding it. It was all so highly improbable.

And that she would go to such lengths to try to gain her inheritance back, and use some of the funds to ensure her mother's release from an asylum, was impressive if somewhat foolhardy. Indeed, it all came down to a box…a box that would magically solve the predicament she was in. When in truth, it was Sebastian who had the power to solve it. It was he who could make all of her problems go away. But how to help her without denting that pride of hers? How to help her when this was never part of their agreement?

'You do not have to do this, Eliza,' he murmured. 'You do not have to go in search of treasure as a way to pay back the debt.'

'Oh, and how am I supposed to pay it back?'

'I do not know but as I said we can discuss this further tomorrow at your house. We can come up with a plan, a proper one.' One that would not lead to possible danger and certain disappointment, he thought to himself.

'I realise that the plan I have devised must seem very lacking to someone of your estimable intelligence,' she said tartly. 'However, it is the only one that could gain such a large sum of money in under three weeks. Besides, I do believe that there is something in this box. Legend has it that the Bawden-Trebarr treasure is so vast it's actually priceless.'

'Then I shall ask again why it hasn't been found before?'

She leant forward, and her face was so close to his that he could easily count the freckles dusted on her nose and cheeks. 'Because the box is actually a conundrum, Sebastian. It serves to guide us to the source of the treasure through a cipher or a puzzle. And this is only after it has been opened, which, as you know, I have managed to do just now.'

'Even so, perhaps we can come to some other agreement.' Eliza's brows shot up behind those round spectacles of hers, her brown doe eyes looking even larger as she stared at him in astonishment. Quite frankly, he didn't blame her for it. She could easily interpret what he conveyed to mean another agreement, one that might take advantage of her reduced circumstances. 'Whatever you're thinking please do refrain from doing so, as I didn't mean anything that might be construed as taking advantage of your situation.'

'Oh, and what might that be?'

'I am not proposing that you pay back the debt by

agreeing to any indecent arrangement. I would never propose *that*, Eliza.'

Sebastian watched as she flushed, her face suffused with a dark pink hue. 'No, I can't imagine I am the type of woman who'd ever inspire that particular proposal from a man.'

Good God, was the woman *disappointed* that he hadn't suggested she become his...mistress as a way to pay back the debt? She couldn't be; it was too damn ridiculous if she was. 'Would you like me to propose that to you?'

'Did I say that?' she murmured, leaning forward as did he, her eyes dropping to his lips. 'I only mean that whatever this other agreement of yours might be, the last thing it could ever be is something as outrageous as you proposing I become your...your...'

'Mistress?'

'Yes,' she whispered.

'Well, I hope it's because you believe me to be a principled man who would never demean a woman in your situation in that manner.'

She shook her head. 'As I said, it's because I would never be a woman who might inspire such a scandalous proposal in the first place.'

He raised a brow. 'Ah, so you believe yourself to be undesirable?'

'Perhaps but it is of no matter.'

'No matter?' He was leaning forward so far now that her lips were mere inches away from his own. He cupped her jaw, his thumb tracing her lower lip back and forth, back and forth. 'I beg to differ. And just so you know, I find you very, very desirable, Eliza Bawden-Trebarr.'

Sebastian pulled her the final tiny distance towards him, and watched in rapt fascination as she closed her eyes, her long lashes fanning against her skin, her lips opening a little just to take a small steadying breath in a tantalising wait for his kiss. A very welcome and wanted kiss.

And just when his lips were about to touch hers, just when he could feel her hot breath whisper against his skin, there was an abrupt knock at the door.

Eliza jerked back suddenly as his brother Dominic walked into his office and stopped midstride.

'Ah, my apologies, Sebastian. I didn't know you had…er…company. Good afternoon, Lady Eliza.'

'Good afternoon, Mr Marsden.' Always the possessor of good manners, Eliza rose and curtsied gracefully as Dominic bowed. She placed the box back inside her portmanteau and closed it before looking up again. 'And now that matters have concluded quite satisfactorily between us with our agreement still intact, Sebastian, I would leave you in peace.'

God, the woman was stubborn. 'Wait, Eliza. Before

you go, can I ask you not to do anything about the casket box? Not even to open it until we discuss everything again tomorrow?' Sebastian knew that if he let her go now without securing her word, she would jump headlong into the unknown in pursuit of finding this supposed treasure. And for some reason he wanted to be there for her, just in case she needed him.

Eliza frowned and leant forward and spoke so only he would hear. 'Why? What possible reason could there be for you to help me in this?'

'Because I would like to assist you where I can and because I want you to know that you're not alone, Eliza.'

She gasped softly and stared at him for a long moment as though she were trying to ascertain his sincerity. 'Very well. Until tomorrow.' She nodded before taking her leave. 'Sebastian. Mr Marsden.'

'Until tomorrow.'

Not for one minute did Sebastian trust that she'd be able to keep to their agreement. Even so, he would protect her; he would still look out for her. Sebastian didn't know why he felt this fierce need to protect her, but he did. Perhaps it was, as he'd said, because she was all alone in the world, save a friend or two, but whatever the reason, he felt compelled to do it. He knew he had to.

Chapter Eight

Eliza glanced down at the box on the table in the front parlour of her Chelsea town house the following day and frowned. She had managed to resist the temptation to look inside the now opened box and had gone about her day, seeing to errands, selling off a few more valuables at a pawnshop and even meeting with her father's solicitor. She had certainly not pondered on the meeting that she'd agreed to have later that afternoon in her home with Sebastian Marsden. Well, perhaps that wasn't quite true.

Eliza wanted to keep to the agreement she'd made with him just as much as she wanted to forget that strange interlude when Sebastian had almost kissed her in his office. But when she considered how desperately she had wanted him to and would have succumbed to him so very willingly had his brother not interrupted them when he did, she burned with shame. And all because she had taken offence that she was not the sort of woman who'd inspire a man to propose a dalliance with. To have as a *mistress*. But no, shockingly, she was just such a woman in Sebastian's eyes, not that he would ever suggest such a demeaning thing. And she liked him all the better for it. Since it spoke of an unwavering respect that he held for women, not that she'd ever done much to earn his respect.

And just so you know, I find you very, very desirable, Eliza...

It was simply the most outrageous thing anyone had ever said to her. To *her*, Eliza Bawden-Trebarr. She was definitely not the kind of woman who'd ever arouse such ardent declarations in anyone, especially from a supposed rogue like Sebastian. Yet, he apparently found her *very, very desirable*!

Heavens...the man had shocked himself with that outburst and it had been reluctantly uttered, in any case. But quite apart from that, he had stunned her again and again with his care and protectiveness of her. And it was this along with being so dazed after their almost-kiss that explained why she'd agreed to discuss matters to do with the debt and the box itself the following day.

Yet, as the day progressed, it was becoming increasingly difficult not to be curious and drawn to it like a veritable Pandora's box waiting for her to look inside.

Especially after the length of the time it had taken to get the blasted thing open as well. So just after lunch, when she had entered the room in search of the book she'd left in the parlour, the box beckoned, making her eventually sit down on the wooden chair and tap a tattoo on the round table before reaching for it.

Surely, it would do no harm if she just had a peek. After all, even though he'd asked her not to, she had never actually promised Sebastian that she would not look inside. Yes, there was nothing wrong with a quick glance and it was her box, after all. Holding her breath, Eliza lifted the metal lock hasp, which would open the lid that finally revealed the inside of the Bawden-Trebarr box.

Just like the outside, the inside, too, was beautiful and ornately finished with the same inlays of different wood and decorated with the same colours of the two Cornish houses.

'Ah, I see you've started without me, Lady Eliza?' Sebastian stood in her door frame swallowing up all the available space with his size and sheer presence. 'Well, there's a surprise.'

Her maid Gertie walked up behind Sebastian. 'A Mr Marsden is here to see you, my lady.'

'Thank you, Gertie. I can see that,' Eliza said with a little breathless quality in her voice as she found

Sebastian in her home, albeit earlier than she had expected him.

'Eliza,' he murmured, bowing in front of her.

'Mr Marsden. Good to see you again.' She smiled up at him and gave him a nod. 'Gertie, can you bring in some tea please?'

'Yes, my lady.' Her housekeeper come maid bobbed a curtsy before shutting the door behind her.

'So…' he murmured, his gaze darting around the room.

'So?'

'You just couldn't stop yourself from taking a peek, could you?' His eyes fixed on hers as he shook his head.

'I think we both can agree that I have done jolly well to last this long.'

'Indeed.' He moved to stand beside her. 'Well, what have you found? May I take a look?'

'Believe it or not, I had only just opened it when you er…announced yourself, so we can inspect it together, if you wish.'

'I do wish it.' He took off his black woollen top hat and placed it on the table. 'The possibility of there being a Bawden-Trebarr treasure has certainly piqued my interest as well as my curiosity.'

Eliza gingerly opened the box again and took a closer look. Around the inside edges of the wooden casket box the standards of house Trebarr with a lion and house Bawden featuring an eagle, both with gold bezants in their respective colours, were displayed in each of the four corners. The interior was divided into four compartments of various sizes made from the same wood and decorated in the same elaborate manner. In one, there was an old metal box that fit snuggly inside. Eliza carefully lifted it out and opened it to find medieval hairpins and a long strip of old faded cloth.

'This could be a ribbon or a token. One that possibly my ancestor Elowen Bawden gave her husband, Simon Trebarr. Look, some of the embroidery has remained and in the Bawden colours of gold, brown and blue, and the Trebarr ones in gold, light blue and green, even if it is faded.'

'It seems so.'

Eliza nodded before placing it back and brushing her fingers inside the box. 'Other than that, there doesn't seem to be anything else, apart from this— a battered, empty leather case. How disappointing.'

'Surely, your ancestors would have employed a far more ingenious way to hide clues for their hidden treasure, otherwise it would be far too easy.' He glanced across at her. 'And what exactly are we looking for, anyway?'

As much as Eliza hated to admit it, she rather liked the way Sebastian had said *we* as it spoke of a comradery that she hadn't ever dreamed could exist between them. 'I do not quite know but something that might contain some sort of clue. An instruction of sorts as to how to go about finding it. Not a handful of rusty hairpins and a faded bit of cloth.'

'Don't forget the old leather case.'

'As if I could.' She sighed deeply. 'Do you think there might be any hidden compartments in the box?'

'Possibly, but the whole thing looks to be made out of a single piece of wood, so I don't think that the casket box itself has any hidden compartments. If it does, then it could be somewhere here on the inside.'

Eliza slid her hand inside, brushing her fingers along and into every corner, trying to feel for anything unusual, as Sebastian tapped against the surface to see if there were any hollow spaces. But no, again, there was nothing out of the ordinary. Her heart sank.

'Let me look at that leather case again,' she muttered and Sebastian passed the small square case to her.

Eliza turned over the case that like the box was decorated with the Bawden and Trebarr colours and motifs. And going down its length were the indented marks of whatever had been kept inside the case. How curious. The very shape and design of it seemed familiar to her, making her wonder where she could possibly have seen something like it before.

Sebastian bent his head towards hers as he studied it. 'What do you suppose used to be kept inside the case?'

'I'm not certain but whatever it was must have made those long vertical marks.'

'True enough. The compact little shape reminds me of something you'd find as part of a gentleman's grooming set. I have a similar one that I keep my hair comb inside.'

'Of course, a hair comb! I could kiss you, Sebastian! Those indentations could very well have been made by the comb teeth. And wait…' she exclaimed excitedly as she lifted her gaze to his. 'I saw a beautiful boxwood comb in your office yesterday, which also came from the Cornwall Collection. It intrigued me both when I was viewing it at Gresham College and yesterday as well, because the Morvoren motif was so familiar as were the Bawden and Trebarr colours painted into the wood.'

Sebastian had raised a brow, a slow smile curling around his lips. 'You could kiss me, eh?'

'Oh, I'm terribly sorry. I didn't mean…as in I shouldn't have said that.' She flushed as she took a step back.

'Nonsense. There's no need to apologise. I know how you like to throw yourself at me.' He winked as he placed his hat back on top of his head. 'I'll take my leave, Eliza, and see if I can locate this hair comb at the Trium Impiorum.'

'That's very good of you…but one moment, if you please,' she said, following him outside the room. 'What do you mean, I like to throw myself at you?'

Sebastian had made his way to the front door, his long strides eating up the short distance. 'Never say that you've forgotten how you initiated our first kiss, Eliza. Tut tut.' He grinned as he murmured over his shoulder. 'I'll send word if I locate it.'

'Thank you…and I never initiated anything,' she retorted as he strode out the front door. But of course, she had. She'd thrown herself at Sebastian and surprised both of them with that kiss in the supply cupboard at Gresham College. And had thought of it every single day since. She sighed, giving herself a mental shake before ambling back to the parlour.

Eliza had better things to do than ponder on a silly kiss that only came about because she'd needed to silence Sebastian. And after that, a near kiss yesterday evening in his office. It was best to forget kissing him altogether and put her mind to good use by continuing her search of a possible secret compartment inside the box until she heard back from the blasted man.

However, it was a few hours later when Sebastian finally contacted her. His brief note informed her that he'd been too late as Tristan had already returned all the artefacts from the Cornwall Collection to the museums, collections and private owners who had lent the items, including the boxwood medieval hair comb. The owner of the comb was one Sir Horace Middleton from Green Street, Mayfair, who also happened to be a regular at his club and had been surprised by Sebastian's interest in his beautiful medieval comb.

Drat...

Eliza continued to read Sebastian's missive, which stated that Sir Horace would be happy for him to view the comb, but it would have to be at his home that evening as he was hosting a soiree, which he would be delighted if Sebastian could attend. Sebastian had accepted the invitation on behalf of himself and Eliza, the Countess of Ritton, and asked Eliza if he could escort her there.

So it looked as though she was attending a soiree that evening, one of those affairs that she'd always dreaded when she'd been married. However, Ritton was no longer alive to cause her embarrassment as he'd used to when he openly flirted with any one of his many mistresses in front of her.

Yet, she couldn't quite accept Sebastian's escort, either. Oh, she was naturally grateful for his help that day, knowing that without him, she would never have thought of the case being used for a comb or have so promptly tracked down its owner. But to have him escort her to the soiree? It somehow felt too friendly; certainly too intimate, and after their recent truce and attempts at cordial civility, she felt this might be a step too far.

At times, Sebastian's innate arrogance made her want to hit him over the head, and yet he was also kind and unexpectedly caring, which surprised her more than she could ever say. Especially since those were not virtues she had ever known in a man before. And certainly not in a man like Sebastian Marsden.

And quite apart from Sebastian's inherent kindness were the times in their short acquaintance when he looked at her; when he actually saw her, and made her feel as though she were not invisible, that her views and opinions mattered, even if he didn't agree with them. He made her chest tighten as though she could scarcely breathe. As though it was her heart that ached. Even so, she could never get involved with Sebastian. It was certainly not the sort of thing that she would ever do. Eliza just wasn't that kind of woman—one who'd get into tangles with brooding, handsome gaming hell owners. And she could certainly not encourage anything beyond a friendly acquaintanceship by allowing the man to escort her anywhere.

With that in mind, she sent word to Cecy and asked her whether she was attending the soiree with her brother and if so, whether she could attend with them.

To which she received a reply to say that they were going and that they'd be happy to escort her.

With that arranged, Eliza wrote Sebastian a short yet polite note, explaining that she would meet him at the soiree that evening. And then pushed all thoughts regarding him to one side, setting about getting ready for that evening before leaving to go to Stephen Duddlecott's house so that they could all attend the soiree together.

Her evening dress was not what one would consider to be in the height of fashion, but she looked well enough in a simple pale duck egg satin silk with a fitted bodice, sitting just off the shoulder with a draped neckline, and a skirt of contrasting striped silk and a pleated underskirt that poked from beneath the scooped hemline. She wore small flowers in her hair along with crystal pins and had her hair arranged in the new French style, having one lock of her pale fair hair curled and placed over one shoulder. She decided to forego her spectacles in the hope that it might render her a little more feminine than usual, although it did make it difficult to see all around her with clarity, so she placed them in her mother's small evening purse to use later when needed. Along with her white gloves and a single black ribbon at her neck with her mother's locket dangling from it, Eliza had completed her toilette and had then dashed to Cecy's wearing her black velvet evening coat. It was a good thing that she didn't attend many evenings such as this soiree since this was one of only two evening outfits that she still owned; the rest having been sold to pay off Ritton's other markers all over town.

Eliza arrived at Sir Horace's house in Green Street sometime later, along with the Duddlecotts. They were ushered into the main reception salon where she was introduced to Sir Horace by his sister, Mrs Linden-Brown, who then took Cecy by the arm to discuss something of great import. With Sir Horace and Stephen Duddlecott taking their leave briefly, Eliza stood alone at the furthest corner of the room, watching the many guests arriving and mingling together, the low hum of chatter filling the salon. She grabbed a flute of champagne from a passing servant and took a long sip to steady her nerves before tapping her toes to the rhythm of the music played by a string quartet. She could do this; she could wait in this room, mingle and chat to the crème de la crème of what society had to offer before having to meet Sebastian Marsden. Eliza knocked back the remainder of her champagne before taking another flute from yet another servant. God above, but this was not going to be as easy as she had initially thought. It had been such a long time since she'd attended a society event such as this and she'd hated it just as much then as she did now.

'Ah, here you are, Eliza.' Of course, there was only one man who spoke to her in that informal manner and that was Sebastian.

He had appeared beside her from out of nowhere without her noticing. But then again, most things were a little hazy and not because she'd consumed too many glasses of champagne but because she wasn't wearing her spectacles. Even so, how did the man constantly do that? It was astonishing that such a large, tall man was able to prowl around like a lithe panther, so effortlessly without gaining notice. It was quite a skill indeed.

'Good evening, Sebastian.'

'And a good evening to you, too, my lady,' he drawled, shifting a little so that he now stood in front of her, bowing and keeping his eyes trained on hers.

Her heart gave a jolt as she took in the way he looked, dressed in his fine evening attire of a fitted fine wool black tailcoat, with black waistcoat and tailored trousers and a pristine white shirt and bow tie. His dark hair was slicked back, making his chiselled features even more prominent, even more striking. And for Eliza to notice this without her spectacles was quite remarkable. But then, she had never thought to see him dressed so, packing all that masculine brawn and sinew into such elegant finery. God, he was so impossibly handsome it made her inhale softly. No wonder the man caught the attention of every woman in the room. He was that magnificent. Indeed, Sebastian Marsden looked every inch the earl that he had been born to be. But no, another man filled those illustrious shoes now. She gathered herself together before speaking again.

'I am glad to see you here.'

'I'm very happy to hear that, although I must confess,' he said, dropping his voice to a low murmur. 'I was surprised that you declined my escort here tonight, Eliza. May I ask whether it's because of who I am? One of the notorious Marsden Bastards?'

Sebastian might have delivered this quip in his usual detached manner, but Eliza would never dream of hurting his feelings, even inadvertently. It wasn't in her nature to do so.

She snapped her eyes to meet his. 'Of course not. That would never have entered my head.'

'Then it was because of my notoriously amoral club?' His mouth turned upwards at one corner but she somehow sensed a tension emanating from him. Did he think that she felt he was somehow beneath her?

'If you must know, Sebastian, I was nervous about coming here tonight. I haven't been out in society much since Ritton's death and well, even when he was alive, I never particularly enjoyed evenings such as this.' She took a deep breath. 'So, I thought it more

prudent if I came with my friends then draw any unwanted attention if…if I came…'

'With me?'

'Yes.'

He inhaled before speaking. 'And if *you* must know,
I do not usually attend society events such as this, either. They make me come out in a rash and I avoid
them at all costs.'

She turned to face him. 'So how is it that you agreed
to come to this soiree, Sebastian? Especially since social gatherings are, as you say, not to your taste.'

'And now you know all about my tastes? But then
again, perhaps you do,' he murmured in a low voice,
making her feel a little warm and a little breathless
in her fitted dress, which suddenly felt too tight. He
sipped the champagne from his flute, watching her
before continuing. 'Sir Horace frequents the club reg-
ularly and like many men of his ilk extends invita-
tions to me and my brothers, hoping to get into our
good graces so that we might extend his credit in the
process. Poor Sir Horace. I cannot imagine his sister
is too thrilled about my presence here.'

Eliza was suddenly annoyed on Sebastian's behalf
for the injustice that society matrons like Sir Horace's
sister directed at him. How dare they when they knew
nothing about him, other than the fact he was declared
illegitimate after his father's death and that he'd had

to make his own way in the world. If anything, there was much to admire in a man like Sebastian Marsden. Resilient, brave and honourable. 'Oh, hang the sister. Women like her love to look down their noses at anyone who they deem beneath them. But you are never that, Sebastian.'

'I never took you to be such a fierce protector.' His brows shot up. 'And of someone like *me*. Whatever happened to those famous good manners of yours?'

'Having the night off.'

He chuckled, shaking his head. 'You need not worry as I don't care for the opinions of old tabbies such as Sir Horace's sister. Besides, this is the first society event with mixed company that I've had the pleasure of attending,' he remarked sardonically.

'Riveting, isn't it?'

'Indeed,' he said, taking another sip of champagne. 'But still, I also hate the idea of becoming an object of curiosity. Like you, I would rather avoid that unwanted attention.'

She smiled up at him, understanding his meaning, knowing that he had done this for her. So that she could get another chance to study the medieval comb at the earliest convenience. 'Then I thank you for coming tonight, Sebastian, when you really didn't have to. When you could have asked for a private viewing another day. When you could have avoided this evening.'

'But then that would have taken more time and knowing you a little as I do, I expect that you might have done something impulsive to get hold of the comb again, since you seem to have an uncanny ability to get yourself into all sorts of trouble. And frankly, I could not afford that risk, since I have a vested interest in you finding the treasure.'

'You do?'

'Certainly. I am a man of my word, after all.' He flicked his gaze around the room before glancing back in her direction. 'But if you continue to smile up at me in that way, Eliza, we are going to get far more of that unwanted attention that we're both trying to avoid.'

'Oh, yes, of course… I'm sorry,' she said, flustered and looking away. 'Well observed.'

How mortifying to be found admiring Sebastian so openly that it had to be pointed out to her by said man.

'It's one of my many…er…talents.' He coughed, clearing his throat. 'And yours, too, I should imagine, to be able to see without your spectacles. May I ask why you have forgone them this evening?'

No, Eliza did not want to explain her vanity, knowing that it was quite laughable for her to want to appear far more than she was.

'No reason,' she muttered, feeling a little exposed to Sebastian's scrutiny. And just like that she wished in part that she was doing this on her own, without

Sebastian's help. For one thing, she was finding it difficult to be around him, with this unwelcome attraction simmering between them and bubbling up to the surface constantly. It made her forget herself when she had more important things to consider. And second, she didn't want to explain, nor reveal, more about herself to him. It wouldn't look well on her.

Eliza took a step away, wanting a little distance just for a moment, but did not see a servant carrying a tray of champagne flutes by her side and collided into him, making the poor man stumble back. He would also have fallen over had Sebastian not helped to steady him. The flutes of champagne, however, did fall, crashing to the ground.

*Oh dear...*so much for not wanting to draw attention to herself!

Sebastian bent down to the floor to help the servant, seemingly finding it difficult to stop himself from laughing.

'Do you mind?' she huffed, lowering herself to help him with clearing up the broken pieces of glass.

'Not at all.' He chuckled. 'I do not know how it is that you manage to go on when you stumble from one scrape to another.'

'Oh, very easily. I live to be the source of your entertainment, especially since I *stumble from one scrape to another*,' Eliza muttered, smiling apologetically at the servant who was trying to get both of them to leave it to him. Sebastian held out his hand to help her rise back to her feet.

'Thank you,' she said as she ran her hands down her dress, smoothing any creases and smiling inanely at some of the guests whose attention they had roused with the unfortunate accident.

'Apologies, Eliza, I shouldn't have laughed,' he said from the side of his mouth.

'Oh, do not worry. I'm quite used to making a complete fool of myself.'

'I wouldn't say that,' he said softly. 'You just have a knack for it. Besides, you wouldn't have collided with that poor fellow if you hadn't forgot your spectacles this evening. Where the devil are they?'

'I didn't forget them,' she said through gritted teeth as she stepped back behind a huge potted plant, hoping it might hide her. 'I chose not to wear them.'

'And why would you do that?'

She grimaced. 'It seemed far more fitting at a society event, and without them I also look more inconspicuous.' As well as looking more feminine, something she wouldn't dream of disclosing to Sebastian.

'Fitting?' Sebastian stepped back as well, to stand beside her once again, and inclined his head in greeting at a few of the guests who caught his eye. 'It isn't very fitting to stumble about into poor, unsuspecting servants, when you can barely see. Or is it the large quantity of champagne you've guzzled down that has you so unsteady?' he teased.

'Must you plague me like a bad smell?' she whispered.

'Bad smell, eh?' he murmured, his brows furrowed in the middle. 'That's not what you said before. I believe you quite liked my...er...smell.'

Oh, God, she did. Sebastian's usual delicious scent of sandalwood, bergamot and lemon had been enticing her as it wrapped around her senses, making her feel a little light-headed, or perhaps that was indeed the champagne? Either way, she didn't have time for it.

'I did.' She grabbed another flute of champagne and after giving Sebastian a defiant look, swigged the whole lot in one gulp. 'But now I find it a bit cloying.'

'Is that so? Well, in any case, I feel it best to keep a close eye on you, just so you don't tumble into any other unsuspecting guests or servants.'

'So that I don't make an idiot of myself, you mean?'

'Indeed.'

'What would I do without you?' she muttered sardonically as she tried to place her flute on the side table and missed. Had it not been for Sebastian's quick hands catching it before it fell down, it would have crashed to the floor.

'I simply don't know,' he said, placing the flute carefully on the table before looking her up and down. 'Besides, you don't need to forgo your spectacles, Eliza. I find that they add a certain charm to your person that I must admit I rather like.' The backs of his fingers touched her gloved hand accidentally as they stood side by side.

Eliza swallowed, feeling a little breathless. This was the way it was with Sebastian Marsden. One moment she was grateful to him for his kindness, the next he was exasperating her with his annoying habit of watching her intently and constantly challenging her, and then finally he had to say something wonderful that stunned her completely.

He thinks I have a certain charm? And he rather... likes me?

Well, she could quite easily wrap herself in the warmth and tenderness of such words. Ones that made her feel like she was cocooned against the harshness of the world around her. She smiled up at Sebastian, wanting to be held in those muscular arms of his.

'Although it would also help in your endeavours if you could actually see where the devil you're going as well,' he added.

Or perhaps not...

God, the man was infuriating when he pulled and

pushed her emotions this way and that; she had no time for any of this.

'Well, as I said, I wouldn't know what I'd do if you weren't here, Sebastian. I'd probably fall flat on my face.'

'Very probably,' Sebastian agreed. 'By the by, I'm not the only one here tonight who has been watching your every move.'

She frowned. 'What do you mean?'

'There on the other side of the salon. But I suppose if you'd not forgone wearing your charmingly practical spectacles, you might be able to recognise the blighter who's been giving you daggers from a distance,' he said. 'I must say, he looks remarkably like your late husband.'

'Ronald Carew…' she growled in irritation. 'The new Viscount of Ritton.' And a major pain in her backside. The man had persistently attempted to see her in the past few weeks but Eliza had no interest in being accused, yet again, of stealing from the Ritton estate. Of all the bad luck to encounter him here, however. This night was beginning to go from bad to worse!

'Has he been giving you trouble, Eliza?' Sebastian said in a clipped tone as she looked up to find that all prior amusement had been replaced by an implacable coldness in his eyes that made her shiver.

'Nothing that I cannot handle,' she said, trying to placate the large, suddenly outraged man beside her. She felt strangely humbled that he felt this protective of her and could not think of the last time anyone had acted that way on her behalf. Still, she didn't need to drag anyone else into her battles. 'Please, Sebastian, there's nothing you need to worry about.'

'Very well, but do let me know if the man causes you any discomfort.'

'Thank you.' She sighed deeply. 'For now, I would rather not have to encounter him.'

'Understood.' Sebastian nodded. 'What ho, Sir Horace, old chum. How are you? Lovely evening.'

Sir Horace raised his pink-hued pudgy face from a short distance away and ambled towards them.

'What in the blazes are you doing?' she uttered from the side of her mouth.

'I believe I'm killing two birds with one stone. Keeping away unwanted men and getting you the chance to view your medieval comb, Eliza,' he said, winking at her.

How was it that she'd almost forgotten about the real reason she'd come to this soiree? Most likely because of the man who stood beside her, who made her feel all kinds of emotions that befuddled her senses.

Well, no more. Eliza could not afford to become diverted from her endeavours. Especially not by Sebastian Marsden, even if the man meant well.

Chapter Nine

Sebastian felt Eliza's nervousness as she stood beside him. And as well as that, he had sensed her unease at the possibility of coming face-to-face with the new Viscount Ritton, which was quite surprising. It was not something that he had expected from her and he decided to get one of his men to enquire into that situation at a later time. Still, he'd be damned if he allowed anyone to believe they could cause Eliza more distress. The woman had had enough of that from her late husband.

'Try to smile, my lady. Sir Horace is about to reach us.'

'I am smiling,' she insisted through a fixed grimace.

'Really? Is that what you call it?'

'Yes!'

'Try and recall that beguiling smile you gave me a moment ago. The one where you looked so enthralled with me.'

'I was never enthralled with you!' she denied in a heated whisper.

'Were you not? My mistake. It must have been something else entirely that made you blush in that endearing way.' He nodded at Sir Horace. 'Ah, Middleton, good to see you again. May I introduce the Countess Ritton to you?'

'Her ladyship and I were already introduced earlier, Marsden.' Sir Horace sketched a formal bow and smiled pleasantly from one to the other.

'Indeed, Sir Horace, I'm delighted to be invited to your soiree and to have had this opportunity to meet you in person.'

'And I, you, my lady. I'm glad that you are out in society again after the premature demise of your husband after falling off his horse. Terrible accident.'

'Thank you,' she murmured.

The man turned to Sebastian. 'I must say I'm very glad that you accepted my invitation, Marsden. There's a small matter that I would like to speak to you about in private. At your convenience, of course.'

And there it was. The trade-off that Sir Horace was seeking in exchange for allowing them access to his precious comb. It was always the way with these men who frequented his club. Why else would the man have insisted Sebastian attend this frankly boring soiree? They sensed a bargain could be made in gaining more credit, or for markers to be written off, and thought a glass or two of champagne would seal the deal. In this case, however, Sebastian was prepared to acquiesce to the man's demands as he wanted Eliza to ascertain whether the comb was important to her search or not.

'Certainly, Sir Horace. You can come by the club to-morrow afternoon and we can discuss your...er. small matter then.' He gave Horace Middleton a speaking look, warning him not to mention any of it to Eliza.

'Capital.' He beamed. 'Capital.'

'And as to the other matter we spoke of, Middleton?'

'The other matter?'

'Yes. I was telling Lady Eliza of your vast collection of Devon and Cornwall-related artefacts.'

'Oh, yes, I have a bit of soft spot when it comes to Cornwall as my old mother was from that part of the world.'

'What a happy coincidence eh, my lady?' Sebastian slid his gaze briefly to Eliza's in feigned surprise before addressing Middleton again. 'For Lady Eliza is also keen on old medieval relics and artefacts.'

Eliza smiled. 'Yes, I suppose I am.'

'It must be because Lady Eliza hails from the county itself just like your dear mother, Middleton, and as a

Bawden-Trebarr, my lady is naturally drawn to all things Cornish. Do I have the right of it, my lady?'

Sebastian gave his head a tiny shake when he saw a slight look of panic enter her eyes. She turned her head and smiled again at Sir Horace. 'Yes, yes, of course. For that very reason, Mr Marsden.'

'Bawden-Trebarr?' Sir Horace's red face screwed into a scowl. 'Did you say Bawden-Trebarr?'

'It was my maiden name, Sir Horace. I am, in fact, the last of the Bawden-Trebarrs.'

'Are you indeed?' Sir Horace suddenly beamed at Eliza. 'By Jupiter, but of course! That must be the reason for your interest in my boxwood hair comb. Allow me to show it to you. Please come this way. You, too, Marsden.'

Sebastian fell into step beside Eliza as they followed Sir Horace out of the main salon in silence and strode along the hallway and down the sweeping staircase, entering a room on the ground floor.

They followed him inside a plush, well-stocked library filled with many leather armchairs and rows upon rows of bookcases groaning with first editions and huge dusty old tomes. The roaring fire in the grate along with the oil lamps dotted around the room gave the impressively huge space a snug warm glow.

'There,' Sir Horace said, steering them towards a glass cabinet set against the furthest wall in the room.

'This is what I believe you were seeking, my lady. A comb that is believed to have been gifted to Elowen Bawden by Simon Trebarr when they were bound in marriage, bringing your ancestors together, my lady.'

'Thank you, Sir Horace.' Eliza smiled, putting her hand to her chest as she looked at the beautifully crafted medieval comb that had brought them to this soiree. 'It is indeed very thrilling to see something so precious.'

'Yes, it is.' He chuckled. 'Hasn't this turned out well?'

'Very well. But it seems you have rather overwhelmed Lady Eliza, Middleton.'

'I have, I have,' he said, putting his hands on either side of his hips, evidently very pleased with himself. 'It is like rolling back the hands of time when one looks at something like this.'

'I believe so, Sir Horace, thank you.'

'My pleasure, my lady.'

Just then the door of the library opened and a servant came in and glanced around until he saw them together at the far wall. 'I'm sorry to intrude, Sir Horace, but you're wanted in the main salon by the mistress.'

Meaning the man's sister, whose idea this evening's soiree probably was, wanted Sir Horace to be beside her attending to his hosting duties rather than showing them his treasured artefacts.

'Go ahead, Sir Horace, but if you'd allow Lady Eliza just a little more time to appreciate the comb, we shall follow you in a moment or two,' Sebastian said with an implacable smile.

The man nodded as he turned to leave. 'Take all the time you need, my lady. Marsden.'

The door shut, leaving Sebastian and Eliza in the library alone. For a long moment she just continued to stare at the hair comb—such an innocuous everyday item—and wondered how this could in any way shed light on the whereabouts of the Bawden-Trebarr treasure. If it even existed.

Eliza sighed deeply. 'It certainly seems to be the one we've been seeking.'

The only noise in the room that could be heard was the occasional crackle of the fire spitting and hissing in the fireplace.

'I believe it is.' He frowned, looking across at her. 'However, I did think you might be more excited to find it again.'

'Oh, I am, thanks to you and of course, Sir Horace.' She turned slowly towards him. 'But what I want to know is what you negotiated with him to facilitate this viewing, Sebastian. And before you deny you did such a thing, remember that I was once married to a man who used similar stratagems in his dealings to get around bargaining away markers that he owed. Not that Ritton was very good at it.'

Of course, Eliza would see through his ruse with Middleton. The woman was whip-smart, but she was also impulsive, chaotic and disorderly, which strangely enough he also liked about her. It somehow made her far more interesting.

'I know you must think that I am interfering, Eliza, but I believe I was thinking of you and finding a solution to the problem at hand—namely getting hold of the comb and finding more clues to your quest.'

'And I thank you for it but I would still like to know the terms you set with Sir Horace.'

'I believe that is between Middleton and myself.'

'You understand then that it puts me in a very difficult situation, Sebastian. I cannot have you negotiating such terms without my knowledge.'

He sighed irritably. 'Eliza, the debt that Ritton left you, which you're hoping to repay, is already a considerable amount. I thought to lessen it by making my arrangement with Horace Middleton privately. It was in no way meant to put you in a difficult situation, as you put it.'

'That is indeed very thoughtful of you. However, it would also make me even more beholden to you than I already am.' She shook her head. 'And I cannot allow that. If this…this collaboration between us is to work, then we need to be honest in our dealings.'

The truth was that he couldn't help coming to the woman's aid like some knight in shining armour. Yet, Sebastian could not understand why he wanted to. Aside from the visceral attraction that he felt for her, which still confounded him, he couldn't comprehend this need to help, assist and to protect. It was damned inconvenient!

'Very well,' he ground out. 'Our dealings will henceforth be honest and transparent.'

'Thank you. And the amount you negotiated with Sir Horace for us to have access to the comb?'

'Eliza…'

'The amount, Sebastian, if you would be so kind to tell me.'

'Five hundred pounds.'

She gasped. 'That is…quite a steep sum for a private viewing, if you do not mind me saying.'

'It is not just for a viewing. Sir Horace has agreed to sell us the comb, and will therefore bring it with him to our appointment tomorrow.'

'I see. Well, again, I must thank you for your foresight, Sebastian, although I am at a loss to understand why you'd undertake such an agreement with the man and think to keep it from me.'

It was a good question. Why did he care? He came

back to this question again and again and he still did not know the reason. Yet, he did care. The very fact that he had even attended an evening such as this, that made him feel exceptionally uncomfortable in his own skin, especially since he was forced to be amongst the very society that he always despised, even though Eliza had surprised him earlier by coming to his defence against anyone who might look down at him, made him realise the extent to which he did indeed care about Eliza Bawden-Trebarr's situation.

'What with your appreciation of old relics and artefacts, I thought you'd want to have the comb tucked back in its rightful place in its case inside the casket box. And I told you, I have a vested interest in you finding this treasure, if it exists. As I can get the debt paid and you can have your castle and estate back.'

'Very true. I'm grateful for your intervention, but you will add the five hundred pounds to Ritton's debt.'

'It is not necessary, Eliza.'

'On the contrary, it most certainly is.' She choked out an unsteady laugh. 'I don't have much left, Sebastian, but I still have my pride.'

'And you know what they say about pride?'

'That it comes before a fall?' she scoffed. 'Oh, I know. I have fallen many times and am prepared to fall and fail again, if it means that I can hold my head up while I attempt it. So, you will add the sum to the tally of what I owe you, if you please.'

'Very well.' He exhaled in resignation.

'Thank you,' she said, her shoulders sagging in relief as she slipped her hand in his, 'for making this all possible.'

'My pleasure.'

He swallowed uncomfortably, realising then how important it was for this woman to have this one hold on determining her own future when she'd been powerless to stop everything and anyone from being taken away from her before. Something he knew that she had in common with his own mother after his father's death. Was that why he found it imperative to help and protect Eliza when he himself had been powerless to do so for his own mother? In truth, it was likely the reason why he went out of his way to help Eliza, even if she wasn't always the easiest to deal with. But then, neither was he.

They descended into a silence but unlike before, the tension from the room seemed to drain away. In fact, the silence was now more companionable than anything else.

'Is that some kind of writing on it?' Sebastian asked as he picked up a magnifying glass left on top of the glass cabinet and passed it to Eliza. 'Just there.' He pointed at one of the intricate carvings on the hair comb.

Eliza nodded, squinting behind the magnifying glass. 'Yes, they're engravings with each of the family mottos on them. The one on the left is from house Bawden, with its motto of *karensa a vynsa cevatys ny vynsa.*'

The way she pronounced the words as they softly rolled from her lips sent a bolt of lust through his blood. He gave himself a mental shake. 'What does it mean?'

'It's Cornish for *love would, greed would not.*'

'And the Trebarr motto?'

'It's *Franc ha leal atho ve.*'

'In Cornish as well?'

'Indeed, it means *Free and loyal am I.*'

The two mottos couldn't be more different.

'Of course, they are quite…different from each other.'

'That's just what I was thinking.' He frowned. 'They seem to contrast one another, greatly.'

'I suppose that's true. Yet, perhaps complement each other, too.'

'Ever the optimist.'

'Not always. However, I like to think that the Trebarr ambition for greatness was tied to their honour and loyalty to one another. That it was this that actually made them great, especially when it was given freely.'

'And what of the Bawden motto?' Sebastian asked. 'Do you believe that love can conquer all while eliminating greed? Whatever that means.'

'No, I admit the Bawden motto has always stumped me. If anything, it's far more open to interpretation.'

'You've obviously had more time to ponder on it. However, its very vagueness is what makes it open to how you want to define it. For instance, it's unclear whether the motto is referring to courtly love, family and kin love or even love of one's country.'

'True.' She nodded. 'But that is the beauty of both mottos. On their own they're fine and estimable, I suppose, but together they're strong, remarkable, powerful and complete one another in every sense.'

He glanced over at her and noted her wistful expression. 'I can imagine how you took delight in having all the family stories passed down from your mother.'

She nodded and smiled absently. 'And my father, who was also a Bawden-Trebarr but from a different, more distant, branch of the family. Their marriage was to preserve the family name, and continue the longevity of future generations. Much good it did them with me as their only surviving child.' Sebastian had not known this. Indeed, when Eliza had said earlier that she was the last of the Bawdens and Trebarrs, she had meant it literally. 'In any case, as far as Elowen and Simon and their two great houses go, I believe they must also have completed one another for here is yet another example of their love for one another,' she said, lifting her eyes to his.

'Behold, a comb.'

'Not just any comb but one that was commissioned specifically to be given as a token of love.'

'A happy story, then?'

She shook her head. 'Not quite. There was a time before the union of Elowen Bawden and Simon Trebarr when the two families contrasted in every sense. They were essentially mortal enemies.'

'Mortal enemies, eh? You have a furtive imagination, Eliza.'

'It is true. The hatred that the Bawdens and the Trebarrs bore for one another was the stuff of legend.'

'So, you're saying that Elowen and Simon were star-crossed lovers?'

'They were. They married against the wishes of Elowen's father. Against the wishes of their clan, their kin,' Eliza revealed with a faraway smile on her face. 'My mother did used to fill my head with stories about their love, which was wondrous, overcoming all of adversity. In fact, I think that was the real legend of the Bawden-Trebarrs—the everlasting love between Elowen and Simon. A love for all time.'

'Very Romeo and Juliet.'

'With the exception being that their union did not end in tragedy but a long and gloriously happy life together.'

'Ah, so not a cautionary tale like you mentioned before.'

'No, not for them.'

'So they did have their happily-ever-after,' he murmured.

'Yes. Although they had to go through much strife and difficulty before they did.' She sighed and shook her head. 'In any case, all that tosh about finding one's all-consuming, everlasting true love like Elowen and Simon did built up in my head, and I admit it was something that I longed for myself when I was younger. I truly believed in it. But after my marriage to Ritton I realised it was not for me, after all. That what made Elowen and Simon's story unique was that they were exceedingly lucky to have found one another. Not every person has the same fortune in finding it. As it happens, very few do. A very lucky few.'

'I must say that for the life of me, I can't imagine a woman like you with a man like Ritton,' Sebastian said with a frown. 'Why did you marry the blighter?'

He wondered whether she was going to ignore that impertinent question but eventually she answered, with resignation and dismay.

'It seems very shallow of me but it was because he was a viscount, because my parents—in particular, my father—wanted me to. Because Ritton showered me with so much attention and could be, believe it or not, very persuasive and charming. Oh, when we courted, in those early days, he was attentive, charismatic and amiable. But it was all an act. The moment we married and he got his hands on my dowry, he changed overnight. He was hostile, aggressive and cruel. And he enjoyed nothing more than humiliating me as he often did in society, by his mockery of me, or by parading his paramours about town, lavishing them with expensive gifts and making my life as miserable as possible. At first, I believed it was my fault for being unfeminine, as he accused me of being, so I would try to please him. I tried to be a good wife to him but nothing I did was ever enough.'

God, but Ritton was fortunate that he was dead and did not have to face Sebastian now. Justice would certainly have been meted out to the man if he had been. In truth, the viscount had been nothing but a pathetic bully. Even so, it was now the second time tonight that Eliza had referred to herself in such unflattering terms. A terrible thought nagged at him.

'Tell me, was it Ritton who insisted on the removal of your spectacles at functions such as this?'

She raised a brow in obvious surprise. 'How did you know?'

'A lucky conjecture.' He took her hand in his. 'But know this, with or without your spectacles, you're beautiful.'

'Oh, you jest, Sebastian.'

'I speak in earnest, Eliza,' he murmured, lifting her hand to his lips. 'You are indeed a uniquely beautiful woman.'

'Thank you,' she said as colour flushed into her cheeks and down her neck.

'Perhaps it's a bit forward of me to say so. However, it is the truth.' He shrugged, feeling that he might have overstepped again. He had to keep reminding himself that he mustn't get too close to this woman, as that would undoubtedly complicate their arrangement. 'And you never know, Eliza. You might marry again.'

'Marriage? Oh, I think not.' She shook her head. 'I think I have had my share of that. And besides, I am not the sort of woman who should have ever wed, Sebastian. In truth, I believe that I would've been far happier had I remained a spinster.'

'You cannot think that just because you were once wed to Ritton, Eliza. The man was never worthy of you.'

'No, he wasn't. I do believe that there are some people who are lucky enough to find that elusive happiness when they meet another person who completes them. But mostly they don't.'

'I thought you believed in that cautionary tale between star-crossed lovers but it seems that you're a romantic, Eliza.'

She gave a short laugh. 'Don't say it as though you have a bad taste in your mouth.'

He shrugged. 'It might be because I don't think that notions of love have anything to do with marriage per se.'

Mutual respect in one's alliance would have been sufficient had he been getting leg-shackled, as he would have once been expected to as the heir to the Harbury Earldom. But no longer. Besides, love was not an emotion that had ever held much sway with him since it left one far too exposed, far too vulnerable. He doubted he was even capable of truly loving another now, as the harshness of his life had shaped him to be quite a different man—one who'd had to learn to be ruthless in order to survive.

'Yes, that's true. I don't mean that love is a necessary component for a successful and happy marriage. Only that for me, after all the years that I had to endure living with Ritton, nothing now would entice me back to the altar. So you see, I am resigned and know that marriage is not something that is destined for me, as it was for my ancestors.'

Sebastian exhaled heavily and wondered how it was that they were here on this evening, at this soiree, in this room, staring at a medieval comb, confessing such intimate and personal things to one another. 'It is not fated for me, either. Perhaps once it was, when I was destined for…for another life. A boy who would grow to be someone else with a name so powerful, revered and commanding. One that would have made me into a very different man to who I am today.'

'But why would that difference in who you are now make you believe that you are fated to be alone?'

'I never said anything about being alone, Eliza,' he said wryly. 'Only that I do not believe in the institution of marriage itself. It's not for me.'

And never will be. Sebastian had vowed after the death of his mother that he would never be part of something that could cause the suffering and destruction of a helpless woman. And for what? His father's belief that he was above the law, that he could be so reckless and stupid as to forget something as important as a drunken night that had ended with a clandestine marriage to a young tavern maid at Oxford? A careless act that would later wreak havoc on his family, his wife of twenty years, his heirs.

'But what if you wanted to start a family? You would not want your children to suffer the ignominy of…of…'

'Being born as bastards?'

She caught her lip between her teeth and looked up at him. 'Yes, I suppose. Not that I would ever think of you as such,' she added quickly.

That made him want to smile; this woman who was so always forthright about everything she said and did, caring not a jot for the opinions of others and what they thought of her after her treatment at the hands of her worthless husband, which had undoubtedly made her stronger. Yet, she felt the need to shield him from the unpleasantness and shame of his birth. It touched him more than he could say. That she said this without even a trace of pity humbled him far more than she would ever know.

'That is what I am, in the eyes of the law,' he said, gently reaching out and running a finger across her cheek. 'And all because my father forgot that he had married another woman before marrying my mother.' He shrugged, dropping his hand and wondering why this conversation had suddenly turned to topics that made him so intensely uncomfortable. Still, he felt compelled to explain. 'I cannot ever begin to comprehend how someone could forget something as important as that and yet my father did. The folly of youth, I suppose, and believing that he was in some way invincible, that his actions would not come back one day to haunt us all.'

'I'm so sorry,' she murmured, placing her small gloved hand on his arm.

He swallowed uncomfortably. 'I doubt my father intended for his family to pay for his misdemeanours in the cruellest of all possible ways and yet it did. It left many scars. My mother, for one, never got over the shame of it.'

Sebastian's gaze dropped to her hand as he felt her squeezing his arm gently. 'Your poor mother.'

'Indeed,' he said, giving her a weak smile. 'And yours, Eliza.'

'Yes, they both seemed to have paid heavily for the misdemeanours and sins of their husbands. In my case, my father was far too dazzled by the prestige and supposed honour of Ritton's ancestry. Yet, he failed to see the man behind the title. He failed to see how venal, cruel and ultimately pathetic the man he'd bound me to was.'

'And as your father, he should've protected you.'

'As yours should have protected you—all of you.'

Sebastian nodded. 'So, you see, I, too, am resigned to what fate threw at me.'

Eliza lifted her hand from his arm and slowly peeled off both of her gloves, before cupping his jaw with her bare hand. A jolt of heat coursed through him, pooling in his groin. He looked down at her large eyes filled with concern and tenderness, wanting to touch her but knowing that if he did, he would not stop from wanting more from her. 'Yet, even with all that adversity, Sebastian Marsden, you still made a huge success of your life and those of your younger brothers. You rose to the challenge of rebuilding your life, which you did so…so very admirably.'

'Is that a compliment, Eliza Bawden-Trebarr?' he said, unable to keep a slow smile from curling around his lips.

'What if it is, Sebastian Marsden?'

'What if…' he murmured softly, dipping his head and touching his lips to hers, gently, reverently, as though he was testing the softness of her mouth, reminding himself again of the feel of her. Blast and damnation, but ever since that first time he'd kissed Eliza in the store cupboard at Gresham College he had wanted to do it again. And again. And again. Sliding his arm around her he pulled her closer as he deepened the kiss.

Chapter Ten

Eliza felt as though she was falling down, down, melting into Sebastian's kiss, as he slanted his mouth across hers over and over again. He wrapped his hand around her head, cradling it lightly, as all her senses heightened and she felt every little touch, every caress. Her whole body seemed to be ablaze, her clothes so tight, so constricting. She wanted to rip them all off. And then tear off his clothing as well, so that she could press herself close to the man, feel the pounding of his heart next to hers. Good Lord, but Eliza must be losing her mind. She did not believe that she was but heavens, she couldn't think very clearly at that moment.

His other arm drew her even closer and she went willingly. Eliza realised that she was trembling a little.

'Are you cold?' he asked as he nipped the shell of her ear.

'No,' she moaned, tipping her head back, giving him greater access to her flesh. 'But oh, yes.'

'Which is it?' His fingers traced a trail down her neck and across her bodice, his mouth following the same path. 'Yes or no?'

'Must you ask questions at this time?'

She felt his smile against her skin before he answered her. 'Yes. With you always, yes.'

Eliza wound her arms around his neck and drew him down as she went up on her tiptoes. 'How can I be cold, when you make me burn as much as you do?'

She pressed her lips against his and kissed Sebastian Marsden with all her being, as she threaded her fingers through his hair. It seemed that was all the encouragement he needed. He touched his tongue to the seam of her lips before deepening the kiss more by sliding it inside her mouth, devouring her. She matched every move, every flick, slide, nip of his lips, mouth, tongue and teeth and heard him growl in his throat. It was devastating, shocking, delicious and unlike anything she had ever experienced before. As though neither of them could get enough of one another. His one hand in her hair, loosening her tresses, with tendrils tumbling around her face, her pins falling out and scattering all over the floor.

'Burn?' he whispered. 'I make you burn?'

'Yes, oh, yes.'

He kissed her mouth again but this time taking his time; slower, gentler, far more languid as though there was no urgency, and time simply stood still, which of course it hadn't. They were in the library of Sir Horace Middleton's house. In the middle of his awful soiree.

She pulled away slightly and sucked on her swollen lower lip as she stared up at him.

'What is it?' he asked.

'Nothing, I just… I cannot… I mean I…'

'There you are, Eliza.' Cecy's voice sounded from across the other side of the library. 'I've been looking for you everywhere. And here you are… Oh, my goodness.'

Eliza screwed her eyes shut and pulled away abruptly, knowing that it was too late. Cecy had obviously seen her in Sebastian's arms, in such a shocking and scandalous manner. How awful must it look to her friend, as though they were engaged in a sordid *affaire*. But then they had been devouring each other's mouths only moments ago so Cecy had every right to be shocked. And although Eliza was a widow and was therefore allowed certain freedoms that were usually denied a young unmarried debutante such as Cecy, it was still unbecoming to be caught in this manner. She turned and gave her friend a weak smile and felt her cheeks burn with embarrassment.

'Oh, Cecy, how fortuitous,' Eliza said lamely but,

in all honesty, she still felt so dazed from those earlier melting kisses that she couldn't think of anything else to say.

'Yes, very fortuitous,' Cecy said from across the room, with her hands behind her back, looking at her feet. Thank goodness Cecy had found them on her own and had not come with a gaggle of guests. That was the last thing she needed. 'I came looking for you, Eliza, because Stephen is desirous to leave, if that… that is amenable to you?'

'Yes,' she practically squeaked, wanting to be far away from this awkwardly difficult situation that she'd been discovered in. God, how mortifying. She half turned and curtsied at Sebastian before striding as fast as she could towards Cecy. 'Good evening, Mr Marsden.'

'Before you leave, my lady, you might want to take these.' His voice hoarse and raspy. Good, at least he was just as affected as she was by all that had transpired between them.

Eliza stilled, took a deep breath and turned back towards the man who was holding her gloves in one hand and a couple of her silver-and-diamante hairpins in the other. She felt herself flush profusely, even more than before. Rushing back, she went to take the items from his outstretched hand. But when Eliza reached out and touched his much larger hand, it closed around hers so briefly that if her senses hadn't been so heightened already, she might have missed it. Her eyes shot to his for just a fleeting moment and she saw the smallest of smiles, lopsided and frankly boyish, playing around his lips. His eyes glittered with unbanked passion and bemusement before he let her hand go and bowed in front of her. Eliza turned and dashed back to her friend, knowing that this evening had not gone the way she'd imagined. Not at all...

The following day, Eliza kept on reliving that kiss, or rather those hot and passionate kisses, she'd shared with Sebastian Marsden in Sir Horace's library. It had come about so unexpectedly after they had shared such intimate and personal stories about their pasts and after discussing the Bawden and Trebarr mottos for goodness' sake. How did it go from that to Eliza throwing herself at him so ardently, so eagerly, and practically pawing at the man? Yet, Sebastian had seemed to be just as affected by her, too. And that was something that Eliza could not comprehend. That she could have such an effect on a man like Sebastian Marsden was frankly extraordinary. Yet, it appeared to be true. After all, had he not declared that he found her desirable? That he thought her...beautiful?

But what now? Where did it leave her with paying back what she owed him so that she could regain her estate? In very murky and uncharted waters. Eliza did not know where she stood on these important matters with him. It confused her beyond measure with her own feelings about him in total disarray. Lord knew that she was attracted to him but what woman would not be? He was the epitome of powerful, handsome masculinity. And with that confident air of self-assurance he had, oozing with natural charm and intelligence, Sebastian Marsden was the most fascinating man she'd ever met.

Still, Eliza could never forget that she had once trusted another handsome, amiable young man. And that had not ended well. While Sebastian was a vastly different man to Ritton, could she believe that he'd be true to his word and assist in getting her mother out of the asylum and continue to help her as he had been doing? Indeed, she was not even certain why he was helping her—apart from having a *vested interest* in Eliza finding the treasure to pay back the debt. He'd even arranged to pay Sir Horace Middleton for the medieval comb behind her back so that she wouldn't need to worry about owing more to him. Why would he do that? It humbled her that he would care but it also made her uncertain and unsure how to proceed with him.

She lifted her head at the sound of a commotion outside in the hall. What on earth…?

Eliza raised her brows and shot up to her feet, having been staring out the French doors and into the small lawned garden for the past few minutes. The sounds of raised voices got louder before the door violently swung open and Ronald Carew stormed in with Gertie following behind him, wringing her hands. 'I am so sorry, my lady, but his lordship would not accept that you were not receiving visitors today.'

The young viscount swung around to face her. 'I'll be damned if you think that I will not be received by you, Lady Elisabeth. After weeks of turning me away as though I were nothing but dirt underneath your shoes.'

'Thank you, Gertie, it's quite all right. His lordship will not be staying long. You may go but leave the door open, if you will,' she said with a smile, before turning her attention back to the viscount. 'How dare you presume to think that you can just storm into my home and terrorise my servants?'

'Had you the decency to receive me earlier, then we would have avoided this, madam.'

'Decency, you say? After this behaviour, I cannot and will not account for any unpleasantness that you have caused.'

'You forget yourself. I am now the head of the family, Lady Elisabeth.'

'And you appear to have forgotten that I am no longer a part of it.'

'You are still the Countess of Ritton, Lady Elisabeth, and as such you will behave accordingly.' He moved close to her, crowding her, his foul breath upon her. 'I want to know more about my cousin's debts, which I have inherited. I cannot believe that you would've been blind to them.'

'I care little for what you believe. And as for Ernest's debts you'd best meet with the estate lawyers and Ritton stewards instead of harassing me.'

'And yet, I cannot help but think you've been hiding something,' he said pointedly, his lips curling into a sneer.

She swallowed uncomfortably, wondering how in heaven she was going to get the man out of her house. Just as she was about to come back with another rejoinder, she heard a voice near the vicinity of the door.

'Am I interrupting?'

Thank God Sebastian was standing by in the door frame, his features schooled in steely, implacable composure. But she had never, however, seen him like this…as though he was holding on to his anger with a tight leash.

'How good to see you, Mr Marsden,' she said in a shaky voice. 'My late husband's cousin, Viscount Ritton here, was just about to leave.'

'Ritton,' Sebastian said with barely concealed coldness, his indignation emanating from his powerful frame. 'Move away from Lady Eliza, if you will.'

Ronald Carew pulled back but kept his eyes fixed to Eliza's. 'I cannot believe that you would entertain a man who beggared the estate of the viscountcy. Yet, once again, I find you in such familiarity with this… this scoundrel, just as I happened to witness at the Middleton soiree. It is utterly shameful.'

'Get out.' Eliza had had enough of the entire Ritton family, wanting nothing more to do with any of them.

'This is not over, Lady Elisabeth,' Carew muttered as he made his way towards the door.

'Oh, I think it is,' Sebastian retorted, brushing a bit of lint from his coat as he blocked the door with his frame. 'I will not hear of you pestering Lady Eliza again, Ritton. Do you understand?'

'Are you threatening me?'

'No, it's just a friendly reminder.' Sebastian glared coldly at the man before moving aside for him to pass through. 'But you would do well to remember it, Ritton.' The much smaller man must have recognised the intent in Sebastian's voice as he gulped before nodding, unable to say more. 'Good, I am so glad we understand each other.'

They were left in silence, Eliza reeling from the dreadful man's departure.

Sebastian looked soberly at her. His eyes now far more guarded and cautious than the last time she had seen him. 'Are you all right, my lady?'

'Yes, thank you.' She pasted a bland smile on her face as she addressed her maid, who was now hovering by the door, clearly still in shock from everything that had transpired. 'If you can bring the tea through, Gertie, thank you.'

'Certainly, my lady,' she muttered before bobbing a quick curtsy and leaving the room, closing the door behind her.

Eliza turned slowly to face him, rubbing her now throbbing forehead. 'I am glad that you're here, Sebastian. It seems that I'm always in debt to you in more ways than one.'

'It's nothing, I assure you. But if that bastard comes here again, especially when you're alone, then I want you to send for me.'

'I shall, thank you.'

'You know I cannot bear men who believe they can bully and abuse women into submission.'

Eliza blinked up at him and tilted her head, wondering whether he was referring to his mother. After all, only last night he had mentioned that his mother had not been well protected after his father's death. Did Sebastian believe that he'd failed to do so when he'd been nothing but a boy himself? Was that why he had continually wanted to help and protect her? Because somehow Eliza's situation resonated with what had happened to his own mother? Possibly...

But oh, her heart went to him, this proud, gruff, honourable man, who was nothing like the scoundrel that men like the new and not improved Viscount Ritton wanted to paint him as.

'No, neither can I, Sebastian. They are all cowards—as is Ronald Carew. And I would prefer not to think of the Ritton name any longer.'

It was a relief to have Sebastian arrive at her house when he did, even if it was awkward seeing him again so soon after the intimate kisses they had shared yesterday evening. At least after Ronald's outburst, she would be spared from discussing what happened between them.

'They seem to be rotten to the core in that family. Every other male worse than the one preceding them,' he said irritably as he dragged his fingers through his hair. 'I'm glad that you're no longer part of them.'

'As am I.' She nodded, her shoulders sagging a little as she turned to face him. 'Please, do take a seat. I am happy to see you, Sebastian, but I did not expect to see you so soon after...last night.'

She felt a blush creep up her chest and flood her cheeks as she waited for the man to speak. And yet, he didn't. For a long moment he stared at her and then without preamble, Sebastian took out a small velvet box from the pocket of his grey woollen overcoat and held it out to her. Eliza tentatively stepped forward and had to stop herself from leaning into the gorgeous lemon-and-sandalwood scent of his that always managed to wrap itself around her as though it were casting some indefinable spell on her.

Frowning, she took the velvet box from him and placed it on the table before opening it up. Taking a small surprised breath, she stared at the medieval boxwood hair comb.

'I see that your meeting with Sir Horace went well.' She flicked her gaze back to Sebastian's and smiled. 'What would I do without you?'

'I only did what most men would do, when they are in the position to help a lady.' He shrugged, looking a bit sheepish.

'Oh, I am not certain there are many men who would.' But then there were not many men quite like Sebastian Marsden. 'Thank you…again.'

That he'd done this for her made Eliza feel a lick of warm gratitude trickle through her and something else, something far more intimate and tender.

'You're quite welcome.' He seemed a little uncomfortable as he nodded towards the medieval comb and the Bawden-Trebarr casket box that she'd left on the table. 'Well? Are you going to inspect the comb?'

'Of course,' she replied as Gertie opened the door and brought over the tea tray laden with a steaming teapot, cups and saucers and a few lavender-spiced biscuits that she'd baked earlier that morning. 'Thank you, Gertie. How do you take your tea, Sebastian?'

'A drop of milk and no sugar please.' He took the cup that she passed to him, their fingers brushing briefly, sending a frisson of awareness up her arm. 'So, is there anything you can decipher from the comb, Eliza?'

She turned the comb around in her hand as she looked closely at it from behind her magnifying glass that she'd picked up from the table. 'No, not really. It is just a comb albeit a beautifully crafted one. I cannot make anything else out, apart from the front being slightly different in design than the back.'

'May I take a look?' he asked as Eliza passed the comb to him, their fingers skimming against each other again.

Goodness, but the way her pulse skittered whenever they touched was outside of enough! She really had to get a hold of herself around Sebastian as this would not do at all.

'Oh, yes, you're right. The two sides are very subtly different in design. I wonder why?'

'It is curious because the craftsmen certainly went to the trouble of making both sides of the comb look exactly the same.' She glanced up at him and pushed her spectacles up her nose. 'But other than this, I cannot see anything else out of the ordinary.'

'What about if you put the comb back in the original case and then inside the casket box. Perhaps something might present itself then?'

Eliza did as Sebastian suggested but sadly still, she could think of nothing. In fact, there was seemingly nothing more to it. She slumped indecorously on the chair beside the table and rubbed her brow for a moment. 'It seems that there's nothing about the comb that indicates how we should proceed.'

'No, it doesn't seem so.' Sebastian stood as he ran his fingers through his hair. 'Perhaps it was one of the other empty compartments that would have contained the clues needed.' He crouched over her, and lifted the leather case out of the box before removing the comb to inspect it once again.

'Perhaps.' Eliza shrugged before straightening in her chair as she suddenly pondered a far more intriguing possibility. 'Or perhaps not. May I have the comb, Sebastian? I would like another look at the differing designs on either side of it.'

Wanting to avoid yet another touch of his hand against hers, Eliza somehow managed to miss the comb as he passed it to her. She watched motionless as it fell and hit the side of the metal magnifying glass on the table.

'Apologies, Eliza,' Sebastian murmured.

'No, no, it was my fault.' She frowned, annoyed with her clumsiness. 'But no harm done. It's still in one piece.'

'Not quite.' He prised the comb from her fingers and turned it backwards and forwards. 'Look, there is now the smallest of gaps between the two sides. It must have come away when it hit the magnifying glass.'

'Yes…but wait, of course!' she exclaimed. 'That's the reason why the two sides have a slight difference in design.'

He nodded, understanding her. 'Because they are two different pieces stuck together to make it look as though it was made from one solid piece of wood.'

'Which means that this very small space in the middle, where you have all the intricate work, with the Bawden and Trebarr mottos engraved, is actually… hollow.'

'Brilliant.' Sebastian grinned. 'And it raises the question of why your ancestors wanted this beautiful comb to have a hollowed-out bit in the middle.'

'Are you thinking along the same lines as me?'

'I would say yes, if you're thinking along the same lines as me.'

She nodded excitedly. 'They wanted to hide something in the hollowed-out part.'

'Precisely.'

Her smile slipped from her face. 'However, to find out what that may be, we'd need to fully prise the comb open. And we cannot do that, as it would damage the comb, Sebastian. After all, it is an important piece of my heritage that you paid a considerable amount of money for.'

'Ah, but who said anything about damaging it? With any luck we'll open it and see if there's anything inside the comb. Afterwards, a craftsman can carefully restore it, as long as the two sides remain in one piece and don't break off. The difficulty will be the delicate comb teeth.'

'And how exactly are we to do that?'

'Watch. Like this.' He started to feel his way around the edges before fetching a small, jewelled dagger from a sheath strapped to the inside of his trouser leg. When he glanced up and caught Eliza's quizzical stare, he shrugged. 'It's an old habit from being a gaming hell owner. I never leave the club without it.'

'Yes, one never knows what dangers one might find in the sleepy streets of Chelsea.'

'True,' he said as he continued to feel his way forward, running his fingers and the tip of the blade around all the edges of the comb. 'The sleepy ones are always the worst.'

She chuckled softly. 'Any luck?'

'Just one moment. I think that there's something right here and...' Sebastian ran the small dagger over the edges again, hoping it might loosen the wood before placing it back in its sheath. 'It is slowly coming apart. Here, give me your hand.' He grabbed her hand in his absently and drew her fingers along the edge. 'Can you feel it?'

Eliza did feel it. She felt the warmth of his large hand covering hers. She felt the same spark of attraction, as she did every time they touched. And it was just the same as always; as it was last night at the soiree. With that came the flood of memories of being in his arms, being pressed against him and having his mouth on hers. Just the thought of it and Sebastian's nearness was beginning to make her feel too warm and breathless. But judging from his eager reaction to show her the opening of the comb, he was clearly unaffected by touching her. But then why would he be? Sebastian Marsden could have any woman he wanted, as a lover, a mistress or for a short dalliance. Had he not already explained that he would not remain alone despite vowing never to marry? There would certainly be no shortage of women vying for his attention. Even at the soiree, Eliza had noticed women young and old trying to garner his attention or catch his eye. And why did that thought give her such misgivings? Why did the thought of the man being with another woman make her feel so desolate...so jealous?

Because in a matter of time, that would be precisely what he'd do. He would be with another. Indeed, there would soon be no reason for them to continue to spend any time in each other's company. Which was just as it should be. After all, Eliza had come to him so that she could try to get her estate back, so that she could help secure her mother's release. And she would do well to remember that.

'Yes, it is the smallest of narrow gaps,' she muttered. 'But it is coming away, Sebastian. Do we need any other tools? I can ask Willis, my housekeeper's son, if he has anything that might work better than a mere dagger.'

'A mere dagger, you say.' He gave her a swift shake of the head before resuming. 'It's a beautiful piece studded with jewels on the hilt and the finest sharpest blade. I tell you that it is more than up to the task of prising this small sliver of wood open.'

She smiled. 'Ah, so you are not so immune to such artefacts from a bygone era, after all. Where did you get it from?'

He didn't answer. Instead, a muscle jumped in the corner of Sebastian's eye as he continued to work with his dagger against the wood, carefully so as not to break anything off. After a long moment he answered her. 'My father. He had three individually handcrafted daggers made for each of his precious sons,' he said bitterly. 'And in truth, it's the only thing we have left from him. That we managed to keep as they were legally ours and did not belong to the Harbury estate. So, yes, this dagger is definitely from a bygone era.'

Eliza stilled his hand by placing her own on top and giving it a squeeze. 'I can see why you would choose to take it everywhere you go.'

'Can you?' he asked.

'Yes,' she said, pulling out her mother's locket from around her neck. 'As it's the same reason I carry this with me everywhere I go.'

Sebastian paused and looked up at her. 'What is it that you're trying to say, Eliza?'

'That by always carrying your dagger, it's as though you're carrying a small piece of your father with you.'

Sebastian stared at her, his gaze penetrating, unfathomable as it flashed with some unknown emotion before being masked over, barring her from seeing any more. He turned away and continued to work in silence as Eliza watched him, mesmerised by the dextrous and efficient way he worked methodically but relentlessly to loosen and prise the comb open.

She hadn't known this about Sebastian Marsden.

That he carried the one thing he had left from his father. The very man who had lived so recklessly, so carelessly, that he hadn't realised that he'd been a bigamist and had plunged his whole family into absolute disaster after his death. This was what Sebastian carried about with him. A gift. Yet, he'd claimed that he hated the idea of relics and artefacts from the past. He'd even mocked her for doing so…yet he carried this. Why?

'Don't get any ridiculous notions in your head.'

'I cannot know to what you are referring.'

He sighed before turning his head around. 'Do not get any sentimental hogwash into your head because I can tell that is exactly what you're doing, Eliza Bawden-Trebarr.'

'I wouldn't call it sentimental hogwash per se.'

'Oh, but I would.' He took a long moment as though weighing up how much he was willing to say, and how much he wanted to conceal. 'The truth is that there is no real reason why I carry this dagger wherever I go, other than I like it. Apart from being exquisitely made, the dagger is versatile. Note what I am currently using it for. And it's practical. But other than that, it holds no value to me.'

'Despite your father gifting it to you?'

'Despite that.'

Eliza didn't know why but she didn't quite believe

him. There were plenty of daggers that he could own that were just as versatile, just as practical, but it was this one that he was attached to. And although he might not want to admit it, she couldn't help thinking that it was precisely for sentimental reasons that he carried it wherever he went. Because it reminded him of a man whom he'd loved but had been ultimately disappointed by. He'd left Sebastian not only to fend for himself after the death of his mother, but caring for his younger brothers as well.

Sebastian made one last flick of the wrist before placing the comb on the table.

Carefully, he used the tips of his fingers to prise the wood open very slowly and as he lifted his dark gaze to Eliza, he smiled. 'Well, can you see anything between the two?'

'I am not completely certain yet but yes, I think there's something there.' Eliza grabbed a small teaspoon from the tray and using the round tip of the spoon placed within the opening, she started to carefully drag out whatever was there.

She paused then glanced up at Sebastian for a long moment before taking a deep breath and pulling out the edge of what looked like a folded piece of vellum. She exhaled long and slow as she teased the remainder out and held it gingerly in her hands.

Very carefully, she unfolded the old vellum in case

it crumpled and disintegrated before they'd even had a chance to see what was written on it. Taking another deep breath to steady the butterflies in her belly, she placed it on the table and raised a brow. For there, on the decayed piece of vellum, were faded, strange markings all over it. Whatever could they mean?

'It looks like a parchment with some sort of message inscribed on it.'

'I believe so.' She nodded. 'Or possibly clues to direct one to the Bawden-Trebarr treasure.'

Sebastian smiled. 'Then it seems as though the legend was true after all.'

'Yes.' She lifted her eyes to meet his. 'It seems that it was.'

Chapter Eleven

Sebastian paced back and forth under the great pillars at the entrance of the British Museum, waiting for Eliza to finally arrive. They had agreed to meet at the museum after finding the folded parchment hidden inside the comb the previous day, but she was more than half an hour late. Where on earth was she? He knew how impulsive and single-minded Eliza could be once she had the bit between her teeth, and she certainly had that now with this new discovery. What if the woman reneged on their meeting and decided to continue on her own? What if she had got into another difficulty just as she'd done yesterday, when he'd walked into her parlour to find Ritton attempting to intimidate her? The man had been lucky that Sebastian had not tossed him out on his backside, as he'd wanted to. But he'd certainly got a rude awakening last night when Sebastian had entered the viscount's venerated home and gave him another friendly warning that if he ever spoke to Eliza again, let alone came within a hundred yards of her, his life wouldn't be worth living. As usual with bullies, the man had spluttered and whimpered but eventually agreed. Good. Sebastian would not allow Ritton or anyone else, for that matter, to hurt her. He paused midstep.

When had Eliza become so…so precious…so vital to him? Even thinking about the woman in such terms knocked the air out of his lungs. The truth was that Sebastian liked her…he liked her a lot, even if that surprised him more than he could say. And as he'd admitted to her himself, he found her desirable and was finding being in close proximity to her increasingly difficult. Especially now that he knew the feel and taste of her mouth. She had somehow gotten under his skin and lingered there. And he could not help any of it just as he could not help the sun from rising.

However, that did not mean that he was no longer frustrated by her. How in the name of all that was holy had she not got into trouble before he'd met her, he would never know—even when she decided to wear her spectacles, as she should. And yet, he just couldn't help himself; he liked Eliza…very much indeed.

'Good morning, Sebastian,' she uttered from behind him. 'Are you going to continue to pace in that inordinate manner? For I must say it is making me feel quite giddy.'

'It doesn't take much to make you giddy, especially if there are any poor, unsuspecting servants around.' He turned to face her, removing his hat and inclining his head in greeting. 'I hope you're well on this fine morning, Eliza?'

'Thank you, I am, and I hope it finds you in good spirits as well.'

'It does,' he murmured as he tucked her hand into the crook of his arm and started for the door to the entrance of the museum. 'I do hope you do not make a habit of being late for appointments, however, as we continue to work together.'

'Try as I might, it is one of my many flaws.'

'I can hardly believe it.'

They walked together through the huge wooden door and into the black-and-white marble-floored foyer with tall ceiling, arches and pillars in the classical Grecian design.

'I must admit that what I am intrigued by is why you'd want to work with me, why you'd want to help. I know that you have said something about having a vested interest in me finding the treasure. Yet, in doing so, you would lose my Cornish estate that you had designs on building a few hotels on. It's something that I have been wondering about, Sebastian, as I cannot understand why you would choose to lose all that.'

It was something that he could not understand, either. But then by helping Eliza, he would still have a reason to be close at hand, should she need him.

'That is exactly the point, Eliza,' he said gently. 'I'm now in the enviable position of being able to choose, to be able to do as I please. And yet, through no fault of your own, you do not have that same choice.'

'Few women do, Sebastian. Of any station.'

'I realise that. Which is why I want to redress the balance, I suppose. I… I cannot stand the injustice of it.'

'Very noble of you.' She looked up sharply at him, pushing back her spectacles as she realised her mistake in using that damned word. She quickly added, 'In the truest sense you are indeed very noble and honourable. Indeed, the most noble and honourable man of my acquaintance.'

He shrugged. 'Not bad for a bastard gaming hell owner.'

'But you are far more than that, Sebastian.'

Was he? Is that how Eliza saw him? More than the mere parts that made him who he was? He strangely liked to be valued by her.

'Cease your praise, my lady, or you might put me to the blush.' He grinned. 'Besides, you'll make me forget the news I bring you, regarding your mother.'

'My mother?' Eliza halted and glanced up at him

eagerly. 'What? Oh, what has happened? Please tell me, what news?'

'It's nothing of note yet, but I've managed to ask the asylum she's at to review her case.'

She blinked several times at him before a slow smile spread on her lips. 'Oh, Sebastian, you have my eternal gratitude. Thank you.'

'There's a long way to go. However, I'm hopeful that this is the first step in getting her out of there.'

She grabbed both his gloved hands in hers and squeezed them. 'How can I ever repay you?'

This was something that Sebastian could not and would not think about. Not at this moment in time when everything between them was as tenuous as it was. He preferred to worry about that at another time, when they both might know where they stood with each other.

'I believe that parchment we discovered yesterday might hold the answer to that,' he said flippantly as they walked inside the main entrance hall and into the huge galleried rooms.

'Touché.' She laughed as they began to stroll side by side again, stopping occasionally to look at some of the exhibits. 'And thank you again. It's most welcome news.'

He shrugged. 'I did promise to help, if I could.'

'You did. And in return I wish to honour my promises just as well.'

'I am certain you shall do your utmost to.'

She raised a brow. 'You make it sound as though you doubt my sincerity.'

He gave her a pointed look. 'Quite the contrary. I don't doubt it but you do realise that you're pinning all your hopes on what you might find on that vellum inside your portmanteau.'

'It is all I have, Sebastian. That and my wretched pride.'

'I know it. It's the same pride that refused to allow me to gift you the hair comb that I bought from Sir Horace, and the same pride that would also refuse me, should I choose to give you back your ancestral estate, which I have the power to do.'

'Of course not. I could never accept that.'

'Indeed. So, you see, I have to help you find the treasure. I have to help you get back your crumbling old castle. There's no other way,' he drawled. 'Now, where to, my scholarly bluestocking? I still do not know why we are here.'

She paused midstep before lifting her head. 'We're here to decipher the inscription on the vellum. But oh, Sebastian, look…look around you and take this wondrous place in. It really is the most magical of places.'

'If you say so. You know my opinions well on the subject of knickknacks from bygone eras.'

She sighed. 'It is a shame that I cannot convince you of the splendour of some of the exhibits here.' She pointed at a huge familiar stone. 'Take for instance the Rosetta Stone there. It looks like an ordinary slab of stone but look closer and what do you see?'

'Strange inscriptions, and if memory serves from those days at Eton, one column that looks vastly similar to some of the Greek we used to learn.'

'Exactly. The significance of this stone is that because of our understanding of both the Greek and Demotic inscriptions on either side there, scholars were then able to decipher the Egyptians' hieroglyphs. Those strange markings there.'

'Fascinating.' It genuinely was. Sebastian could admit to being impressed with the large stone, especially the Egyptian hieroglyphs that had Eliza in raptures. Not that he wanted to dwell on other things that had the woman in raptures, namely their heated, intimate kisses and those soft moans that escaped her lips. He gave himself a mental shake. 'So, you're interested in this unusual Egyptian language, then?'

'Yes, aren't you?'

'Well, I cannot say that I have given it much thought.'

She stopped to address him. 'Don't you see that

with the Rosetta Stone, scholars were able to unlock the hieroglyphs and understand so much about this ancient civilisation that would otherwise have been closed off to us? It is this that interests me. The fact that this unremarkable-looking stone manages to link us to the past. It tells us about how these people lived thousands and thousands of years ago.'

'While I can comprehend how thrilling such a thing is, I fear that I will never be interested in anything that links us to the past. I rather prefer to live in the present and firmly believe that the past belongs in the past.'

'Ah, but without it how can one learn and move forward?'

'Like many things, one step at a time, Eliza.'

She frowned. 'You and I are never going to agree on this, are we?'

'I don't suppose that we shall.' He flicked his gaze around the place. 'No, sadly, this dusty old place does little for me, interesting as the Rosetta Stone is. Indeed, I cannot recall ever coming here unless I was forced to.'

'Which you were not on this occasion. You need not have accompanied me, Sebastian.'

No, he did not need to have come here. There were a million and one things that needed his attention, and traipsing all over London, following Eliza on her quest, was certainly not one of them. It amused his brothers, especially Dominic, immensely. The jibes he'd had to listen to the past few days regarding following his bluestocking around apparently like a lost puppy was outside of enough. But cool and collected, he never rose to it, knowing it would only confirm their beliefs regarding Eliza. And in truth, Sebastian could have got one of his men to keep a close eye on her but had wanted to do it himself.

'True.' He raised a brow. 'But I insisted on coming.'

'Yes, you did.' She nodded. 'And I could hardly forget your opinions on this *stuff*, with the exception of your practical and versatile dagger. Why it practically makes you come out in a rash.'

He gave a short laugh and shook his head. 'How well you seem to know me.'

'I do.' They stared at one another for a moment before Eliza coughed, clearing her throat. 'Anyway, we haven't come to look at the many wonderful exhibits but to look at some old Celtic and Cornish inscriptions that I need to check against the markings made on the vellum.'

'Yes, and I assume it's well protected somewhere in that overly large portmanteau?'

'Yes, it is. And what is wrong with my practical and versatile portmanteau?'

'Nothing except you always seem to carry the whole world and everything you own in there.'

His jest was met with a small smile. 'That's possibly because everything I own can fit quite neatly inside it, Sebastian.'

Implying that her worldly possessions consisted of so few items. He could kick himself for his thoughtlessness. Damn it, but it didn't seem right that a woman like Eliza should be reduced to this. It did not seem right at all. Even when there were many women and children littered all over the city in far worse circumstances than Eliza. And while his natural instinct was to help many of those in need, it was this one woman who presently seemed to matter to him. And for reasons he could still not fathom.

'Eliza, I did not mean…'

'I know.' She nodded. 'Come, we need to get to the first floor, and by the by, Sebastian, were you aware that you just called me *your* scholarly bluestocking? That you used such words?'

Naturally, Eliza would notice his mistake and rather than pretend that she'd misheard him, insist on finding out more.

'I had not noticed.' He turned to her and gave her a bland smile. 'It must have been a slip of the tongue. Come along, then. Let's see about these Celtic and Cornish inscriptions of yours.'

They continued to the side hallway that led to the stairwell and ascended the stairs in silence. On reaching the first floor, they moved from room to room until they eventually reached the one space that housed the exhibits dedicated to Celtic, Brittonic and Cornish artefacts dating back over a thousand years. Eliza then moved into the next smaller antechamber just off the room.

'Where are you going?' Sebastian asked. 'I thought we'd come to look especially at the Celtic and Cornish room?'

'Not quite,' she said as she moved towards the lone man, evidently a steward working at the museum. The smaller antechamber housed many rows of desks, with oil lamps over each one and chairs beneath each desk. 'We've come here for something very specific.'

They reached the steward, who was standing beside a small desk with an opened tome on top. He gave them a curt bow before speaking. 'My lady, you have only one hour before I come back for it. Please take care and keep the oil lamp away from the book.'

'I shall, thank you.'

Eliza waited until the steward left and lowered herself onto one chair as Sebastian sat beside her. 'So, would you like to explain why we are here and what we are doing?'

'Certainly. This—' she pointed at the huge book '—is the *Vocabularium Cornicum*, a twelfth-century Latin-to-Kernewek or rather, Cornish, glossary. It will help us decipher the transcript of the message in the vellum.'

'Wait one moment, Eliza.' He turned to her. 'Last time we looked at the vellum together, there was no message that I could see. Just a load of faded jumbled-up words that made little sense. Please do not say that it was this…this Kernewek, or Cornish language?'

'Well, yes, it is all in Cornish but no, that's not what any of the jumbled-up words were.'

Eliza took the vellum from her portmanteau and smoothed it out flat on the desk and then got out her large magnifying glass and a sheet of foolscap. She started to read from the glossary and make notes on the foolscap using the inkwell and quill that had already been provided.

He frowned. 'I don't comprehend.'

'The jumbled-up words—that is exactly what they were, Sebastian.'

'Were?'

'Yes, and now they're not.' Eliza had her head down as she continued to look through the glossary and then make more notes on the foolscap. 'I managed to decipher the message into legible Cornish. All I need to do now is translate it into English—hence the need for this glossary.'

'Allow me to understand you, Eliza. You have already deciphered the vellum? When did you do this and…how?'

'I did it yesterday evening after you left, knowing it was a good use of my time to decipher the message before coming here.' She lifted her head and glanced at him. 'And as for the how…it was really quite simple once I realised that the first and last letter of each word had been replaced by one letter sequentially before the actual one. So, any word starting with the letter *b* for example in the text was actually starting with the letter *a*. And so on.'

'That's brilliant, Eliza,' he said, smiling at her and shaking his head in amazement. 'Absolutely brilliant.'

'Thank you,' she said, giving him a bashful smile. 'It's something I quite enjoy doing, actually. Deciphering and decoding manuscripts.'

'I'm impressed.'

'Easily so, it seems.' She chuckled, dismissing his compliment at hand, which bemused him slightly.

Eliza did not seemingly know how take flattery, which once again showed the extent that she had been spurned and overlooked by those who were supposed to cherish her so. He hoped that at least her friends, such as Miss Cecily Duddlecott, did. She seemed to be just as uniquely different as Eliza.

'So, are you going to tell me what the translation says?'

She nodded. 'Look through the magnifying glass, Sebastian. The first line is *Rag karrow Bawden ha Trebarr.*'

'And that means...?'

'"For the love of Bawden and Trebarr,"' she said, pointing at the second line. 'You can see that I have deciphered the second line into Cornish, too. *Ny dal keles man an pyth a thue gvelis veyth.*'

'Yes, I see that,' he said, looking at both the original vellum through the magnifying glass and the line that Eliza had written out after it had been decoded. 'And have you worked out what it means yet?'

'Yes, it says, "it must not be hidden at all. What shall come shall be seen."'

'Very cryptic and vague as that could refer to anything.'

'True, but if we manage to work out more of the translation then perhaps we have a better chance of making sense of the message.'

Sebastian rose and took off his hat and his grey superfine coat before sitting back down beside her, pulling the chair closer to hers. 'Tell me what you would like me to do to help, Eliza.'

She smiled at him, covering his hand with hers. 'Are you certain that you want to spend your time in this dusty old place when you have far more important matters needing your attention?'

He returned her smile and nodded. 'I am.'

'Very well,' she murmured, holding his gaze for a long moment before glancing back down at the vellum. 'In that case, let's both look for the words in the glossary so that we can translate them together.'

Together... Now there was a word he'd never been comfortable hearing about himself in connection with another. And yet, this time it did... It made him feel like a part of something. Something that stirred deep inside his chest, unequivocally different and unknown.

He swallowed uncomfortably, unable to say more, pushing away those unwanted feelings and pulling his focus back to the task at hand. 'So, where do we start?'

'From the beginning,' she said, catching her bottom lip between her teeth, as she did whenever she was excited by something or other.

They worked tirelessly and in silence, trying to piece together the message bit by bit, translating the Cornish painstakingly into English, so that finally they had the message written out.

'There, I think we have it.'

'I believe we do,' she said, nodding absently. 'And so, *nyns yw. Dh'aga gemmeres dh evos own rag y dhewgh wir yn pub redya*, means...'

'"Lest you go astray from where you should always be."' He frowned. 'What do you think it's saying here?'

'That perhaps when you're in need and are far from home, which in my ancestors' case would be…'

'Trebarr Castle.'

'Exactly, and then the next line, *gwrewgh fowt ow owr y'ma*, means…'

'"Seek my heart." Or in this case, perhaps it means to seek the treasure?'

'I believe it might.' She nodded. 'And then *ha teuth yn-mes*.'

'"And go abroad"—from Trebarr, one would assume.'

'Yes. And the next line seems to elaborate on it. *Mes an kribow Trebarr dell dy grendrevethoryon gol in dhe voyowgh*.'

'Which means, "from the coastline of Trebarr into your neighbour's palms."'

'And, *gweres ha pwegh dodh mos theni ow splaneth war-lergh an gwarri dheag*.'

Sebastian read the next translated line. '"Seek and you shall find my heart beneath the sacred oak tree." So again, I would surmise that the heart in this case must be a reference to the Bawden-Trebarr treasure.'

'As would I and it's evidently buried beneath a great oak, in a neighbouring land near Trebarr—possibly their ancient enemy's. The Bawden land became part of their estate after Simon and Elowen's union.'

'That sounds plausible. And the next line is?'

'Tragyas bys yn fy unn y dhewlangterdhe Elowen bys Bawden.'

'Which means, "forever in my heart, oh, daughter of Elowen of Bawden." That is directed solely at you, Eliza…'

'Indeed. I have goose bumps just reading it,' she said softly. 'It's incredibly touching. Exceptionally moving.'

He smiled. 'As you should. And finally it ends with *Rag karrow Bawden ha Trebarr*, just as it did at the beginning.'

'"For the love of Bawden and Trebarr…"'

They both sat in silence for a long moment, pondering on everything that they had uncovered together. Sebastian read through the message again and again. It was all quite astonishing—this voice from over four hundred years ago, speaking to them as though they were right there in this room. It sent a shiver down his spine. He glanced sideways at Eliza, who had tears in her eyes, staring at the words, knowing that it was her this message was for—to the daughters of Elowen of Bawden…

And though Sebastian would like to believe that he had been of some help in uncovering the hidden faded words on the vellum, it had mainly been Eliza who had instigated the search. She had been the one driving it. It finally made sense to him now why she admired artefacts such as the Rosetta Stone, since they allowed her to appreciate how, in some way, everyone was linked to one another. How the knowledge of a language could break through the veil of misunderstanding and the unknown, allowing us to make sense of it all. This was what she wanted to be able to uncover and learn. And it was this that she had tried to make him understand; tried to reason with him to see the importance of being able to unlock the secrets of the past because by doing so one could gain perspective, knowledge and insight.

And suddenly, Sebastian understood Eliza's fascination with the past was because of moments like this. Moments that made her comprehend who she was and where she came from. Moments that must now vindicate all she had believed about herself. And to think he had once mocked her for her overzealous interest and diligence regarding this quest, questioning her reasoning. It made him feel ashamed. But it also made him experience an ache somewhere deep inside his chest.

'You should feel very proud of yourself, Eliza.'

'Thank you.' She turned to him and smiled as she wiped the tears now streaming down her face with the back of her hand. 'But I could not have done any of this without you, Sebastian.'

'Oh, I rather think you could,' he murmured as

he reached out and cupped her cheek. 'You, Eliza Bawden-Trebarr, are capable of anything.'

They locked eyes with one another and slowly, very slowly, moved closer until their foreheads touched.

'So what now?' he asked.

'Now?' she said, gently rubbing her forehead against his, skin to skin, back and forth. 'Now we make plans. We need to start the search for this tree in Cornwall, at Trebarr Castle itself...'

She pulled away slightly and lifted her gaze to his, frowning a little. 'Not that I have any expectation that you would accompany...'

Sebastian silenced her by reaching over and placing one finger on her lips and shaking his head. 'I want to... I want to accompany you.'

He watched, riveted, as she took a small shaky breath before nodding. 'Yes.'

'Yes...' He lifted her chin up with his finger and moved closer to her, his lips touching hers. He covered her mouth with his but just as he was about to deepen the kiss, wanting to taste her again, the steward came back into the room, making them pull away from one another abruptly.

'Are we finished here, my lady?' the man asked Eliza as she dropped her head and looked away.

'Yes... Yes, I suppose we are.'

Which could not be further from the truth, for Sebastian knew with alacrity that they were not finished at all. If anything, this was just the beginning.

And God help him with that…

Chapter Twelve

Eliza stood on a platform at Paddington the following morning, with her leather trunk as well as her trusty battered old portmanteau. Wearing her fitted military-style jacket, matching long skirt and a smart buttoned-up shirt with lacing at the neck, her mother's onyx brooch at the neckline and a long cloak to keep out the cold, she felt ready to undertake this journey that would effectively take her back to her ancestral home. A figure pierced through the fog of steam from the locomotive engine of the train from the Paddington to Exeter leg of the journey and stepped closer towards her.

Tipping his hat, Sebastian inclined his head in greeting and walked in front of the porter carrying his trunks.

'Good morning, Eliza.'

'Good morning,' she said, staring up at him, taking in his handsome appearance, as well as his impeccable attire.

'I hope you are well,' he murmured, throwing one of his dazzling smiles in her direction resulting, as it always did when he looked at her like that, in her feeling like she'd been struck by a jolt of lightning.

She nodded, unable to say more.

Oh dear, how on earth was she going to cope? The awkwardness of travelling with Sebastian alone, after she'd decided to leave Gertie and Willis at her house in Chelsea, so that no one would think that she was travelling to Cornwall, made her feel uncertain of herself. Again. And while she felt grateful to have Sebastian's protection as he accompanied her on this journey, Eliza had never travelled alone with a man who wasn't her father or husband. Until now. It might be scandalous, even for a widow, but that wasn't the real reason for her awkwardness. No, it was the fact that she would be travelling together in such close proximity with a man whom she was constantly aware of and to whom she was ridiculously attracted.

It was bad enough that Eliza thought about Sebastian constantly. Bad enough that she had to continually push away any lingering thoughts about that night in Sir Horace's library. Bad enough that he tormented her endlessly in those vivid dreams of hers as she tossed and turned at night reliving every touch, kiss and caress. Bad enough that she'd agreed to have him help her at the British Museum of all places. To top it all, Eliza must be addled in the head to have agreed for him to accompany her to Cornwall. Alone. Being with him day and night, night and day, as they travelled to Trebarr Castle. And yet, she had agreed, knowing that his mere presence was comforting, even though her constant awareness of him was frankly exhausting, let alone unbecoming.

Eliza should certainly not be having such lascivious thoughts about him. Indeed, Sebastian made her feel breathless, made her heartbeat quicken and made her pulse hitch whenever he was near. And that was before he'd even lifted his dark, smoky eyes to meet hers, or threw her one of those laconic smiles that transformed his hard, angled features into something so much softer—boyish, even. It sent a tumult of emotion racing through her. That blasted surfeit of emotion, which she'd once mocked him about, was now something that she didn't know what to do with.

How on earth was she to endure being close to the man with the hum of all this unfettered desire between them? She exhaled before retuning his smile. Eliza would just have to keep herself in check around him and refrain from doing anything that might embarrass either of them.

'Well, shall we?' he said, raising a brow as he ushered her to their train carriage.

'Yes.'

They boarded the train and walked down the long, narrow aisle until they found their first-class carriage, as though they were on their way to embark on an elicit *affaire* rather than being on the hunt for Eliza's family treasure. And after Sebastian tipped the porter who'd carried their trunks and put them in the luggage holdalls, they took their comfortable plush seats opposite one another, with a table separating them. After ordering a pot of coffee, they both descended into what appeared to be a comfortable silence, and yet it was anything but. It seemed wholly ungracious to be resentful of the elegant luxury that was afforded her in the first-class carriages, but Eliza would never have been able to sit here had she been on her own. She glanced at the man who sat across from her and knew to whom she should be thankful for this unexpected indulgence and sighed.

Dash it all, she was not as green as all that to believe that Sebastian might want more from her despite all this simmering attraction between them. If anything, Eliza was probably placing too much importance on his attraction to her despite everything he'd said, since a handful of heated kisses was all that had ever transpired between them—which for an experienced, worldly man such as Sebastian Marsden amounted to very little, compared to her. Besides, it was not as if she wanted anything more from him, anyway.

Still, she couldn't help but feel vulnerable and confused. Despite having once being married, Eliza realised that she actually knew very little about men. Not that she'd cared one jot that she didn't. Until meeting Sebastian Marsden. Now all her thoughts were in disarray. All her beliefs about herself shattered and unclear. She was not certain of anything anymore, especially of the man sat across from her, seemingly without a care in the world, reading his newspaper.

But in truth, Eliza owed him so much already. From allowing her extra time to repay Ritton's debt, to purchasing the comb from Sir Horace, to assisting her at every turn—albeit begrudgingly at first after he'd encountered her unexpectedly at Gresham College—to dealing ruthlessly with the dreadful Ronald Carew. And then there was the manner in which he'd insisted on helping her at the British Museum as they'd worked together to uncover the secrets of the vellum efficiently and expediently. It had surprised her. Indeed, they'd made a good team. Eliza had found those quiet moments together at the museum some of the most intimate and riveting moments in her entire life. Especially as Sebastian had shared her joy at finding the four-hundred-year-old message from her ancestors in the vellum. The sheer relief at this discovery had made her feel so emotional that she had not been able to stop the tears from streaming down her face. And when she'd looked up, it was Sebastian who had been there for her. It had been Sebastian who wiped away those embarrassing tears. It was Sebastian who had eventually congratulated her and who had then kissed her. And it was Sebastian who was now accompanying her to Cornwall, wanting to see this quest to the end, as he'd put it. Eliza did not dare hope for more but this uncertainty made her feel uneasy as well as putting her on edge.

'May I ask you a question, Sebastian?' she said, leaning forward.

'Mmm?' he muttered from behind the newspaper.

'I am, as you know, grateful for your escort but will you not be missed? Do you not have matters to see to at your busy club?'

'Would you rather I wasn't here?' He folded back his paper and gave her a shrewd look. 'With you?'

'No, of course not.' She took a sip from her coffee cup before returning it to its saucer. 'It's only that I do not know how the Trium Impiorum will get on without you.'

'Be easy, Eliza, the club is in good hands. Dominic, Tristan and my major-domo are overseeing everything while I am away.' He sighed. 'But that's not what you are asking, is it?'

She swallowed uncomfortably. 'You must admit that…that travelling alone together is highly irregular. It's really not the done thing.'

'No, I don't suppose it is. Indeed, I was mildly surprised that you decided to travel without your maid.' Sebastian raised a brow. 'But do you care? Do you truly care what anyone might think about us?'

'No,' she said, shaking her head. 'Not at all… Well, actually, perhaps a little.'

'What is it that worries you?'

'What if someone should recognise me or you, travelling together…alone?'

'That's highly doubtful,' he drawled as he resumed reading his newspaper.

'Or perhaps recognise our names?'

'What has suddenly got you into this state?' He pushed down his paper and frowned. 'Our names? Well, then, from this moment forth we shall be known as Mr and Mrs Weston—a boring and sedate married couple. Does that suffice?'

She flushed at the idea of being *Mr and Mrs* anything with Sebastian.

'No, it does not… Mr and Mrs Weston—of all the nonsensical ideas.' She lifted her head to find him grinning at her. 'Oh, you were jesting.'

'I was.' He nodded. 'Do not worry yourself unnecessarily, Eliza. Be easy, take in the passing scenery, take a nap but whatever you do, try not to fret.'

She sighed. 'Yes, I suppose you're right.'

They fell back into silence as Eliza looked out the window, taking in the beautiful countryside and rolling hills as the train had left the dirt and grime of the city. And apart from a few short exchanges, they remained in quiet contemplation as the steam train continued its journey southwest to the coastal city of Exeter. As dusk settled, and the rain thrashed against the window with the wind howling outside, her eyes closed gradually with the monotony of the train travel lulling her to sleep.

It seemed as though it was only a moment later when Eliza woke with a jolt as a soft caress grazed across her cheek. 'Wake up, sleepyhead. We have arrived in Exeter.'

'Oh,' she said, stifling a yawn behind her gloved hand. 'We arrived far sooner than I thought.'

'Oh, yes, very swiftly done,' he muttered sardonically. 'It's only taken a mere eight hours to get to Exeter. With many hours to go until we venture further west.'

Eliza rose but could not contain another yawn, making Sebastian smile at her, shaking his head. 'Come along, Eliza, before you start dozing off again.'

They disembarked and collected their trunks but after discovering that all further trains were suspended from departing that evening, Sebastian and Eliza knew that they would need to secure overnight lodgings in Exeter.

Heavens above.

This was precisely what Eliza had been concerned about, not that she didn't trust Sebastian. It was more that she did not quite trust herself around the man than anything else. She followed him out of Exeter St David's station and waited to hail a carriage before driving through the city trying to find a hotel or inn. Yet, each and every one they stopped at had no rooms to accommodate their needs until they drove to the Half Moon Inn on the corner of High Street and Bedford Street in the centre of the city. But even here, they were full to the rafters. The only availability the Half Moon had was just one bedchamber, which Sebastian and Eliza agreed to take, otherwise even this would soon be taken by someone else as well. Which meant of course that Eliza's earlier apprehension rose to the surface again. And before Sebastian could answer the innkeeper when he asked for their names, she blurted out: 'We're Mr and Mrs Weston.'

Sebastian turned slowly towards her, his face incredulous.

'What is it?' she whispered from the side of her mouth. 'This was your idea in the first place.'

'I was jesting,' he hissed back.

'Well, I could hardly share a room with you as a single, unmarried widow! What would the innkeeper think?'

'He would think exactly the same as he does now that we're Mr and Mrs bloody Weston.'

'Well, try to be more convincing. Otherwise, I'll die of shame.'

'I'll see what I can do, *Mrs Weston.*'

'I'm glad to hear it, *Mr Weston.*'

The innkeeper showed them to their room as a young lad brought up their trunks behind them.

'I hope the room is to your satisfaction... Mr Weston?'

'Indeed it is. I thank you, and spotless, too, which is a relief as lint and dust play havoc with my wife's incessant snoring.'

Eliza raised a brow. *Oh, it was to be like this, was it?* 'Aha, what a jester you are, Mr Weston, when you know you're a veritable window-rattler yourself.'

The innkeeper looked from Sebastian to Eliza, unsure what to say. 'Well, we do pride ourselves on our rooms bein' as you say, spotless.'

'And it is, my good man. Can you please bring up

a tub and some hot water for my wife to be able to bathe and a maid to help?'

'Yes, sir.' The man nodded after Sebastian placed a few more coins in his callused hands. 'And would you be wantin' an excellent dinner that ma missus of the Half Moon prepared earlier? Steak n' kidney pie and gravy with treacle puddin' n' custard for afters.'

Her stomach made a noise as Sebastian nodded at the man. 'That sounds delightful and with a bottle or two of your finest claret. On second thought, perhaps one.' He looked pointedly towards Eliza. 'Mrs Weston has been known to guzzle the claret as though it's mother's milk. And then she'll have all your patrons complaining with her warbling. Can't have that now, can we?'

The innkeeper looked down at his feet. 'Righto, sir.'

'Oh, and just before you leave,' Eliza said, smiling, 'perhaps a bath for Mr Weston, also? It would be so soothing for my husband's terrible gout.'

The innkeeper couldn't get out of the room fast enough, and he left, hastily shutting the door behind him and leaving the two of them alone in the well-appointed room, with a blazing fire in the hearth adding a welcome warmth, a large four-poster bed taking up most of the room and an armchair beside it. Sebastian leant against the small dining table with his arms crossed over his chest.

'Gout?' he muttered.

She shrugged. 'Seemed like a fair exchange since I guzzle claret like—what was it again? Oh, yes... mother's milk. So charmingly put. And apparently, I snore, too.'

'No, Mrs Weston does. I don't know whether you snore.'

'And I hardly know whether you do, either.'

But soon, they'd both find out, since they were sharing this room. And of course, they both came to that realisation at the same time as they looked away in different directions, unable to meet each other's eyes.

Eliza slumped in the armchair and started to absently tap a tattoo against the side of it.

'May I ask if there is anything wrong?' Sebastian said, watching her from under a hooded gaze.

'Wrong?' She stopped tapping and frowned. 'Of course, there is something wrong. For one, we are now stuck here in Exeter instead of being on a train heading west toward Penwith.'

He pulled away from the dining table and ambled towards her in that easy way of his before starting to remove his overcoat.

'What...what on earth are you doing?'

'Getting comfortable,' he murmured, moving past her to hang it on the coat stand. 'Any objections?'

Yes! she wanted to scream as he returned to sit on

one of the dining chairs, spreading out his long legs in front of him and then crossing them at the ankles as he got *comfortable*. Well, at least one of them was.

'Not at all,' she said instead, failing to keep the irritation from her voice. 'Do as you must.'

'I hope that I'm not making you feel nervous, by any chance, Eliza.'

Again, her unadulterated response would be yes, yes, yes but she schooled her features to being as unconcerned as possible. 'Should I be?'

'Not at all.' He got up at the sound of a knock at the door. 'We are married, after all.' He raised his voice a little. 'Not now, Mrs Weston, but certainly later, unless my gout is playing up...'

Sometimes Eliza could happily throttle the man, he was that annoying. And as if he had an inkling of what was passing through her head, Sebastian winked at her before opening the door, admitting the innkeeper, who came inside the chamber along with a few servants carrying trays of food, setting them on the table. Steaming dishes of steak and kidney pie, bowls of cooked carrots, greens and mashed potatoes, as well as the promised treacle tart and custard, all of which made her tummy rumble from the delicious aromas wafting in the room. Rolls of freshly baked breads with a few knobs of butter were also placed on the table, along with not one, but two bottles of claret.

Ha! And after everything Sebastian had said about her being a claret guzzler!

Sebastian declined the offers of serving them, stating that they'd see to themselves, meaning the servants left with a promise to come back later with the hot water and tub as well as a maid to help Eliza. They descended into another long silence. And were once again alone. Eliza used the time to busy herself with taking off her cloak and military-style jacket, hanging both up on the coat stand, while Sebastian removed the lids from the dishes. She sat down opposite him as he dished out food onto both their plates.

'I hope you're hungry,' he said, passing her plate back to her.

'Famished.' She placed her napkin on her lap before picking up her cutlery.

'Good. Tuck in.'

But Eliza suddenly couldn't eat even though she was holding the cutlery in her hands. Despite the fact that she hadn't eaten all day and was very hungry, she just couldn't do it. Instead, she pushed the plate away and drank the claret, enjoying the dark, fruity warmth of the drink slipping down her throat.

Sebastian lifted his head and frowned. 'What is it? I thought you said you were famished but you seem to be drinking your wine instead.'

'I don't know why I'm not able to eat,' she said.

Sebastian sighed before also putting his cutlery down as well. 'You need not worry yourself about any of these…arrangements, Eliza. Just because we're sharing this chamber doesn't mean that…anything needs to change between us. And if it puts your mind at rest, I'll sleep on the armchair while you can take the bed.'

'Thank you,' she muttered lamely, wanting to say that quite the opposite was true. That she trusted him far more than she did herself. That she would much rather he slept on the bed beside her.

'You honestly didn't expect me to insist that we share the bed, did you?'

She shook her head. 'It is fair to say that my expectations in a situation such as this are very limited indeed.'

How could she say in words that she found her attraction to him to be a highly inappropriate distraction and one that she could hardly afford?

'I wouldn't doubt it but you have nothing to fear from me.'

'I do know that, Sebastian,' she muttered, taking another sip of the delicious claret and holding out her glass for another measure. 'And by the same token, you have nothing to fear from me, either.'

Sebastian let out a bark of surprised laughter before drinking his claret and pouring some more for

Eliza. 'My fear has always stemmed from your unpredictability. Otherwise, I believe I'm safe with you. Now eat.'

He thought that she was jesting with him when she was being in earnest. Eliza might be safe from him but she wasn't quite certain that he was safe from her clutches. Not when she wanted desperately to press her nose to his neck. When she wanted to kiss him again. When she itched to touch his hair, his skin... everywhere. Heavens, but where had these scandalous thoughts come from?

'That is good to know. But in all honesty, Sebastian, when I ventured to the Trium Impiorum all those weeks ago I would never have thought it within the realms of possibility that you would willingly come to the British Museum to help translate the deciphered message, let alone leave London to come to Cornwall with me.'

'Neither did I.' He shrugged as he took another bite of the pie and mash smothered in thick gravy. 'But it is perhaps time that I visited the estate that was given to me in order to settle a debt.'

'Ah, so you do not come for only my benefit but for your own as well.'

'Did I give you the impression that it was purely for yours alone?' he teased. 'After all, I do possess some curiosity about an estate that has inspired so much time and effort to claim it back. And if I like it very much and if I were the unscrupulous sort, then who knows, I might even renege on an agreement made in good faith.'

She laughed. 'Abominable behaviour if that were true, which I rather doubt, as you are not the unscrupulous sort.'

'I'm very glad you think so.' He chewed slowly before swallowing and wiping his lips with the napkin. 'And since you know that I am not to be feared, nor the unscrupulous sort, you should be at ease and eat your dinner, since you're clearly hungry.'

She did as she was told and finally started to eat the hearty food with good appetite. They descended into a comfortable, companionable silence as they devoured every last morsel. And after taking the final bite, Eliza placed her cutlery down and wiped her lips delicately before reaching for the second bottle of claret.

'I hope you're satisfied that my hunger has been satiated?'

It was clearly the wrong thing to say, as Sebastian, who was about to take another sip of claret, stilled, his eyes catching hers, clearly taken aback. His eyes seemed to smoulder then and catch a blaze momentarily as he stared at her intently before he appeared to snap out of whatever it was that had him transfixed. Eliza was not quite certain what had happened but at least she was no longer as nervous of being in this chamber with the man. It all seemed so silly now to have been apprehensive of being alone with Sebastian, when all she had to do was to resist his charms. Which she was convinced she could do, with a snap of her fingers. Eliza licked her lips and reached out for the now practically empty bottle.

'Except perhaps for this empty bottle of claret.'

'Because we have guzzled it all. I did tell the innkeeper what Mrs Weston was like.'

'You did.' She leant forward and gave him a saucy wink. 'Only because Mrs Weston hopes that by guzzling all this claret, she might not hear Mr Weston's terrible snoring.'

He smiled. 'A veritable window-rattler, I hear.'

'Indeed.' She chuckled.

'In any case, I would like to open the second bottle so that I can gain more courage, but I think I've had enough.'

'I don't quite follow.' He frowned as he lifted his eyes to hers. 'Why would you need to gain more courage? Is this still about you feeling uneasy about us sharing this chamber?'

'No, no, no,' she said dismissively, waving her hand about. It was more because she wanted to pounce on him, which of course she would not do. The thought did make her giggle a little, though, as she envisaged throwing off all caution to the wind as well as her spectacles before leaping into his arms. 'Poor Sebastian. Always so sensible, so honourable, so steadfast, so dependable. And always thinking of others.'

'You make me sound like a bore.'

'No, that would be Mr and Mrs Weston,' she said, shaking her head. 'I doubt one could ever describe you as a bore, Sebastian.'

'What a relief,' he said wryly.

'Yes. But maybe I could do with a spot more claret or perhaps we can get a bottle of brandy instead?' she mumbled. 'I'll have to ask the maid to slip some by when she comes here later. After all, Mrs Weston does have a bit of a problem.'

'It seems Mrs Weston might have something else on her mind?'

'No, no,' she muttered dismissively.

Sebastian caught her hands in his. 'What is this really about? You have been in quite a peculiar mood ever since we arrived at the Half Moon.'

'Must there be something?' she said, pulling away. 'It's not as though I can't stop thinking about kissing you again or stop thinking about what happened in Sir Horace's library that night. Because I can tell you that I haven't given any of it a second thought. And anyway, you know quite well that I am peculiar, Sebastian.'

His eyebrows shot up. 'You haven't given any of it a second thought?'

'Didn't I say so?'

'You did. But now I do feel rather guilty, Eliza.'

'Why so?'

He leant forward as though he were imparting something of great import. 'Because I on the other hand have thought about that night in Sir Horace's library many, many times.'

'Oh.' Eliza opened and closed her mouth several times before finally speaking. 'Very well, then. I've thought about that night quite often, too, if you must know.'

'You have?' He gave her a look of feigned surprise, the vexatious man. 'Quite often, eh?'

'Yes, well done, for making a bluestocking widow feel so marvellously wanted and valued from all your prodigious attentions.'

Sebastian smiled as he reached out and cupped her jaw. 'Oh, Eliza.'

'No.' She stepped back and shook her head. 'No, Sebastian, I do not need your pity just because I cannot stop thinking about that night, about kissing you and about ravishing you.'

A slow smile curled around his lips. 'You wish to ravish me?'

Oh, God, what was she doing being so indiscreet

and disclosing all her secret thoughts to this man? Still, it was always better to let out the truth than to keep it all hidden, wasn't it? Taking a deep breath, Eliza held her head high. 'Did I not say so?'

'Yes.' Sebastian crossed his arms over his chest and pressed his lips together as though trying not to laugh. 'Indeed, you did but I am trying to understand all that you have said. Trying to make sense of what you are about.'

'Have I not made myself quite clear, Sebastian?'

'Yes, but allow me to understand you,' he murmured, prowling towards her with that slightly lopsided grin of his. 'You wish to seduce me?'

'Yes. No.' Her shoulders sagged as she sighed deeply. 'I'm not sophisticated enough to do that, Sebastian. Which was probably the reason I had hoped to gain a little courage with the claret.'

He raised a brow. 'I see. And what did you wish to do with that courage exactly?'

She took a shaky breath just to steady her nerves. 'There's a spot just beneath your ear that I have been wanting to press my lips against since we sat together at the British Museum. I would also like to press my nose to that spot and inhale.'

'You wish to inhale me?' he teased.

'Among other things.' She threw her arms in the air. 'I want to kiss you again and touch you all over and do so many other things that no proper lady should ever know anything about, let alone dream of doing.'

For a long moment he just stared at her, before shaking his head and swallowing. 'Well, this is all rather unexpected, to say the least.'

She exhaled. 'I think I'm a bit overcome at being alone together in the same room as you, Sebastian. I'm not very experienced at such things. You see, I find you equally if not more. A lot more...' She took a deep breath. 'I find you very desirable. But this is not good, Sebastian. You're far too much of a distraction.'

'Because you can't resist me?'

'Of course, I can resist you. I have done so the last couple of days, haven't I?'

'You do surprise me.' He raised a brow. 'And your intent on seduction has been made very clear, Eliza.'

'Oh dear, has it? Please know that I would not necessarily act on any of it. You really are quite safe from me, Sebastian.'

'Am I? You have, after all, made this extraordinary revelation on the very first night we have got to Exeter after forcing us to dissemble as the hapless Mr and Mrs Weston.' He sighed deeply, shaking his head. 'I acknowledge that I have thought about our...indiscretions in the past but now that we're alone in this bedchamber, you spring this on me? How do I know you won't just pounce on me especially since you're bent on seduction?'

She paled as she slouched in the armchair. 'Oh dear, perhaps you are right. Perhaps I'm the unscrupulous sort after all.'

Sebastian chuckled and shook his head 'Wait, wait, I'm… I'm only jesting with you, Eliza.'

Sebastian threw her a smug smile, the fiend, as he leant against the table and watched her from over the rim of his glass. 'I must say, however, that your revelation is rather enlightening. Albeit delivered in your usual blunt fashion.'

Eliza's head dropped forward and she closed her eyes. 'I didn't mean to disclose so much. It's been a heady few days, what with finding the vellum, and then translating it together at the British Museum.'

'Ah, yes, when you wanted to press your nose to that spot beneath my ear and inhale.'

'Will you stop teasing me?'

'Yes, of course, I'm sorry.'

'As am I.'

'No need.' His smile felt suddenly like an intimate caress. 'It's perfectly normal and natural to have such feelings.'

'It is?' she whispered.

'Yes,' he said softy, the teasing glint in his eyes replaced by something far more potent. Far more enigmatic. 'What if I told you that I feel exactly the same as you?'

'You do?'

His eyes raked her up and down as Eliza suddenly realised that Sebastian was also finding it difficult to keep this desire, this want and need, contained.

'Yes.' His smile turned wolfish. 'Come here, Eliza.'

'Why?'

Every scrap of his jesting and teasing had evaporated now. 'Because you cannot seduce me from the other side of the chamber. Although we shall limit this seduction to that kiss you've been thinking so much about.'

Without even realising it, Eliza had risen from the armchair and was moving towards Sebastian, still leaning against the edge of the table. 'I had no idea there could be a limit on seduction.'

Good Lord, had she actually uttered those sultry words?

'What kind of a man would I be if I were to take advantage of you, when you're still not completely sure?'

'An ordinary one.' She tilted her head to the side as she studied him. 'However, I do believe you're anything but ordinary, Sebastian.'

'Thank you,' he muttered wryly, before inclining his head. 'I do try.'

'A little too honourable, perhaps.' She shrugged.

'Is there such a thing?' He cradled the nape of her neck and started to caress her spine with the pad of his thumb in round, circular motions. 'The truth is that I want you, Eliza, very, very badly, but you need to be certain—and not require a couple of glasses of claret for courage—before you come to me.'

Oh, heavens…she took in a small intake of air before leaning into his caress. 'I… I am.'

'Are you?' he said hoarsely.

'Yes,' she murmured, trying to catch her breath.

His eyes darkened as he dipped his head and lifted her chin with his finger. 'Good, because it seems that I'm the unscrupulous sort, after all.'

And with that his lips were on hers, devouring her mouth.

Chapter Thirteen

The knock at the door made Sebastian lift his head and pull away from the woman in his arms, eliciting a groan from her. He'd forgotten about the request of a bathtub, hot water and a maid to help Eliza with her ablutions. He was tempted to tell them to go to the devil but knew that would be unfair to these hardworking souls. So with a reluctant sigh he gently removed Eliza's arms from around his neck and moved away, noting her eyes fluttering open, dazed and slightly confused.

'No, don't go,' she whispered.

He smiled before letting in the maid along with a handful of servants carrying the large basins of hot water and the bathtub. 'I shall see you after you have readied yourself for bed, my darling…er… Mrs Weston,' he murmured with that playful curve of his lips for the benefit of the servants and a heated gaze for Eliza before closing the door behind him.

He exhaled slowly through his teeth and marvelled at how this night had transpired. God, but it was an impossible situation and one that he now wanted to grasp onto with both hands, even though he knew it was best to avoid taking Eliza to his bed tonight. For despite all his assertions, it would change everything between them irrevocably. And yet, it felt as difficult to resist as it would denying himself his next lungful of air. He ran his shaky fingers through his hair as he thought of returning to the chamber. But for now, he would go to the taproom and while away his time.

Sebastian made his way back to the chamber an hour or so later after mulling everything over in his head, knowing full well that he would have to reluctantly withstand Eliza's clumsy attempts to seduce him tonight, thanks to her rather enthusiastic imbibing of the claret. Even so, he had to admit that she was vastly more endearing and adorable than if she'd been a skilled temptress. It flattered and charmed him more than he could say that she would just come out and tell him about her attraction to him. And this was what he loved about her, this innate honesty and forthrightness. She might be peculiar, as she put it, but he was endlessly amused by this quality to her character as it made her unique and interesting.

Sebastian stilled midstep.

What he loved about her...?

Damn but what an unfortunate slip. It was obviously a mistake, after a long day of travelling and the frustration of sharing only a kiss when his body still throbbed for more.

Sebastian clicked the latch of the wooden door open and walked in, closing it behind him. He glanced around the room, astounded at what was before him. For the chamber was now a perfect solace of tranquillity and serenity with the oil lamps dimmed and the fire crackling in the hearth. But far more compelling was the tableau before him of Eliza in her prim and proper night-rail, evidently asleep on the huge four-poster bed.

He stepped quietly towards her and watched for a moment as she slept, making little snoring noises, which made him smile. God, the woman was an enigma. One moment she wanted him so fiercely she was fairly shaking with need, the next she'd obviously collapsed into bed from sheer exhaustion.

With a sigh, Sebastian disrobed, peeling off all the layers of his clothing, washed and used his tooth powder and brush before changing into a loose-fitting cambric sleeping suit. He wore the shirt part as well, despite usually discarding this when he was in his own bed. The last thing he needed was to give Eliza a fit of the vapours from his nakedness, although from his experience of her so far, one never knew how the woman would actually react!

Sebastian got into bed and closed his eyes. As long as he could pretend that Eliza was not in the same bed, then perhaps he might have a small chance of getting some much-needed sleep. Which, of course, proved rather futile as it seemed only a short while later that a small, narrow beam of light poured through the small gap between the curtains, causing Sebastian to wake and feel a solid body pressed against his back and a woman's arm loosely slipped over his waist. Eliza had obviously moved in her sleep and nestled herself against his back, which meant of course that he was suddenly very aware of her soft curves, with only a handful of scant clothing, rather than the many usual layers, separating them. A bolt of lust coursed through him.

He exhaled a shaky breath as he felt himself harden. What on earth was the woman trying to do to him? Kill him on the spot? He was just a red-blooded male, not a saint. Very carefully, he removed Eliza's arm from his person and shuffled along until he reached the edge of the bed, so that his back was no longer touching her front. But just as quickly as he'd untangled himself from her, she moved in small increments until she was once again pressed right up against him.

Dear God, what new hell was this? Sebastian could

either endure this ordeal and make sure he kept his hands firmly to himself, or he could try to move her back to her side of the bed and likely wake Eliza in the process. Or he could quietly remove himself from the bed altogether and still possibly wake Eliza! He could feel her soft, breathy snores against his back, making him smile despite this awkward predicament. *How very like Mrs Weston...*

In the end he elected to stay put and live through it, hoping that Eliza might eventually roll back to her side of the bed, instead of attaching herself to him.

And yet, she did not move again, remaining stuck to Sebastian like glue as he closed his eyes for a short time only, knowing it wouldn't be long until he'd need to get up.

He woke up again some hours later when he felt Eliza stirring behind him.

'Oh,' she eventually said in a rather muffled voice. 'Oh...oh dear, I seem to have moved across the bed so much that I've grossly invaded your privacy, Sebastian.'

'And a good morning to you, Eliza.' He smiled inwardly as he slowly turned around to lie on his back. 'And yes, it seems that you have.'

'Yes, good morning.' She shot upright into a sitting position next to him, pulling the coverlet up to conceal her form, despite the fact she was wearing that hideous night-rail, which covered every inch of her. 'Oh, Lord, and after I promised that you'd be safe from me...'

'Just as I promised that I'd sleep on the armchair.'

'Which was never necessary as this bed is big enough for the both of us. That is, if I'd remembered to behave with more decorum. I am sorry, Sebastian.'

'For what, exactly?'

'For everything,' she muttered, rubbing her fingertips against her forehead in that familiar way of hers. 'For my indiscretions last night, for practically throwing myself at you and for using you as a human coverlet. I have never behaved in such a brazen and wanton manner before.'

'Yes, you did rather paste yourself to me.' He couldn't help but tease her a little. 'Perhaps you were on the hunt for the sweet spot beneath my ear.'

'Oh, God, I forgot about *that*.' Eliza covered her face in her hands. 'I'm dying of shame. How utterly mortifying.'

'Again, I'm jesting, Eliza. And evidently doing it quite poorly.' He reached out and prised her fingers away from her face and dropped a kiss to the top of each hand. 'Besides, I'm rather fond of your newly acquired brazen and wanton manner.'

'Oh, stop. I embarrassed myself terribly last night.'

'Did you?' he drawled. 'I had not noticed.'

'How can you be so understanding?'

'Easily.' He put one hand behind his head. 'You forget the many things that I also disclosed to you last night.'

She flushed pink in the small area of exposed skin at the top of the frilly collar of her night-rail, the colour spreading up her neck and into her face. 'No, I haven't forgotten.'

'And neither have I, Eliza.' Sebastian laced his fingers together with hers. 'Let's not worry about any of that.'

'What should we worry about, then?'

'At this moment, I cannot think of a single thing.' He caressed the soft skin of her wrist before pressing his thumb across her vein and feeling her pulse quicken. He took a deep breath. 'Instead, we could consider carrying on where we left off?'

This close he could see her take a small intake of breath. 'And where...where is that?'

'That is up to you to decide, Eliza.' He bent his elbow and placed his other hand beneath his head as well. 'You see, I have had ample time to consider your forthright declaration about all the many things you'd like to do to me and find that I am amenable to them all.'

'I see.'

'So, you may continue your pursuit to seduce and ravish me at your leisure.'

'Well, this is an interesting development,' she said breathlessly. 'Especially since I had thought to stop being so brazen and wanton.'

'I'd rather you didn't.' He grinned up at her. 'But the choice is entirely yours, Eliza.'

She stared down at him for a long moment as she deliberated over all that he had said, while he did not move an inch. Eventually, Eliza reached over and brushed her thumb across his lower lip, backwards and forwards and still he did not move, knowing that he would stay true to his word. It was Eliza's decision in terms of what would happen next. As he'd said last night, Sebastian wanted her desperately but it was meaningless if she did not fully embrace the desire she felt for him as well. In that, Eliza had to claim it for herself without being swayed either way by him.

She bent her head and pressed a quick, hard tentative kiss to his lips before swiftly sitting up again, as though she was testing the shape of his lips. She did it again, her eyes dropping to his mouth, taking a big gulp of air into her lungs. She kissed him once more but this time lingered longer, her breath warm as she licked into the corner of his mouth. And still, Sebastian did not move, his hands clasped tightly together beneath his head.

Eliza moved closer and tangled her tongue with his. He groaned as she slanted her mouth across his and kissed him again and again, getting bolder and more demanding. This was what he'd hoped that she would do. Unleash the passion that had always been there, but that she'd locked up inside herself. He'd tasted it before and knew her to be a far more sensual creature then she believed. But this was something she needed to discover for herself. She had to realise that desire was not shameful or embarrassing but natural and wondrous. Or rather it could be...

Sebastian buried his hands into the pillow beneath his head, so that he might refrain from touching her. Not yet, not yet...even though it was killing him that he wasn't allowing himself to take her into his arms.

Eliza pulled away from his mouth and dropped kisses slowly and assiduously all over his face, jaw and down his neck.

'Is that the spot that you've been searching for?' he murmured. 'Is that where you'd like to inhale me?'

'Yes, yes, yes,' she whispered as she rubbed the tip of her nose on that spot beneath his ear before licking and nipping his skin. She moved her way down his neck again, making him exhale through his teeth. 'Your scent here makes me weak at the knees.'

God, she was killing him...

Eliza pulled away to sit up and started to undo the buttons of his shirt, her eyes glazed, her pale blond hair mussed. Had she ever looked more alluring, more beautiful, more enticing? No…not to him. He thought at that moment that she was the most beautiful woman he'd ever known. And once she had undone the last button, her eyes snapped to his. Taking a shaky breath, Eliza drew aside the opening of the shirt to reveal his naked form. She grazed her fingers and nails across his chest and abdomen, so slowly as though she were putting to memory the shape of him. Sebastian hissed as Eliza lowered her head and kissed, licked and nipped his exposed skin, following the trail that her fingers left as she explored him so excruciatingly slowly, he thought he might howl from both excitement and frustration.

He panted as Eliza then lowered herself to lie across him, her face just inches away from his own, and smiled. 'Do you not want to touch me now?'

'More than anything,' he rasped. 'But knowing how you're such a stickler for good manners, I thought to preserve the right of courtesy for ladies going first.'

'Very commendable as well as thoughtful of you, Sebastian.'

'I'd like to think so,' he drawled as he finally pulled his hands free from beneath his head and slipped an arm around her waist, letting his hand move up and down her spine. He needed this damn thick cotton night-rail gone but once again, that would be Eliza's decision.

As if she were reading his mind, Eliza sat back on her knees, keeping her eyes locked on to his. She took a few shaky breaths, her chest rising and falling rapidly as she unbuttoned the mother of pearl buttons that ran from her neckline all the way down to the lace-front yoke. Sebastian's eyes dropped to the exposed skin where the material gaped open, and before he knew what she would do next, Eliza pulled each arm free from the long, billowing sleeves of the night-rail and pulled the garment over her head before throwing it on the floor.

He stared at her, his jaw dropping as he took in Eliza sitting beside him in bed, with just a sheer cotton chemise and a half corset, all of which left very little to the imagination. The woman was all lush curves, long, shapely limbs and soft, soft skin. She was the most sensual creature he'd ever encountered and she was his. At least for now...

She helped Sebastian remove his shirt altogether before climbing over him and straddling him, making him feel every part of her glorious body.

Dear God...

Sebastian cradled her head and pulled her down for a fierce hungry kiss with his free hand as Eliza threaded her fingers into his hair, gripping him tightly and kissing him back with just as much intensity and fervour. She seemed to want and need him with the same fierce desperation as he did her.

He kissed her slowly, tasting her deeply, before holding on to her waist and swiftly flipping them both around so that he was now on top and he had her beneath him. Damn, but he could no longer resist the woman. His fingers skimmed down her front, undoing the laces of the half corset quickly and discarding it. He cupped her small, pert breast in his hand through the sheer cotton chemise and bent his head to lick the underside of her breast, before taking her erect nipple into his mouth and sucking it, making her moan and arch her back. Eliza pushed to sit up and gently swatted his hands away, giving him a coy look before pulling her chemise over her head and throwing it on the floor to join the rest of their garments.

He took in a shaky breath as he looked his fill of Eliza in her glorious nakedness. Damn but she was so adorable if not a little vulnerable as she held her head up and held his gaze, his captivating bluestocking.

'You're beautiful,' he murmured, sinking his fingers into the pale golden hair tumbling down her back.

'As are you, Sebastian,' she said softly, leaning forward to cup his jaw. 'I have never known anyone quite like you.'

He turned his head and kissed the palm of her hand. 'And I have never known anyone quite like you, either.'

They were simple words, honest and true, but in that single moment in time they encapsulated something momentous and significant, something far more powerful than Sebastian could hope to understand... but he would reflect on it later. For now was the time for something else altogether. It was time to feel, to explore, to cherish and to worship...all that surfeit of emotion that they had once spoken of.

He lifted her over him so that she now sat on his lap and smiled at her, kissing her neck, catching her earlobe between his teeth. As his hands roamed over her shoulders and back through the thick strands of her hair.

'Mmm, I want to see whether I can also find the spot, the very spot that had you in raptures.' He nipped and sucked on the long, pulsating vein that ran down her throat.

'But that spot may be quite...quite different to yours.'

'True.' He pulled away and gave her a wicked smile, marvelling at how Eliza could make such an incredibly brazen comment quite unknowingly. She seemed to have no idea of the double entendre she'd made, which delighted him more than he could say. 'Perhaps I should go in search of it.'

'Oh, but that's not what I meant.'

'I know,' he murmured, gently pushing her back

down so that she was lying on the bed again. 'I have become quite good at unravelling your clues and trying to decipher their meanings.'

'Is that so?' she hissed as he ran his hand from the base of her neck all the way down, taking in every curve and dip of her body, skimming her breast and alighting on to the softness of her stomach.

'Yes,' he whispered. 'I have it on good authority that if I were to find what I am looking for then it might unlock many secrets that I have been seeking.'

'Then you should certainly proceed with your search.'

'I intend to.' He lifted her arm and dropped kisses on each finger moving to the palm of her hand, and the delicate soft spot on her wrist. 'No, not quite here.'

He grazed his teeth along her arm, across her shoulders and chest and moved lower, nuzzling his way to her breast, kissing, nipping and licking her. 'Let me see... Could this be the spot?'

'I cannot... I cannot tell.' Her voice was barely audible.

'Then I must ascertain it myself.' He smiled against her skin, before continuing to kiss his way down her body, kissing her stomach, swirling his tongue inside her belly button. 'Mmm, it is not here, either.'

His fingers caressed her body with his mouth, teeth and tongue following the trail left by his hands, before taking hold of her leg, and kissing his way down to the arches of her feet, her ankles, and then moving back up again. He licked into the delicate skin behind her knee and watched as Eliza moaned, thrashing her head from side to side.

'Almost but not quite here, either.'

He flicked his eyes to hers, watching them glitter and darken as he pressed a kiss on the inside of her thigh. 'I feel I am getting close now.'

He turned his head and pressed his face between her thighs, kissing and nipping that sensitive skin there as she arched her back.

'I believe I have found the spot,' he murmured as he gently pulled her legs apart even more and buried his head between her thighs before worshipping her there, making Eliza buckle and scream his name.

Sebastian wanted Eliza to lose herself to this desire. He'd known all along that she possessed a wild intensity and wanted to unleash the passion that he doubted she was even aware of and yet was there, hidden deep inside her very soul. And he wanted it. He wanted it desperately for himself.

Chapter Fourteen

Eliza could not quite comprehend what was happening. What in heavens was Sebastian doing to her? It was as though she had no control over her body as he elicited the most extraordinary sensations again and again and again from her. Every touch, every kiss, every caress, was felt deeply in every part of her. And now he was kissing her, using his mouth, teeth and tongue in the most scandalous way.

Heavens above…

She had no notion that it could ever feel like this and thought she might die if he stopped doing all the clever things he was doing. It was all becoming too much to bear. Far too much…

Eliza moaned and whimpered as she lost herself more and more to this…this forbidden pleasure. It built to a crescendo inside her, before she suddenly screamed, thrashing her head from side to side as she came completely undone.

Her breathing was rasping and coming in spurts as her eyes fluttered open, to find Sebastian now above her, his lips curling into a wide smile. Eliza reached out and placed her hand on his jaw, caressing his face.

'Oh my, that was…incredible.' She took a moment to exhale. 'But I want you. I want all of you, Sebastian.'

She watched as his eyes darkened. 'Are you certain?'

'More than anything.'

Sebastian got off the bed and disrobed completely before returning to bed and moving back into Eliza's waiting arms. His gorgeously strong and agile body covered hers as he placed himself in between her legs. He dipped his head and caught her mouth with his, kissing her hard as he supported himself on those huge arms bent on either side of her. He lifted his head and pinned her with his glittering gaze, making her feel breathless before he entered her body in one long thrust.

Eliza gasped loud as he filled her completely, making her clench tightly around him and closing her eyes as she arched her back instinctively.

'Open your eyes, Eliza,' he demanded. 'Look at me, sweetheart. I want to see you. I want to see every little thing in your eyes.'

She opened her eyes but was unable to utter a word,

never taking her eyes off him as his movements became relentless, quickening the pace with his thrusts. Eliza melted into him with the heady push and pull of their bodies coming together as one. Sebastian rolled them both to one side before flipping them over so that once again he was beneath Eliza and she was straddling him on top. He continued to move inside her as she whimpered and embraced this new perspective from above, liking being in control. She smiled at him—this beautiful man who had desired her, liked her and wanted her as much as she desired, liked and wanted him. They seemed to be two halves of the same coin completing one another in a way she'd never thought possible before—not like this. Not for her... Even in this, he was saying wordlessly that together they were equally matched. It made her feel adored; it made her feel empowered. And it made her feel so much for him that she could burst into joy at this exquisite moment that was theirs.

He had wanted her to come to him with a clarity, so that she was certain she knew what she was embarking on. And now... Now Eliza finally understood what he had meant. Because this was no quick fumble in the dark. This was something else entirely. Something far more potent that needed her to go into it with her eyes wide open.

Sebastian sat up, wrapped his arms around her and

held on to her tightly, taking her mouth in another long, drugging kiss. He increased the pace, penetrating her so deeply that she knew she could not hang on for much longer.

Eliza screamed his name over and over again as she shattered into a thousand tiny pieces, just before Sebastian pulled away from her body and found his release on the bed.

The peace she'd found as she lay in Sebastian's arms was unlike anything Eliza had ever felt before. In truth, nothing that morning was quite like anything she'd ever experienced. It was as though everything that she had once believed and accepted could be possible in a relationship between a man and woman was now replaced by this unfettered newness. Which was something far better, stronger, meaningful and beautiful. Something quite unquantifiable, that she could not put a name to. A word that she could not yet ascribe to this feeling, which nevertheless made her head spin. And it was all because of *him*… Sebastian Marsden. The last man she'd ever have believed she could have such feelings for. And yet, she did…

'Are you well, Eliza?'

'Perfectly so,' she said on a yawn. 'And you?'

'Never better. Go back to sleep,' he murmured. 'It's still quite early.'

'But what of catching the next train? What of getting to Penwith?'

'There's no rush. We can get the next one.' He bent down to kiss her forehead. 'Sleep, love.'

Love?

But of course. That was the elusive word that she sought. The one that matched how she felt about Sebastian Marsden. It was love...she was in love with him. But how could it be true? Could she trust her own judgement when she had erred so badly before with Ritton, when she had also believed herself to care for him? Was it all too soon in any case, to believe that this feeling was actually that profound emotion rather than a momentary sensation of gratification after what had just occurred in this bed? A glorious sensation that would soon pass, in any case. Only time would tell and with these uneasy thoughts running through her head, Eliza drifted off to sleep cocooned in Sebastian's arms.

The next time Eliza opened her eyes, it was to find Sebastian with a towel wrapped around the lower half of his body, secured around his hips. The sight of him with wet hair, evidently after he'd bathed, and peering out the window, made her heart clench tightly. God, he was a magnificent-looking man. In the daylight she could feast her eyes on his taut, rugged body, all sinewy muscle and long, powerful limbs. And to think this was the man with whom she had lain, who had given her the most unimaginably exquisite pleasure. And to whom she had given herself so completely—Sebastian Marsden. A man who was a contradiction in every sense. One who was scandalous and apparently ruthless and hard but just as equally kind, generous and thoughtful, even though he found it difficult to trust or allow anyone to get close to him. Just as she did. This made him flawed in a way that made him real and human. And it was this that she was drawn to. This human and very real side to the man.

Sebastian turned away from the window and caught her staring at him. Their gazes locked and for a long moment all she could do was just stare into those fathomless dark grey eyes. Even from a short distance the intensity and smoulder felt like it could engulf her whole. He pushed away from the wall that he was leaning against and prowled towards her with a smile that promised all manner of scandalous pursuits. A smile that was nevertheless achingly tender, making her feel breathless and a little dazed.

The soft mattress sank down as he sat on the edge of the bed, pressing his lips to hers softly in a long, lingering kiss.

'Good morning,' he murmured, running his fingers through her hair. 'Again.'

'Good morning.' She pulled the coverlet up, concealing herself, suddenly feeling a little shy. 'Again.'

'I hope you're hungry as I have ordered a hearty breakfast to be brought up.'

'I am, thank you.' She frowned a little. 'But should we not make haste to get to the next train heading west?'

'I have already made enquiries, Eliza,' he said, playing absently with a lock of her hair, curling it around his finger. 'The trains have been cancelled this morning due to the inclement weather so there is really no need to rush anywhere. We can get the next train later on in the day.'

'Oh, I see.' She raised a brow and gave him a small smile from beneath her lashes. 'But what will we do to amuse ourselves?'

'I can think of a few things.' He winked before bending down and catching her lips with his, devouring her mouth. Eliza slipped her arms around his neck and pulled him down on the bed with her, as someone knocked on the door.

Sebastian lifted his head and threw her an impish grin. 'Do not go anywhere. I shall be back in just a moment.'

'Make sure that you are.'

Goodness, who was this wanton, sultry woman that she had become? Eliza barely recognised herself anymore. She watched as Sebastian rose, threw on his shirt and long robe, and ambled across the room to open the door to a couple of servants carrying trays of food and tea for them to break their fast. They set the trays on the table before leaving the room, just as Eliza got out of bed and walked towards the veritable feast.

'Did I not ask you to stay abed, Eliza?'

She shrugged. 'You're familiar with what I'm like, Sebastian, and know that I'm not very good at taking instruction or doing as I'm told.'

'Quite. I'm exceedingly familiar with you, love.' He smirked as he approached her from behind and wrapped his arms around her waist. 'And I have never met with a more exasperating woman than you, Mrs Weston.'

'You…you wretch, Mr Weston.' She feigned mock outrage at his not so loverlike words as he laughed, pressing a kiss to the side of her neck. 'Here I thought you were the most wonderful man in every possible manner, yet you disparage me so abominably.'

'Shocking behaviour,' he murmured as he kissed her along the length of her neck. 'It's just as well, then, that I like you as much as I do.'

Her breath hitched at his admission. One that Eliza was certain he hadn't especially wanted to make, judging by how he'd just stilled behind her, his arms that held her to him, slackening. Sebastian had also once again called her *love*. Had he realised this, too? What did it all mean? Eliza stepped out of his embrace and poured tea into two cups before turning around and offering one to Sebastian.

'I like you very much, too.' She smiled, hoping that this would dispel the sudden tension in the room. 'Very well indeed. In fact I… I.'

I feel an emotion far greater than mere like.

'In fact you…?' he repeated.

I love you… Eliza had already realised the truth of her errant feelings but before she embarrassed herself more, she tried to think of something else to say.

'In fact, I am enjoying our time together greatly, Sebastian,' she said lamely, knowing that it was as though she were describing a society function rather than their far more scandalous diversion. 'I'm glad you came with me to Cornwall.'

'As am I,' he said. 'But you make it sound as though there is a limit to our time together.'

'Ah, but you said yourself that there was a limit to seduction.'

'Indeed, but perhaps I was wrong.'

She shrugged. 'If you say so.'

'Oh, believe me.' He gave her a heated look. 'I do.'

Eliza gave him a small smile, which he returned before they sat down and filled their plates with eggs, slices of ham, toasted bread and local Devon butter.

The silence between them stretched as they ate and pondered on everything that had occurred between them since they had arrived at the Half Moon. It was not easy being in such close proximity with him in this chamber with all of this tumult of emotion that she had to prise apart and decipher, hoping to understand it all. Eliza could do with being alone, even for a short moment or two just to think about her feelings for Sebastian and all the implications. Yet, at the same time, she could not bear to be anywhere but in this room…with Sebastian.

'You're doing it again, Eliza.'

She lifted her head and frowned. 'Doing what?'

'Pushing your food around when you're clearly hungry. You seem to do that whenever you're agitated, or thinking of something or other.'

'It does seem that I cannot do more than one thing at a time,' she admitted wryly.

'May I ask if anything is the matter?'

Yes. What do I do when all of this is over? When we get back from this visit to Trebarr Castle? What happens to this newly found attachment between us? But more importantly, what do I do with all of these feelings that I have for you when you have said in the past that you do not believe in love?

Eliza had always been so vigilant to shield herself from hurt, building walls to protect her bruised and battered heart only to have those walls smashed to pieces with her heart now belonging to Sebastian, anyway. And without the man even knowing…unless she told him now. Yet, she felt exposed, vulnerable, unwilling to put herself in a position that might end in heartache and disappointment. She couldn't do it… not yet, anyway. And might he not think that she was trying to manipulate him and use this tentative attachment between them as a way to get around the debt that she owed him? God, it made her feel wretched contemplating all of that.

'I wondered what would happen if I…if I were unable to pay back Ritton's debt?'

Eliza had always had a terrible knack for blurting things out without always thinking them through. It was something that had always managed to get her into so much trouble in the past. And with that one question she'd suddenly made everything that she had shared in this room with Sebastian feel a little sordid and wrong…when in truth it was quite the opposite.

He gave her an implacable look. 'Is that what has really been worrying you, Eliza?'

'No, yes… I do not know.' She sighed, shaking her head. 'I just do not know what to do with any of it.'

'Any of what?'

'These feelings that I have for you.' She made herself look up and meet his implacable gaze. 'This surfeit of emotion between us.'

Sebastian did not say anything for a long moment, watching her from over his cup of tea before he sighed, his eyes softening. 'Must you do something about it? Now?'

'I would like to know…' She took in a deep breath before continuing. 'I would just like to know how things stand between us, after everything we have shared. After last night and also this morning.'

'I do not know the answer to that myself, Eliza, except to say that my feelings for you are unlike anything I've ever known before. I have nothing to compare to it.'

Her heart made an erratic beat. 'You don't?'

He smiled and shook his head. 'No. And it scares me as much as it clearly scares you. But I want to see what happens and where it takes us.'

'As do I.' She realised then that this would be enough. It was enough that Sebastian felt this much for her. She would follow him anywhere and see where it would take them. Eliza would rather have this honesty from him than any declarations that were untrue. But dear God, it scared her as it evidently did him. Something that neither of them had ever expected.

He reached for her, cupping her jaw and brushing the pad of his thumb along her cheek. 'Even so, I want you to know that I care deeply for you and would have no more talk of the debt that Ritton owed me. You, Eliza, have never truly owed me anything. Now eat.'

Sebastian might believe that now but would he always think that? Because in truth she owed him far more then he could ever know. And because of that Eliza knew that she had to find the treasure. Otherwise, the Bawden-Trebarr estate and Ritton's debt would always come between them.

Sebastian had been on the brink of telling Eliza what he truly felt—that not only did he feel deeply for her but that he was falling in love, an emotion that only a few weeks ago he would have laughed at and dismissed. How had everything changed so much in such a short time? It seemed so improbable, inexplicable and frankly unbelievable and yet it was true.

And yes, it made his head spin, scaring the hell out of him. He did not know what to do about any of it... not yet. All he knew was that he wanted Eliza. He wanted her ardently and with a passion that he could not quite comprehend himself. But he would... He would find a way through this so that he could keep her in his life somehow.

Eliza rose and held out her hand to him before taking him wordlessly back to bed where once again they made love. This time it was achingly slow and languid and tender as every exploration, every touch, every kiss, was heightened before they succumbed to the heady insatiable desire burning between them. Afterwards, when they were sated and replete, their bodies tangled together, they just held each other. Held each other in the quiet solitude while the rain thrashed against the windowpane outside.

Sebastian pulled the edge of the coverlet over them and tucked his hand beneath his head and wondered whether he'd ever felt this sanguine…this content.

No, never.

'What are you thinking?' Eliza turned her head and pressed a quick kiss on his chest before nestling against his shoulder.

'Ah, so now you wish to know my every thought as well?' he teased.

'No, keep them. I was just being curious as always.'

'But I like your curiosity and how you're intrigued by the world around you.'

'Do you now, Mr Weston? It seems that you are quite captivated by me.'

'It seems that I am.' He smiled as he dropped a kiss on top of her head. 'Have you always been so curious, then, about everything around you?'

'You mean, have I always been a bluestocking?' she murmured. 'Yes, I suppose I have. As a child I was always in a rush to learn more, to discover and to read as much as I could and I never changed the older I got. I always wanted to find out about anything that I did not quite understand, even in areas of academia that were deemed unsuitable for a young and impressionable woman, much to my father's dismay.'

'He did not approve?'

'No, he was incandescent with his censure and disapproval of me. That was why he forbade me from attending Oxford, even though I managed to pass the entrance examination. It had been a dream of both Cecy's and mine, ever since we met at Ravendean's School for Young Ladies many, many years ago as girls. But my father had other plans for me, and pushed for an alliance between Viscount Ritton and myself while Cecy… Cecy attended Oxford without me.'

'I'm sorry, Eliza. That must have been very disheartening.'

'It was.' She shrugged. 'But there was no point clinging onto the past and what could have been, so I made the best of what I had, which in fairness was very little.'

'I'm sure that was difficult,' Sebastian said as he absently threaded his fingers through her hair. 'You must have had regrets.'

'Too many but to no avail,' she said sadly. 'We must do what we can to move forward in life and live with what fate throws at us.'

This was something that Sebastian knew he did frequently—cling onto the past until it became fetid, seeping into his very soul. 'I know but with the best will in the world, however, it's not always easy.'

'No, it's not.' She paused a moment before continuing. 'Just as it must have been difficult for you when your life changed irrevocably.'

No, it had never been easy and at times Sebastian felt the darkness would consume him, but eventually he'd learned to let go of so much that once had him shackled to his past. Yet, some of it would always remain. Always...

'My father's death changed everything irrevocably, as you said, and for so long it was difficult to accept the truth of that.'

'I can understand that you did something far greater, Sebastian. You survived and made something of yourself despite it all.'

'I had no choice in the matter. And after my mother's death, my brothers and I were completely on our own.'

'That could not have been easy.'

'It wasn't,' he said bitterly. 'She was a gentle, kindhearted soul and she was crushed after my father's death.'

This was not quite what Sebastian had thought they would be discussing in the aftermath of intimacies with Eliza, and yet, he was doing so, anyway. There was a rightness about sharing his feelings with her about that terrible time, when he'd never acknowledged them to himself let alone anyone else. But then Eliza Bawden-Trebarr was not just anyone.

'I'm so sorry.' She cupped his jaw, caressing his face. 'Was it long afterwards that you started the Trium Impiorum?'

'Not exactly. The money that we had ran out soon after my mother died, so I did all manner of jobs to keep us from ending up in the workhouse. From working in a Thames shipping yard, to working as a tosher, just to put food on the table and be able to pay for the roof over our heads. Eventually, I found a job as a clerk in a solicitor's firm, which brought in a steady income. But it was all a million miles away from what I had been destined for—becoming an earl,' he said with a shake of his head. 'Dominic and Tristan also worked once they were old enough, although, I made sure to get tutors for Tristan when funds allowed since he showed an interest in more scholarly pursuits, and he eventually went to Cambridge.'

'Oh, Sebastian, you really are the very best of brothers.'

'Tell that to Dom and Tristan.' He snorted. 'Anyway, it was hard, it was gruelling, actually, but we did it.'

'And so, you eventually saved the funds to be able to buy the gaming club?'

'Not quite. My father had made provisions for my mother and my two younger brothers, should anything happen to him. Provisions that were unentailed from the Harbury estate. However, my uncle Jasper, who became the Earl of Harbury after my father's death, contested this, too, and it took years to resolve. By then my mother had been dead for a number of years and we had all but forgotten our old lives. So, you can imagine our surprise when we found that we were actually due the unentailed portion after all, despite everything my uncle had done to prevent that eventuality. And with the money safely in our pockets we stuck up the proverbial two fingers at him and all the rest of the aristocracy by opening the Trium Impiorum.'

'And thank God for it.'

'Indeed. It's still going from strength to strength.'

Eliza turned her head and pressed a kiss to his chest. 'You should be rightly proud of your achievements.'

'I am but I can never forget the way it all came about. I can never forget that it was from that moment after my father died. And try as I might, I cannot get away from how it has made me feel so damn resentful.'

'I understand, Sebastian, but how could you resent

the life that had been yours for the taking, when it was not your fault that you were forced to make it into something else?'

'Because it had all been a lie,' he said on a sigh. 'Everything to do with my father and his lofty Harbury title had been a lie. Everything. It was as though my brothers and I were given the key to the kingdom and told that all its riches were ours to take, and just when we reached out to claim it, it was all snatched away. And then to make matters worse, we had to endure the shame and disgrace of my father's sins—most of all my mother, who gave up on life altogether after her whole world shattered. And I was too young to do anything about it.'

'I'm so sorry,' she muttered, lifting her head and supporting it with her bent arm. 'But your father's sins, although terrible and painful, were, I dare say, never intentional. I doubt he ever meant for any of you to suffer in the way you did.'

'What difference does that make, Eliza? We suffered, anyway,' he said bitterly.

'It makes all the difference,' she said, gently laying her hand on his chest, over his beating heart. 'Don't you see that your father was a man who unintentionally hurt his family with a terrible mistake that he'd made? I doubt he'd ever wanted that to happen.'

'No, of course he didn't.'

'Because he must have loved you all so much,' she murmured, brushing her fingers across his chest. 'And somewhere deep down inside you have always known that, Sebastian.'

'What?' His brows furrowed in the middle as he flicked his gaze at her. 'What do you mean?'

'Think on it, Sebastian. Why else would you keep on your person a jewelled dagger that your father once gifted you, which, while practical, could have fetched you a pretty penny when you were so desperate for funds?' Before he could respond she continued with her bold assessment. 'And why would you use the sums from the money he left you and your brothers to create The Trium Impiorum, even if you believed he might have disapproved of it—which you have really no idea of knowing, by the by. Your father might even have approved of what you and your brothers did, after the manner in which you lost the Harbury estate and were made to accept the ignominy of being declared illegitimate.'

Sebastian blinked in surprise. How could this woman know any of this when she had no prior knowledge of who his father was? And yet... And yet, what Eliza had said somehow resonated with him, and was far closer to the type of man his father had been than the one Sebastian had inadvertently fabricated in his head so that he could throw all his frustration and his resentment at it. It was as though he had forgotten. Or perhaps chosen to forget who his father was because he couldn't bear thinking about the past. Because in truth, his father *had* loved them, all of them, and would never knowingly have subjected his wife and his sons to the pain and hardship that they had endured after his death.

He suddenly remembered more as memories of that time came flooding back. His mother's complete devotion to his father's memory even after the revelation that he'd been a bigamist had been astounding. As well as how she would never allow Sebastian or his brothers to disparage their father in front of her. Perhaps Eliza, with her usual astuteness, had been right. Perhaps his mother had died of a broken heart. Perhaps his mother would have given up on life, anyway, because she missed her husband terribly after his death. In the aftermath of their spectacular fall from grace, she had been subdued, and Sebastian had always thought it was because of the shame she had felt. But their mother had been made of hardier stuff than that. She wouldn't have cared what people said; she would have held her head up and behaved with her usual grace. It must have been that she was suffering from the unbearable pain of losing her husband, someone she'd loved so desperately. And when she'd caught a fever in that terrible winter, she had just faded away…

Sebastian turned and kissed Eliza on her head. 'How is it that you can see things in such a singular manner?'

She looked surprised. 'I cannot say.'

'I can. You're simply a marvel, Eliza.'

Perhaps that was one of the many things he loved about the woman. She constantly surprised him with her forthright and passionate manner. Indeed, Sebastian had realised this about Eliza from their first encounter—that she was unlike anyone he'd ever met before. Perhaps he'd sensed it from all the letters she'd bombarded him with before demanding that he meet her, and why he'd sat purposely in such darkness the first time she had come to the club unannounced. To try to intimidate her, to try to scare her into leaving him alone. But she'd seen through all of that in her no-nonsense manner. She'd seen through his darkness and she had seen…*him*. And it was this that had intrigued Sebastian. He had been drawn to the light she seemed to carry in her very soul. And as he lay next to her, he realised with unease that he always would.

Chapter Fifteen

By nightfall, Sebastian and Eliza had caught the later
train to Penwith, in Cornwall, and had hired a carriage from the station that would take them to the
Trebarr estate. With the journey from the station eventually taking them off the main roads to pathways that
gained them access into the rugged and wild terrain of
this part of Cornwall. As the carriage trundled along,
Eliza sat at the edge of the seat waiting for that first
glimpse of the incredible ruins of Trebarr Castle with
bated breath, unable to contain her excitement.

And then suddenly, as they turned a corner and
drove past a wooded thicket, the clearing opened up to
reveal the beautiful old ruins bathed by the moonlight
casting shadows and light all around it. Eliza sucked in
her breath and asked to stop the carriage. She climbed
down and raced across to the castle ruins with Sebastian following in pursuit behind, calling her name.

God above, but she had been waiting so long to set

eyes on this place again. It had been too long. Far too long since she had been here as a little girl clutching onto her parents' hands as they explained the importance of it to her.

'It's just as magnificent as I remember,' she murmured once Sebastian caught up with her. 'Perhaps even more so.'

Sebastian looked around the huge area and nodded, catching her hands into his. 'Yes...yes, it is.'

'Over there is the main castle keep where they would have had the main solar chambers and where the lord and lady—Simon and Elowen—had their living quarters.' She pointed at the large building made from local stone. 'And that there on the raised plinth would have been the Great Hall where they would have enjoyed many banquets and celebrations. It's actually very well preserved if you would like to have a look?'

'Shall we not return in the morning when we might see everything better? I would hate for you to slip on one of those cracked steps and fall and hurt yourself, Eliza.'

It was far more prudent to come back in the morning light but Eliza just could not wait to have a look around. 'I will be fine, I promise.'

'Very well, then, in that case, wait right here while I go and fetch the oil lamps from the carriage to help light the way.'

Sebastian climbed over the boulder and back onto the pathway to the carriage before returning with a couple of hand-held oil lamps in bevelled glass from the carriage, pressing one into Eliza's hand, who had for once done as she was requested and waited for him with a huge smile.

'Show the way, my lady.'

They walked hand in hand, holding up their respective oil lamps as they climbed the stairs leading to the Great Hall. Eliza pushed the ancient wooden door open with a creak and they were plunged into further darkness apart from the light provided by the oil lamps, which they shone around the chamber trying to see the old hall.

'Incredibly, the roof stands but it looks as though it would need some repair.' Sebastian nodded up above while holding out the oil lamp.

'The repairs should certainly be made on what is otherwise an excellent example of a hammerbeam roof, which is actually older than the one at Hampton Court Palace.'

'Interesting.'

'As the current owner of this estate I'm glad you think so.' She moved towards the faded muralled wall. 'Beautiful… Look, Sebastian, can you see what is on this wall? The Bawden-Trebarr standards in their respective colours.'

'It seems to be a replica of what we found inside the box.'

'It is,' she said softly, wanting to take in all the finer detail and intricacies of the design. 'With both the Bawden and Trebarr mottos entwined. *Karensa a vynsa covatys ny vynsa.* "Love would, greed would not…"'

'And the Trebarr motto of *Franc ha leal atho ve.* "Free and loyal am I."'

Eliza spun around to face Sebastian. 'You remembered the motto and in Cornish as well?'

'I did.' He smiled sheepishly as she approached him. 'Since it was important to *you.*'

'Oh, Sebastian.' Eliza placed her gloved hand on his gorgeous face. 'I… I…'

She loved him. More than anything in the world Eliza wanted to tell him at that moment and in this place—this hallowed place, the very hall where her ancestors came together. She wanted to make him see everything that she held in her heart. And tell him that she cared for him, that she loved him, but the words felt as though they were stuck in the back of her throat. She opened her mouth to try again…

'Oho…who goes there?' A man's voice boomed from the other side of the hall.

Sebastian moved in front of Eliza to stand tall in a protective stance. 'I am Sebastian Marsden, current owner of this estate. And this is Lady Eliza Bawden-Trebarr, who I have accompanied here. Who are you?'

The short and rather rotund man came forth and looked up at Sebastian and frowned in surprise. 'Bawden-Trebarr? Did you say Bawden-Trebarr, my good sir?'

'I did.'

'Bless my soul, a Bawden-Trebarr has come here at last.' He clapped his hands together and bowed to them. 'Yer very welcome here, my lady. And yer, too, sir. Come please. Yer must come to the Sailor's Mermaid, the local pub in these 'ere parts where yer'll both be the guests of honour, so yer will.'

Eliza and Sebastian followed the man, Silas Brunde, a steward of the estate, in the carriage that carried their trunks back onto the main path and to the nearby hamlet of Trebarr, which consisted of a handful of small stone-terraced cottages with just one detached building—The Sailor's Mermaid—along with a smithy and a row of shops overlooking a small village green. They could hear the raucous revelry inside the pub, and when they entered, following Silas inside, it seemed the whole pub turned to look in the direction of the newcomers. Yet, the moment Silas Brunde announced who they were, there was a hushed silence before the pub suddenly erupted into cheering.

The pub was filled to the rafters with people who

shook their hands as they were ushered to a small central table. Tankards of beer and ale were brought over to the table forthwith, and a couple of musicians playing the flute and fiddle resumed making their merry music, while the revellers stamped their feet, danced and sang along.

'I had not expected such a welcome as this,' Eliza muttered to Sebastian over the din; the first words she'd spoken to him since that stupendous moment in the Great Hall when she'd wanted so desperately to tell him of her feelings. The moment had obviously passed but she hoped to get another opportunity to tell him later.

'Yes, I believe they are exceptionally glad to have you among them, Eliza.'

'Me?' she said in surprise. 'Don't you mean you? After all, you are the owner of all this.'

'Who knows, by tomorrow when we start digging for your treasure, there might be a new owner. Or rather the rightful owner of the Bawden-Trebarr estate.' Sebastian held out his tankard of ale to her, which she clicked hers to in a toast.

'I'll drink to that.'

'Then here's another toast, Eliza,' he said, holding out his tankard. 'For tomorrow and everything it brings.'

'For tomorrow,' she murmured as she slammed her tankard against his.

* * *

But the following day did not quite turn out exactly as either Eliza or Sebastian had hoped. When Eliza had woken up in the bedroom of one of the widowed Trebarr tenants who had insisted on having Eliza stay at her house, unlike Sebastian, who'd made do with one of the rooms at the pub, she had been filled with so much optimism for what that day might bring. But she could not have known then how badly it would turn out.

After breaking her fast at dawn and meeting Sebastian along with a few farmhands who'd volunteered to help them dig near the largest and most magnificent oak trees and woodland that the deciphered and translated vellum had mentioned, it soon became clear that they did not know exactly what they were doing. Each dig proved fruitless and soon the excitement and heady anticipation of finding the Bawden-Trebarr treasure that the vellum alluded to fizzled into a damp squib. All that they had achieved was lots of unsightly deep holes in the ground everywhere.

Eliza, however, could not stop even when the day was almost ending and she was tired and exhausted in every way because of their failures. She would not and could not give up as it would mean giving up on so much more than just losing the estate.

'I believe we should stop for today, Eliza.' Sebas-

tian came upon her wearing work clothes, his shirt-
sleeves rolled up to reveal those hard-working arms
of his. 'The light is starting to fade and many of the
farmhands have decided to stop, too, as they need to
get up early for their work tomorrow morning.'

Eliza wiped the sweat from her brow and looked
up in dismay at the area around them. 'I understand
but it must be here. It must.'

'The treasure, if it is still buried, could be anywhere, though,' he said gently. 'It was always going to
be a huge challenge to find it, even if it was still here.'

Sebastian was right, of course. This had always
been a fool's errand, and the proposal she had presented to him had always smacked of desperation. It
had been a mad scheme but she had followed it blindly,
willing it to happen as she pushed for it relentlessly
and refusing to listen to the voices of reason around
her. God, and she believed herself to have a scholarly
mind—a bluestocking, who was analytical and ratio-
nal in her findings, yet she could not even see what
was before her eyes at how ridiculous this all was.
That this whole search was hopeless. And despite all
their findings, it had always been so.

'I think I've found summat, my lady.'

Sebastian and Eliza exchanged a surprised look
before quickly making their way toward the young
farmhand who had called out to them. They crouched

down on the grass beside him as he dragged out a large wooden box.

'Well done, Sam,' she said as she studied the box, trying to tamp down her excitement, knowing full well that this could be yet another false hope.

'Well?' Sebastian murmured. 'Shall we open it?'

Eliza nodded as he brought a crowbar to break through the wooden box. Once the lid broke open, they looked inside to find it filled with earth and old straw, but something else was hidden in its depths. Something that was wrapped in very old material. They set it on the ground and began to untie the knotted ends, letting the material slide down to reveal yet another box—a box identical to the one that Eliza had. The Bawden-Trebarr box.

'It exists.' She sat back on her feet and exhaled slowly through pursed lips. 'I cannot believe it actually exists.'

Sebastian smiled at her and nodded. 'Yes, it seems that it does. And it seems that just like yours, it needs the correct seal to open it.'

Eliza nodded before fetching the seal that Tristan Marsden had surreptitiously allowed her to bring on this expedition, so long as she brought it back in one piece. Taking a deep breath, she placed the metal seal in the centre of the box and pressed, listening to the familiar click as it slotted into place before releasing the metal lock. She opened the lid of the box but unlike the one in her possession, this one was completely empty. Whatever had once been there was now gone. Lost through the annals of time.

They both stared at the box for a long moment, neither wanting to admit defeat.

'I'm sorry, Eliza.' She heard Sebastian murmur from beside her as he reached over and covered her hand with his, giving it a squeeze.

But her mouth was too dry to respond other than to nod lamely, and being filled with a huge sense of disappointment as it all came crashing down around her.

'It doesn't matter, Eliza. Not now,' Sebastian said as her eyes filled with tears.

Was he mad to think that? Annoyed with herself, Eliza wordlessly gathered the seal and stuffed it back inside her portmanteau irritably as she rose and threw the empty box aside. Sebastian moved to follow her. 'Did you hear me, Eliza? I said it matters not that we were unable to find the Bawden-Trebarr treasure. Not to me.'

'That speaks well of you, Sebastian, but it matters very much to me,' She said bitterly as she continued to march away from this clearing with Sebastian following behind her. 'And this does change everything.'

He was upon her so quickly, stilling her by her elbow. 'How so? I fail to understand you, Eliza.'

She spun on her heels to face him. 'Can't you see that this failure, this disappointing loss, will change everything? Including what we have between us. Don't you see that this failure would always come between us?'

'No, Eliza. I don't,' he said as he laced his fingers with hers. 'What I believe... In fact, what I know is that I love you.'

What...?

She nearly stumbled backwards with that unexpected declaration. Dear God, but Sebastian's feelings mirrored her own. Oh, she knew he desired her and had said he liked her very well but...*love*? No, she never would have believed it. And declared at such a time as this with the failure of the find still ringing in her head. Oh, what a mess. Sebastian had said that they should see where this...this liaison would take them just over a day and a half ago—heavens, but it felt like a lifetime ago now—and yet it had already taken them here—to precisely nowhere.

She slipped her hand free of his and dropped her arms to her sides. 'I love you, too, Sebastian. More than you will ever know.' Sebastian smiled and stepped forward to reach for her, just as she took a step back and held up her hand.

'But I wish now that I had told you the truth of my feelings back in the Half Moon Inn or when we were standing in the Great Hall of Trebarr Castle yesterday evening, instead of now, in this moment...this moment when everything that I tried to achieve has all been for naught.'

'Come now, does it matter, after we have told each other our innermost feelings? I love you and you say you love me—which, by the by, is the most wonderful thing I have ever heard. Surely, that is all that matters?'

Eliza hugged her arms around herself, suddenly feeling very cold. 'I wish that were true but it cannot be.'

He frowned. 'I don't comprehend you, Eliza.'

'Don't you see that the failure of today changes everything between us?' she murmured softly. 'That my inability to regain this estate by paying back Ritton's debt will now and forever cast a doubt over everything between us? We can never come together in whatever this is between us, as equals, which for me was of the utmost importance.'

He moved towards her. 'I don't give a damn about the Bawden-Trebarr estate—it's yours with my compliments,' he ground out through clenched teeth. 'And I don't care about the debt. All I care about is you, Eliza. *You*, for the love of God.'

Eliza reached out and cupped his jaw as he turned his face and pressed his lips in the centre of her palm.

'But don't you see, Sebastian, that you will one day wonder about the timing of this disclosure? You will wonder whether my love for you had been an attempt to manipulate you in some way just to gain back this estate.'

'You would think so little of me?'

'Of course not.'

'Good, but let's for the sake of argument address your rather arbitrary assumption. Allow me to ask you whether you are trying to manipulate me in gaining the estate that I'm freely giving you, anyway. So, are you, Eliza?'

'No, Sebastian, I am not.'

'Then what is all of this about, sweetheart?' he said on a frustrated sigh.

'All I know is that perhaps not now, not even tomorrow, but someday that niggle of doubt would surface, Sebastian, and I cannot bear to lose your good opinion of me, your respect and even your love.'

He had once had those very doubts when he'd asked what her game was. Would his concerns not resurface again in the future? Eliza had no way of knowing but knew it would destroy her if she were to lose his trust. In any case, what could she bring with her into this union? Nothing. Which meant that they were set to be unequal from the very start. It raised the very important question—what kind of future would they have, then?

'Eliza, I…'

She silenced him by placing her finger against his lips and shook her head. 'I want to come to you. I want to be with you, but on an equal footing, even if our laws and our society do not quite accept that yet. This is who and what I am, Sebastian—a woman who believes in what Cecy and I set up in The Women's Enlightened Reform Movement.' He smiled briefly at that. 'But how can I come to you if this…inequality, this disparity, stands between us? How?'

Eliza gave him a small, sad smile before turning on her heel and leaving him to ponder on everything that she had said, striding quickly to get away from this place.

Chapter Sixteen

It had been the most arduous journey back from Cornwall early the following morning accompanied by Sebastian. Eliza had spent the night shut inside the old widow's cottage, needing time and space with all her thoughts running around her head, not knowing if she was making the greatest mistake of her life in stepping away from a future with Sebastian Marsden. Neither had spoken very much outside of the usual pleasantries as they travelled back to London via Exeter, but this time without the overnight stop. Thank goodness as Eliza would have found that an impossible intimacy. It was unbearably awkward as it was to travel in such close proximity to Sebastian when what they could both do with was having some time apart. And yet, Eliza felt that her heart was shattering into tiny little pieces, anyway, especially the closer they got to London.

By nightfall they had reached Paddington and after

Sebastian had dealt with a message that had been waiting for him on arrival, they hired a carriage to take them to her town house in Chelsea. Strange but it seemed after everything that she had been through she was right back where she'd started from.

'I want to thank you for everything that you have done for me, Sebastian,' she said as the carriage came to a stop outside her house, and she swallowed uncomfortably as she held out her hand.

He took her proffered hand and pressed a chaste kiss on the back of it. 'You might want to thank me for something else, Eliza.'

'What do you mean?'

'Go inside and find out,' he murmured before tugging her back by her fingers. 'But know that this, Eliza Bawden-Trebarr, is by no means over.'

He gave her a quick, hard kiss on the mouth before jumping out of the carriage and helping her down, walking her to her door. After her trunk was also delivered, he made a curt bow and got back inside the carriage, leaving her bewildered. Good Lord, what had he meant about this not being over? And what did Sebastian mean when he told her that there might be something she'd want to find inside the house?

As if to answer her question, the front door swung open and Eliza's mother stepped out onto the porch and ran towards her, enveloping her in a tight embrace.

Oh, God, this was what he'd obviously meant. Sebastian had told her that he would help her with her mother's plight and he had not let her down. It made her want to weep when she considered everything that he'd done for her, time and again.

Oh, Sebastian...what am I going to do about you?

It was over two weeks since Eliza had seen him. Two weeks since she had looked on that beloved face and spoken to him. Oh, she had sent several missives to him, thanking him effusively for the safe return of her mother, which she later found out was partly due to Sebastian's reaching out to his cousin, Henry Marsden, the new Earl of Harbury, which she knew in her heart he would never have done if it hadn't been for her. And wanting to do this one service for her.

And then to add more fuel to these feelings of being beholden to Sebastian, he had reverted all ownership of the Bawden-Trebarr estate back to her, just as he'd said he would. She had tried to return it to him, but it came back yet again with his solicitor's letter including the landowner's registry seal on it. It was now Eliza's legally and there was little she could do to change that. All of which made it difficult to know what to do about Sebastian Marsden and her feelings for him. She could not go to him as she desperately wanted to because of all the things she had said to him in Trebarr that night. The reservations she'd had about the inequality of their alliance, as well as these feelings of inadequacy over her failure to find her own way out of her problems, had not diminished. Not by any stretch.

But dear Lord, how she ached to be near him, to talk to him, to touch him. She was heartsick and nothing, it seemed, would mend it.

'Are you even listening to me, Eliza?' Her mother's words broke through her musings.

Eliza blinked and took a sip of tea before returning the cup to the saucer. 'Pardon, Mama, I was not attending.'

'No, you were not, dearest.' Her mother frowned as she set her teacup on the small table in Eliza's back parlour and watched her for a long moment. 'Is this still about your Mr Sebastian Marsden?'

'He is not my Mr Sebastian Marsden.'

But he should be, he should...

'You and I both know that is a lie, Eliza,' her mother said quietly. 'Do you love him?'

'Yes, Mama.'

'And he loves you?'

'Yes, I believe so.'

'Then why have you been moping about the place for two weeks? Why have you kept away from him since you parted?'

'Because I wanted to be with you, Mama. You cannot know how much I have worried for you. How much I missed you. It's my greatest joy to have you back with me, safe and sound.'

'And mine, too, dearest. And yet it would never have been possible had it not been for your young's man intervention.'

'I know,' she uttered bleakly. 'I know.'

Her mother reached out and slipped her hand over hers. 'Eliza, do not mistake strength for being prideful.'

Prideful? Is that what she was being?

'It is far more complicated than that, Mama. I am indebted to Sebastian in a manner that would always come between us. It would always cast a shadow on how we came to be together as a man and a woman and it would compromise my values and beliefs in the suffrage of women.'

'Very admirable, Eliza, but consider that Mr Marsden has not asked you to compromise your values and beliefs, as far as I'm aware.'

'No, of course he hasn't.'

'And yet, you seem to believe in the notion of coming together as a man and woman, as you rather vulgarly put it, in terms of a monetary equality when you should be thinking of equal minds, equal values and equal hearts, which from my understanding seems to have been the case between you and Mr Marsden.'

Eliza covered her face with her hands and shook her head. 'I wish it were as simple as that.'

'Tell me, Eliza, is this more to do with being afraid to commit to Mr Marsden because of what happened with Ritton?' *Yes, no, she was no longer certain.* 'Because if it is then you need to find your courage and fight for this love of yours. For it is a rare thing and not something that comes along too often in life.'

'Perhaps I don't have the conviction left to fight for anything.'

That was certainly true. Eliza herself had never believed that she would one day find someone and be loved by him in return. After Ritton, she'd thought any chance would be elusive, practically out of reach for someone like her. And yet, she had found it in Sebastian.

'You are scared, Eliza, and I can understand why. However, that is not the woman you are, especially as the descendant of all those women who came before us, namely Elowen Bawden-Trebarr.'

'I know that, Mama, but I'm not certain whether love can be enough, as there are too many challenges, too many obstacles in the way for me and Sebastian.'

'Then find a way, dearest.'

'I thought I had,' she said sadly. 'I thought that if I'd found the Bawden-Trebarr treasure when we went looking for it then at the very least, it would have been something.'

'May I see the vellum that you and your Mr Marsden discovered together?' She smiled up at her daughter. 'I still haven't seen it despite the exciting story you regaled me with about finding it.'

'Yes, of course. I'll fetch it now.' Eliza rose, leaving the room momentarily before returning with both the vellum and the transcribed translations, and held it out for her mother.

'Thank you,' the older woman said as she scanned her eyes over the vellum and the translation. 'Well, it seems that you have both done a thorough job here.'

'Yes, we…we worked well together,' Eliza muttered as she slouched back on the chair. 'But it all came to nothing when we went looking for the blasted oak tree that the vellum refers to on the Trebarr estate.'

'What did you say?' Her mother froze and lifted her eyes to hers. 'You looked for it by an oak tree on the Trebarr estate? In Cornwall?'

'We did, but to no avail.'

'Oh, my sweet girl, I don't think the Bawden-Trebarr treasure was ever in Cornwall, but in Devon,' she said earnestly. 'For it was in Devon where Simon and Elowen pledged to be together, so therefore that's where the treasure, if it's still buried, would be.'

'I don't understand—why Devon?'

'Because that was where Elowen Bawden was escorted to by Simon Trebarr no less, as she was promised to another man. But just before he left, Simon told Elowen of his love and begged her not to marry the rather odious Sir Roger Prevnar and that he would be waiting by an old oak tree in a small woodland on the edge of Dartmouth, if she would choose him instead. And so he waited and waited. And on the morning of Elowen's wedding to Sir Roger, she absconded from his castle and met Simon underneath the old oak tree that I'm certain the vellum refers to. That is where they pledged their love to one another. So you see, the tree was…'

'In Devon and not Cornwall.' Eliza stood abruptly, shaking her head. 'Oh, Mama, do you know what this means?'

Her mother frowned. 'No, dear.'

'It means that I must be away to Devon on the very next train,' she said excitedly.

'But dearest, please wait…'

Eliza, however, had already left the room, needing to quickly stuff a few things together in her handy portmanteau. Her mother's explanation of the whereabouts of the treasure propelled Eliza into action, and once again, she soon found herself boarding the next train from Paddington heading to the southwest in search of the Bawden-Trebarr treasure, praying it hadn't been ransacked already...

Sebastian had been brooding for over two weeks now, ever since he'd returned from Cornwall in a dark mood, flitting from a bleak cloud of despair to anger to an ache deep within his chest. He couldn't quite believe the turn of events that had led to his estrangement from Eliza and all because of her pig-headedness in needing to pay back Ritton's debt. God, as if he cared about that!

However, in quiet contemplation, Sebastian recognised that with everything that had transpired between them ending in the disappointment of finding nothing in Cornwall, Eliza needed time. Time to come to terms with her feelings for him. And time to know what it was that she wanted. But what if she truly believed that they had no future despite their confessions of love for one another? What if she was adamant that he had no place in her life? Good God, he would have to convince her, woo her, anything to make her realise that he wouldn't give her up without a fight. He'd meant every word when he told her that he meant to keep her... And yet, if she had truly decided against a future with him then wouldn't he have to accept that, let her go and get on with his life without her?

Damn it, apart from those very proper letters filled

with gratitude for everything he'd done, he'd not heard from or seen her in over two weeks. How the hell was he supposed to get on without her? How? She had barged into his life in a whirl, upending everything in it and then she'd left it in exactly the same way. Exasperating woman. If only she would burst into his office and demand something outrageous again from him.

Sebastian rubbed his brow, knowing the truth of it was that he missed her terribly. He missed her so much it actually hurt. A knock at the door snapped him out of his reverie.

'Come in.'

His major-domo opened the door and walked in. 'Lady Bawden-Trebarr is here to see you urgently, Mr Marsden. Shall I see her in?'

Eliza? Here?

'Of course!' He stood and started to pace the room before turning around to see that it was not Eliza but her mother who had been ushered into his office.

Tamping down his disappointment, Sebastian bowed. 'My lady, it is a pleasure to see you. How may I be of service?'

'Good day, Mr Marsden, I am sorry to come here unannounced but I thought you might want to know that my daughter has once again left London in search of the Bawden-Trebarr treasure, if it is even still there. On account of what I told her.'

What the hell has she done now?

'What did you tell her, my lady?'

'That the treasure had likely never been buried in Cornwall but Devon, a woodland on the edge of Dartmouth, to be exact. And oh, Mr Marsden, she left so soon afterwards and all alone. I cannot help but feel concerned for her well-being.'

'But why would Eliza do that?' he thundered, unable to keep the anger from his voice, even in the presence of Eliza's mother. 'Why would she not ask for my help?'

'Perhaps because she believes she has already asked too much of you. Because she has something to prove to you. With Eliza, it could be anything.'

'Yes, it could.' He exhaled irritably. 'And I presume you would have me follow her, my lady, despite Eliza's rejection of my suit?'

'I would, yes.' The older woman's sad smile was so reminiscent of her daughter's it made his heart clench. 'My daughter loves you, Mr Marsden, but after her marriage to her late husband, she lost who she was for a long while. Until she met you. But I also believe she is also unsure as to whether she is truly worthy of you.'

Sebastian felt as though all the air had been knocked

out of his chest. 'Unworthy of me? But I'm… I'm the one who is…'

'Illegitimate?'

'Exactly.'

'That is not something that would make one jot of difference to Eliza, Mr Marsden. You must know that about her by now.'

'I do.' There was never any question of whether Sebastian would follow Eliza Bawden-Trebarr. 'I shall go on the next train, my lady. And I shall find her. Of that, you can be assured.'

'Thank you. That would ease my worry.' She smiled. 'I do not like to think of her being alone. And you know Eliza has always been so alone, especially during her marriage to Ritton. My husband never should have pushed for the match.'

He nodded, unable to say more. Sebastian sprang into action and after assuring Eliza's mother that he would find her and bring her back home, he rushed to get the next train from Paddington, knowing that she was probably one train ahead of him.

Thank goodness that the journey to Dartmouth in Devon had not taken as long as when she had travelled to Cornwall a fortnight ago, but it had still taken the better part of the day by the time she'd arrived. Eliza had, however, decided to wait to venture to the small woodland that her mother had described lying northwest between Dartmouth, near Bayard's cove, and the old remains of Stromley Castle, until the following morning, which was quite unlike her. So after organising the hiring of a vehicle and a man to help her with the dig, she set off after breaking her fast, eager to find out whether the Bawden-Trebarr treasure was still buried where her mother had believed it could be. Devon…it had always been in Devon that the Bawden-Trebarr treasure had been hidden and specifically under an old oak tree on the edge of Dartmouth—if indeed it was still there.

A little while later they entered the small wooded area and Eliza began to search for the largest, oldest oak tree, as a dense fog wrapped itself around her legs, making visibility a little harder. Pushing her spectacles up her nose, she looked and felt her way along so many trees that did not quite fit the description her mother had given, dismissing them all until she encountered an old majestic-looking oak. She let out a shaky breath as she felt her way down the gnarly bark of the ancient trunk, knowing that it must be this one.

With the decision made and with the assistance of the hired help, she started to dig close to the tree but not too close that they'd damage its ancient roots. They hopefully wouldn't need to dig around the perimeter of the tree as her mother had been adamant that the site would most likely be north of the tree itself, away from Dartmouth and facing the clearing closest to the remains of Stromley Castle.

'I think we might need another spade, Mr Jenkins,' Eliza muttered, wiping her brow.'

'Very well, miss, I shall return with one from the cart.'

Eliza continued to dig before she heard Mr Jenkins return. Crouching on the ground she started to pull out a long, spindly weed with her bare hands. 'I shall take that,' she muttered, holding out her hand without bothering to look back and grabbing hold of the smaller spade that the old man had fetched for her. 'Thank you.'

But then she heard a vastly different voice to the kindly old man behind her. 'You're welcome.'

Eliza dropped the spade and spun around to find Sebastian Marsden crouching low behind her.

'Hullo, Eliza,' he drawled. 'Fancy finding you here.'

She stared at him for a long time, drinking in the sight of this beloved man. 'What… What are you doing here, Sebastian?'

'Looking for you.' Even his voice made her pulse quicken.

'You were?'

'Yes.'

For a long moment Sebastian and Eliza were rooted to the spot, neither of them saying anything.

'Are you… Are you well, Eliza?' He eventually broke the silence.

'Yes.' She noticed the dark circles underneath his eyes and the thin white lines at the corners of his mouth. He looked so tired and weary as he rose and stepped closer. 'I am well.'

'Good.' He exhaled an irritated breath before turning around to look at her with an irate gaze. 'Because perhaps now you might like to explain what the hell you're doing all the way out here, on your own?'

Oh dear…

'I assume you must know that since you're also here, Sebastian.'

'But why, Eliza? Why would you not ask me to accompany you?'

'Surely, you must know that I had to do this on my own.'

'Do I? You and your pride, Eliza Bawden-Trebarr,' he said, shaking his head as he turned his back on her.

'I'm truly sorry, Sebastian,' she said, moving to stand behind him and placing her hand on his back.

'What for, exactly?'

'For doubting you. For doubting myself.' She sighed as she gently pulled him around to meet her gaze. 'And I'm sorry for causing you pain. I… I thought if

I could give you something in return for the debt then I could… Then we could start afresh. Be together as equals.'

'Good God, Eliza, it was never your debt to pay back. And Ritton should never have used your ancestral estate to pay the damn thing in the first place. Don't you see? The estate has always been yours. Always.'

'What about the debt?'

He pulled her close to him and looked down at her. 'That will now pass onto the new viscount. And if he promises never to come within a hundred yards of you then I might consider it paid.'

'But, Sebastian…'

'This is not up for debate, my lady,' he murmured, brushing his knuckles down her cheeks. 'Don't you see? All I have ever wanted is you, unencumbered by any land, debt, castle or even treasure. Just you, Eliza.'

'I want you, too,' she murmured as her eyes filled with tears.

'Good, because I'm yours. I have been from that first moment you came tearing into my office. And if you'll have me, I want to be yours in every way possible.'

'You want to marry me?'

'I want to marry you.' He nodded, catching her lips

with his before lifting his head, his eyes glittering with such tenderness. 'Will you have me?'

'Yes… Yes, I think I shall have you.' She felt her heart might burst from happiness. 'I love you, Sebastian.'

'I love you, too, Eliza. Always.'

As Sebastian bent his head to kiss her, Eliza pressed her finger on his lips. 'There's just one more thing you might like to know. I believe I might have found something under this tree.'

'Oh, God, Eliza.' His shoulders shook from mirth. 'Whatever am I to do with you?'

'Love me.' She grinned. 'But in the meantime, help me retrieve the box I found.'

'Gladly.'

Under the same tree where her ancestors had pledged to be together hundreds of years ago, they eventually unearthed a box buried deep within the earth. Inside the box, they discovered a small pouch tucked into the furthest recesses and within that, they found two gold-and-emerald rings that must have once belonged to Simon and Elowen. Smiling up at one another and using the same rings, Eliza and Sebastian made a similar promise beneath the same old oak tree. They promised to love and honour each other until the end of their days.

* * * * *

MILLS & BOON®

Coming next month

ONLY AN HEIRESS WILL DO
Virginia Heath

Book 1 of **A Season to Wed**
The brand-new regency series from
Virginia Heath, Sarah Rodi, Ella Matthews and
Lucy Morris

Gwen laid down her quill and steepled her fingers. 'This is a surprise, Major Mayhew—although I must say, a timely one. I've been thinking about earlier and—'

'So have I. Incessantly. But I'm in. Obviously I am in.' He suddenly smiled and that did worrying things to her insides. However, if his smile made all her nerve endings fizz, what he did next made them melt. 'I would have been here sooner but I had to collect this.' He rummaged in his waistcoat pocket—this one a vivid turquoise peacock embroidered affair that shouldn't have suited anyone but did him—and pulled out a ring. 'This was my mother's. I hope it meets with your satisfaction.'

She stared at it dumbstruck. Shocked that he had thought of it and yet unbelievably touched that he had. 'You brought me a ring…' She had assumed, when her engagement was announced, she would have to buy her own and that it would be a meaningless trinket—not an heirloom. Not something that meant something to someone. Something pretty and elegant, a simply cut oval ruby the size of her little fingernail surrounded by diamonds, that she probably would have chosen for herself before she talked herself out of it for being too bold.

He shrugged awkwardly. 'It seemed the very least I could do after you proposed.' Then to her utter astonishment he reached across the table, grabbed her hand and slipped it on her finger. 'It fits perfectly. Perhaps that's an omen?' He held her hand while he stared at it, twisting it slightly so that the lamplight caught the stones and made them sparkle. Gwen barely noticed the gem, however, as his touch was playing havoc with her senses.

He let go of her finger and, for a fleeting moment, common sense returned, warning her to yank the thing off and hand it back to him. Except…

It felt right on her finger and she couldn't formulate the correct words to tell him that she had changed her mind. That he wasn't at all what she was looking for, but she hoped he found another, more suitable heiress, to marry as soon as possible. Instead, there was another voice in her head overruling that of common sense. One that was rooting for Major Mayhew, no matter how wrong she already knew him to be.

Continue reading

ONLY AN HEIRESS WILL DO
Virginia Heath

Available next month
millsandboon.co.uk

COMING SOON!

We really hope you enjoyed reading this book.
If you're looking for more romance
be sure to head to the shops when
new books are available on

Thursday 27th February

To see which titles are coming soon, please visit

millsandboon.co.uk/nextmonth

MILLS & BOON

MILLS & BOON
A ROMANCE FOR EVERY READER

- **FREE** delivery direct to your door
- **EXCLUSIVE** offers every month
- **SAVE** up to 30% on pre-paid subscriptions

SUBSCRIBE AND SAVE

millsandboon.co.uk/Subscribe

afterglow BOOKS

Afterglow Books is a trend-led, trope-filled list of books with diverse, authentic and relatable characters, a wide array of voices and representations, plus real world trials and tribulations. Featuring all the tropes you could possibly want (think small-town settings, fake relationships, grumpy vs sunshine, enemies to lovers) and all with a generous dose of spice in every story.

♪ @millsandboonuk
⊙ @millsandboonuk
afterglowbooks.co.uk

#AfterglowBooks

For all the latest book news, exclusive content and giveaways scan the QR code below to sign up to the Afterglow newsletter:

SCAN ME

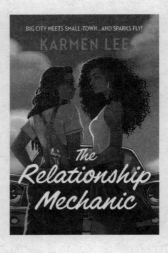